Thank You for Readi

Enjoy!

Joy Harding - Augus.

M000286299

BOUNDARY WATERS SEARCH AND RESCUE: BEYOND BELIEF

BOOK ONE IN THE BOUNDARY WATERS SEARCH AND RESCUE SERIES

BY

JOY HARDING

ISBN 978-1-63630-787-9 (Paperback)
ISBN 978-1-63630-788-6 (Hardcover)
ISBN 978-1-63630-789-3 (Digital)

Copyright © 2021 Joy Harding
All rights reserved
First Edition

All quoted Scripture except where noted is from the New American Standard Bible, Copyright 1960, 1962, 1963, 1968, 1971, 1972, 1973, 1975, 1977 by the Lockman Foundation—a Corporation not for profit, La Habra, CA All rights reserved.

This is a work of fiction. Names, characters, businesses, places, events, locales, and incidents are either the products of the author's imagination or used in a fictitious manner. Any resemblance to actual persons, living or dead, or actual events is purely coincidental.

All rights reserved. No part of this publication may be reproduced, distributed, or transmitted in any form or by any means, including photocopying, recording, or other electronic or mechanical methods without the prior written permission of the publisher. For permission requests, solicit the publisher via the address below.

Covenant Books, Inc.
11661 Hwy 707
Murrells Inlet, SC 29576
www.covenantbooks.com

Dedication

First and foremost, I dedicate *Boundary Waters Search and Rescue: Beyond Belief* to the Master Artist. It is my prayer that I have transcribed His inspiration with honor.

Second, I dedicate *Boundary Waters Search and Rescue: Beyond Belief* to a remarkable group of people. To Dan, my husband, and to Wanda, my mother, thank you for being my first readers. Thank you, too, for your encouragement, for proofing my work, and for your comments. To DKBB, my amazing editor, thank you for your patience, your focus, your gentleness, and your time. Thank you, too, for comparing my writing to one of my favorite authors—generous praise that made my heart happy. To my beta readers, Christine Brings, Darcy Buch, Carol Kronholm, and Donna Liljegren, thank you for your faithfulness, for your time, for answering my sometimes-vague questions, for catching gaps, holes, and contradictions in the plot line and for your kindness. Thank you, too, for growing fond of my characters, that means the world to me. I am beyond grateful!

Finally, a huge thank you to my readers. May you be blessed. Enjoy!

In gratitude,
Joy

For Jack and Liz

In Christ alone my hope is found,
He is my light, my strength, my song
This Cornerstone, this solid Ground
Firm through the fiercest drought and storm.
What heights of love, what depths of peace
When fears are stilled, when strivings cease
My Comforter, my All in All
Here in the love of Christ I stand.[i]

TABLE OF CONTENTS

PART 1

By Divine Appointment

CHAPTER 1

〜

THE GATHERING STORM

Listening to the wind howl, Dr. Jack Lockwood was grateful for the solid walls surrounding him. He'd been particular when he'd built his half-log home outside of Ely the year before. Northern Minnesota was no place to dabble with flimsy siding and unreliable heat. As was his habit, he'd done extensive research. Then he'd spent the extra money and installed geothermal heat and electricity powered by sun and wind.

Looking around the room, Jack was pleased with his choices. The generously sized kitchen and the living area with its wood stove flowed together to accommodate gatherings of friends. His study and a full bath shared the front of the house with the dining area. The loft and bath upstairs housed guests—with plenty of room even when his brother's family of six visited. The master suite was at the back of the house and included a library with a sitting area, his bath, and his bedroom. In this area, his private sanctuary, he departed from common sense just enough to include a wood-burning fireplace. He knew that conventional fireplaces sucked up more warm air than they provided, but he just couldn't build a northwoods home without a fireplace that burned real logs. This one was a work of art, constructed with local river rock by a stone mason from Ely. Jack's years in Montana and Colorado had convinced him that the loss of heat was worth the ambiance and smell of a crackling fire. It also helped resale value, especially when it came to city dwellers with romantic notions of moving to the country.

Jack jumped when the two-way radio in the study emitted its distinctive warble. His cell phone sat silent on the desk, but in this remote location the reception could be dicey, especially when the weather was bad.

"Dispatch to Lockwood, over."

Jack wondered at the note of urgency in Dan's tone. It wasn't even 6:00 a.m. and his friend and business partner already had his knickers in a knot about something. "Lockwood here. I'll be leaving shortly." Jack frowned when Dan didn't reply immediately. "Dispatch, did you copy?"

"Yes, I copy." Dan sounded a bit disgusted. "Jack, have you even looked outside since you woke up?"

"Of course I looked outside," Jack sputtered. "I know it's snowing, but this is Minnesota. It snows. I know how to drive in this stuff and Hildy will make it through anything." Hildy—short for Hildegard—was Jack's large four-wheel drive SUV. Outfitted with medical equipment and supplies as well as rescue gear, it had thus far proved adequate for everything Minnesota had thrown at him.

"Trust me when I say it *is* a big deal and it's not just the snow," Dan countered. "The predicted front hit earlier than expected and now it's stalled right over us. Up until a couple of hours ago this stuff was coming down as freezing rain, to the tune of about two inches of solid ice coating everything. Since then we've had about six inches of heavy wet snow, and it's not going to stop anytime soon. Gale force winds are causing white-outs across the entire region, and wind chills into the double-digit below zero range. Trees and power lines are down from here to the Canadian border and south to Duluth. So stay put!"

Jack glanced out the window. It was dark outside—not surprising since sunrise was almost two hours away. "Hang on a sec," he told Dan. Dropping the microphone on the desk, Jack pulled open the front door, couldn't see much through the storm door, so he pulled that open. The raw wind nearly blew him back into the house. Dan was right—the wind was strong and was blowing the snow sideways.

Jack stepped onto the porch, but before he finished his second step, he landed hard on his backside, the composite decking so slippery he couldn't maintain his footing. Crawling back inside, he slammed the door, and returned to the radio. "Okay, it's cold and windy out there and you're right about the ice. If I can get to the garage, I'll take the snowmobile. You're going to need all the help you can get. This is going to be a mess."

"Jack!" Dan exclaimed. "I *need* you to stay where you are. It's already a mess out there and you can't help me by wrapping yourself around a tree and slowly freezing to death."

"I can take care of myself," Jack protested stubbornly, "and..." A loud crash shook the house. He ran for the door, then, his lesson learned, he shuffled across the porch and down the stairs, swinging his flashlight. One of the eighty-year-old pines on his property had fallen victim to the wind and was now on the ground and blocking his access road. Driving out was no longer an option, at least not until he could see to run a chainsaw.

After he got back inside, Jack picked up the microphone again. "Dan, are you still there? I lost one of the big trees by the drive. I can't get to the highway, at least not in Hildy. I'll try to get the snowmobile out once it's light."

Dan said something rude under his breath. "I'm here, and I'm getting really tired of repeating myself! Stay home, Jack. I'm not kidding! The National Guard is helping us get people off the roads and every user in the Boundary Waters[1] that's on the books is out and safe. God help anyone who just wandered in without registering at the ranger station. Law enforcement all over the northern half of the

---

[1] The Boundary Waters Canoe Area Wilderness (BWCA/BWCAW) is a wilderness area located in the northern third of the Superior National Forest in northeastern Minnesota. Over 1,098,000 acres in size, it extends nearly 150 miles along the International Boundary, adjacent to Canada's Quetico and La Verendrye Provincial Parks. The BWCAW contains over 1,200 miles of canoe routes, 12 hiking trails, and over 2,000 designated campsites. The BWCAW allows visitors to canoe, portage, and camp in the spirit of those travelers that came before them centuries ago.

Taken from: https://www.recreation.gov/permits/233396

state have closed roads. Once we get everyone to shelter, all we're going to do is stay inside—insofar as possible—until we can safely do our jobs, which according to the weather service is going to be anywhere from three to four days. Harrison out!"

Jack frowned at the abrupt sign-off. Dan needed his help. However, Jack knew enough about survival in these conditions to think twice about disregarding his friend's advice—order. For that's what it had been, an order from the Police Chief of the small town where Jack lived. Still, Jack wouldn't hesitate to disobey that kind of order if he really believed he could get to his snowmobile, start it, and then find his way safely into town under current conditions. He knew the surrounding country well, but if he lost his way in the snow and wind, he would become one more emergency for Dan and the Guard to cope with on a morning that had already stretched them dangerously thin. He also knew that things had to be bad for Dan to request assistance from the Guard—especially when it was only the third week in November.

After pouring another cup of coffee, Jack turned on the television. Although he had electricity and satellite service, he got nothing but static as he flipped through the 101 channels his carrier claimed to offer. Tossing the remote into a basket, he muttered, "So much for that. Guess it's going to be a reading kind of day." With a start, he realized that he'd already resigned himself to staying where he was until the weather abated. Dan knew Jack's abilities. The fact that he'd told Jack to stay where he was drove home how bad the conditions were outside.

Settling onto the sofa in the study, Jack sipped his coffee, relaxing as he watched the swirling flakes outside the window. It scarcely seemed possible that he was back in the middle of a Minnesota blizzard. He'd never expected to be away from the Midwest for so long, but relocating had become part of the pattern of his professional life.

Things might have been different had Ellie lived. They'd both loved the city of Minneapolis from the time they'd arrived, just after they were married, so that he could finish his medical education. Jack remembered their excitement when he'd completed his residencies in emergency medicine and surgical critical care at the University of

Minnesota and found out that he'd landed his dream job as a trauma surgeon at the Hennepin County Medical Center. He'd happily accepted the position and they'd made plans to stay in Minneapolis.

The two of them settled into a comfortable life and had just purchased their first home when Jack opened their door late one November night and a uniformed officer tore his world apart in the space of five seconds. A fiery crash on an icy roadway had taken Ellie without even giving him the chance to say goodbye. The joy and sense of belonging she'd given him were abruptly and irretrievably gone. He'd coped with her death the only way he knew how. He worked harder and longer than anyone on his team to numb the pain of loss.

Jack's hard work paid off, and less than eighteen months later, he found himself the department head for the entire emergency medical unit of the largest trauma center in the state. Although people tried to convince him that the position was an honor, especially at his young age, he'd hated it from the start. He'd been nothing more than a glorified bureaucrat. Even when he did have patients, there was no getting to know them. His time had become too valuable to 'waste' on single-patient care. Somehow, he'd become a medical demi-god directing others without touching the people he saved. Minneapolis and his position at the Hennepin County Medical Center no longer felt like home.

Leaving behind an empty house filled with happy memories and sad, awkward interactions with Ellie's grieving family, Jack had moved on, accepting a position at the opposite end of the spectrum from a well-staffed, well-equipped urban hospital. While many believed the position was a step down for him, the rural practice on the high plains of Montana had been the perfect place to restore his faith in the practice of medicine while soothing his blistered spirit. Doctor Donald Sloan, his business partner, became a mentor of the finest sort—showing Jack what it meant to have the soul of a true healer.

Their practice spread out over miles, and mornings often found Jack in Don's ancient truck, jouncing over gravel roads to remote farmsteads. House calls were still a way of life in this place. His patients had faces and names. Jack knew their families and they'd welcomed him into their lives as both physician and friend.

It was here that he'd met Dan Harrison, the twice-divorced, dark-haired, dark-eyed chief of police of the small town where their clinic was located and also a Gulf War honed helicopter pilot. Early on, when Jack had needed help transporting a patient from a remote ranch, Dan had flown them both to the nearest hospital. After that, the police chief and the department's helicopter became an integral part of their medical practice, allowing them to respond quickly to emergencies in remote locations and to airlift patients whose illness or injuries required care beyond what they could offer.

Months turned into years and Jack never looked back until the day Donald died. A massive stroke ended the older man's life as he was returning home from church one Sabbath morning. Shortly thereafter, Dan left town, accepting a position as a detective in Denver, Colorado. A new police chief took Dan's place, the freeway came to town, they broke ground for a new clinic affiliated with a large health system, and Jack knew that his time in this place was coming to an end. It wasn't home anymore.

Jack was considering a move back to the Midwest when Dan Harrison had called him. The idea of establishing partnerships between law enforcement and physicians had stuck with him. Urban police departments lost too many people to accidents and assaults because of the time lag between the arrival of officers and the onset of medical help. Now captain at one of the largest precincts in the Denver Metro area, Dan wanted Jack to come to Denver and help him create a combined service, first responder program similar to the one they'd formed in Montana. The way Ellie had died—gravely injured and unable to move in the center of an icy freeway—prompted Jack to accept Dan's offer. The pilot program they developed rapidly expanded throughout the Front Range metro area, the numbers of lives the combined service saved speaking for itself.

Jack and Dan worked tirelessly, hiring and training applicants, including established physicians, veterans on the police force, and those fresh from their medical education or the police academy, then sharing their methodology with other cities. But Jack never gave up working shifts on the streets. He was making a difference saving lives, and a part of him felt like he was honoring his late wife by doing this kind of work.

It was just over two years ago that Jack made what he vowed would be his final cross-country move—the move that brought him home to Minnesota. He was by nature an introvert and the older he got, the harder it became to start fresh in a new location.

Ely, Minnesota, was a town on the edge of the Boundary Waters Canoe Area Wilderness. Between its proximity to a wilderness area regularly used by non-experts in outdoor safety and the extreme and changeable weather northern Minnesota was famous for, Ely often coped with injuries and rescue situations unusual for a small town. The local hospital, local law enforcement, and the United States Forest Service had hired him and Dan to bring their expertise to this remote area to create a combined-service search and rescue team dedicated to the Boundary Waters Wilderness.

Thanks to his time at the Colorado Police Academy, Jack carried a badge. He was experienced in police procedure and proficient in the use of firearms, but before taking on co-leadership of the new program, he'd passed a military-caliber training course in outdoor survival and tracking. Dan, who was now the Chief of Police in Ely, had passed the same course and had also earned his EMT certification.

It was interesting that circumstance had brought Jack full circle just as his second half-century of life began. He was again working in a dream job in Minnesota, this time one that combined his gift for medicine, his passion for rescue, and his love for the outdoors. The work was varied and challenging. His team had rescued families lost deep in the wilderness, treating their injuries as they'd guided them out, or set up an evac via helicopter, float plane, amphibious vehicle, or canoe. When he wasn't on call for search and rescue, he enjoyed his position as an emergency medicine physician and trauma surgeon at Ely Bloomenson Community Hospital (EBCH).

The last two years hadn't given Jack any reason to regret the move—not career-wise or on a personal level. As much as he'd enjoyed the mountains, he loved the north country wilderness and

Lake Superior's rocky north shore even more. In the late summer, Dan had married Beth Erickson, an energetic, silvery-blond sprite with bright blue eyes. A full-blooded Norwegian, she owned a local bakery and coffee shop, the Northern Lights Café, in Ely. Jack had rejoiced with them, glad that Dan had finally found someone to share his life after two disastrous early marriages. In his shallower moments, Jack also appreciated that his friend had chosen someone who knew how to make a great cup of coffee.

The three of them were extremely close. They shared a common love of cross-country skiing, climbing, and canoeing that kept them entertained when they weren't working. Their bond was so strong that Jack seldom felt like a third wheel. While he missed having a romantic relationship with a special someone, it didn't leave him aching as it once had, and he was content.

Relaxing deeper into the down-filled cushions, Jack considered going back to bed, but although it was just after five-thirty in the morning, he wasn't very tired. He routinely got up early, went for a hike, or did a cross-country ski circuit before going into work. Jack took fitness very seriously especially given his age and the physical demands of search and rescue. His appearance was an asset in his chosen field. To people in trouble, he looked old enough to have the knowledge they needed him to have and fit enough to guide them through any physical challenges facing them. Right now, he wanted to do the job he'd trained most of his life for, helping those in need. Yet here he sat, sidelined by the weather and a well-meaning police chief.

Jack was still considering his options for the unexpected, unwelcome day off, when a black, furry form jumped into his lap, nearly spilling his coffee. Setting the mug on the end table, he smiled and scratched the green-eyed cat behind her ears. "Well, good morning to you too, Binx. It looks like we're going to have a quiet day together." Jack swore he saw Binx smile as she turned around in his lap precisely three times, then plopped down with a soft "meow." When she started to purr, Jack's eyelids drooped. It was warm and quiet.

CHAPTER 2

A "CHANCE" MEETING

Jack had no more than closed his eyes when Binx did something strange. Instead of cuddling in for a nice long nap, she sat up alertly in his lap, then jumped to the windowsill. Her ears perked up and she stared through the glass, her eyes wide. Then, before Jack had a chance to look outside to see what had captured her attention, she jumped down and ran to the front door. She was making an odd sound—something closer to a growl than a "meow." It was a decidedly different behavior for her. When he didn't get up, she ran back into the study and batted at his hand. He reached down to pet her, but she dodged away and returned to the front door. Something outside had her interested. Jack looked out into the darkness but couldn't see much thanks to the blowing snow.

When Binx started to paw at the wood door, curiosity got the better of Jack. He got up, put on his moccasin-style slippers over his socks and slid into a lined flannel shirt. There was no way he was facing the weather again wearing only a long-sleeved tee shirt. Opening the door, he turned on the porch light, then gingerly stepped outside. Squinting into the snow, he looked left and right down the porch and then out into the yard, trying to see what had captured his cat's interest. All he could see that was out of the ordinary was a pile of snow a couple of feet in front of the steps. It hadn't been there the last time he'd been outside. Unless it had accumulated on the green metal roof before sliding off, there was no reason for a drift to form in that location, particularly given the wind direction.

Shrugging his shoulders at Mother Nature's caprices, Jack turned to go inside, before the rest of him was as wet as his slippers. Before he took a step, a low moan shattered the pre-dawn darkness, a low moan that came from what he'd just determined was nothing more than a weirdly placed snow drift.

Ignoring his wet feet, Jack took the three steps down from the porch in a single leap and brushed at the drift with bare hands. The wind drove icy pellets of snow into his eyes and he kept blinking to clear them. He intensified his efforts when his half-frozen fingers came in contact with cloth. Almost immediately he uncovered a woman in a black coat lying face down on the ground. She didn't move when he touched her. Wet brown hair streaked with silver lay frozen to the back of her head. He couldn't tell if she was breathing.

After checking her spine and neck, Jack tried to turn her over, but she was stuck, frozen to the ground. He pulled harder and this time succeeded in turning her face up. What he saw unnerved him. The woman had a large purple abrasion on her left temple, the two-inch laceration at its center still dripping blood. Freezing blood saturated the collar and upper front of her coat. Even worse, her hands, white with cold, the nails torn and bloody, were duct taped at the wrists in front of her. Looking around, he wondered what in the world he'd stumbled into—an abduction or assault? Kinky sex gone wrong? Industrial accident?

Shaking his head to dispel the increasingly wild theories fueled by hypothermia, Jack tried to think beyond his growing lethargy. His flannel pants and shirt were soaking wet and freezing to his skin and he couldn't feel anything below his ankles. The few feet back to the house seemed like miles. Why hadn't he put on a jacket and gloves? Or real shoes? Because he hadn't planned on finding a body in his front yard. Was that all this was? Trying to keep his own frigid hands steady, Jack felt for a pulse on the woman's neck, her skin colder than his own to his touch. It took time, but a beat and then two fluttered beneath his fingertips. Spurred on by the knowledge that she was alive, he lifted her stiff form into his arms. Slipping and sliding, he barely made it back to his own front door.

As soon as he was inside, Jack kicked off his frozen slippers, moving as fast as his wet socks, icy feet, and the burden he carried allowed. Given the way he'd found the woman, he knew he needed to involve Dan, but first he had to get her warm. After laying her on the bed and covering her with a quilt, he went into the master bathroom and turned on the taps to draw a bath in his free-standing soaking tub, another luxury he'd vacillated over, one that might now save a life. After setting the water at the right temperature, he left it running, grabbed his medical bag from the locked cabinet in his study, and returned to the bedroom.

Jack was feeling the effects of hypothermia after being outside for less than ten minutes in lightweight clothing. The woman in his bed, who'd been outside for who knows how long, wore jeans, socks, sneakers, and a wool turtleneck over her undergarments and nothing in the way of outerwear but a lightweight coat.

Stripping her of her ice-rimed garments, Jack carried her into the bathroom and laid her gently in the warm water. She slid limply down the sloped back of the tub and had he not been holding her; her head would have slipped beneath the water's surface. After a couple of minutes, she still hadn't moved—hadn't shown any sign of life other than her slow respirations and her skin warming beneath Jack's hands. Her pulse remained thready and faint. Angry bruises, stark yellow, green, and purple, covered her pale skin. None of them were as large as the one on her head save one covering the left side of her rib cage. Her breathing grew labored, loud in the quiet room as she struggled to suck in air. Jack was afraid she was going to die in his arms before he even knew her name.

An hour later, she was still breathing, and her core body temperature was approaching normal. Lifting her out of the cooling water, Jack dried her with a warm towel from the heated rack, then dressed her in a pair of his sweatpants, a sweatshirt, and covered her hands and feet with wool socks. After changing into dry clothes, he examined her, then tucked her back into his bed.

She needed transport to a hospital with CT scan and X-ray equipment. Jack couldn't tell if she had a skull fracture or if she'd broken ribs or if she was bleeding internally. She was in shock, her pupillary response indicated a head injury of some kind, bruises covered most of her body, and frostbite whitened her extremities. She could be in or going into hypovolemic shock. He had no idea how much blood she might have lost prior to collapsing in his front yard. She showed no signs of returning consciousness. Finally, he had no idea who she was, how far she'd walked, what her medical history was, or why her hands had been bound. Jack needed help and he needed it soon.

Resting his hand on the unconscious woman's forehead, Jack reassured her, "You're safe. I'll be right back."

"Lockwood to Dispatch, over." Jack waited through several long seconds before he got a response.

"Dispatch, Harrison here." Dan still sounded peeved.

"Dan, I need you to respond whatever emergency medical services are still running to my place. Let them know they'll have to walk the last twenty-five yards. About an hour ago, I found a woman in my front yard. I have no idea who she is, but she's been out in this mess for a while. She's badly injured and unconscious. I found her with her wrists duct-taped together, so this wasn't an accident. I have a description for you, she's about five foot, six inches tall, 140 to 150 pounds, average build, Caucasian, short graying brown hair, blue eyes, I'd say late forties. Any idea of what kind of ETA I'm looking at?"

Impatience disappearing from his voice, Dan responded, "Jack, that's not going to happen. I'll get her description on the wire, but nothing is moving. The National Guard tried Hummers and snow-cats, but they pulled them all in. Between the ice and zero visibility, we endangered more lives than we saved. We got to everyone stranded on the roads that we knew about, but there's no way I can get anyone to you right now. You're too far out of town. Maybe later this afternoon, if the visibility improves. But she's still one of the lucky ones."

"You want to explain that logic to me or to the woman dying in my bedroom? How is she lucky?" Jack snapped angrily.

"At least she has a doctor caring for her—a really good doctor. I'll get someone to you as soon as I can. Harrison out."

Jack stared at the now-silent radio. He knew that Dan was frustrated by the weather and people who were going without needed help because of it. And his point about the woman in Jack's care being "lucky" was valid. But Jack needed the medical technology he generally had at his beck and call. Thanks to his search and rescue position, he had basic supplies here at the house—oxygen, antibiotics, hydration IVs, some medicine—but he was without imaging equipment which meant he couldn't accurately diagnose any possible internal injuries or even determine for certain whether or not she had a skull fracture.

Like the physicians of earlier eras, Jack could only diagnose using the brain in his head, the report of his five senses and, thanks to portable equipment, evaluate her heart. He'd done a physical exam, treated her frostbite, performed an EKG, and started a saline drip. After hesitating briefly, he'd added a rape kit. She would have to decide whether or not to process the forensic evidence if she regained consciousness, but given the way he'd found her, it was better not to take a chance. Finally, he'd started her on oxygen, hoping to ease her breathing. That was it. He'd rendered the aid he could without knowing more of her medical history. Now all he could do was keep her warm and continue with a supportive care regimen. It had worked for physicians before the advent of modern technology, hopefully it would work for him.

Two hours later, late morning by the clock, it was still almost dark outside. Jack sat in the chair next to the bed, watching his patient. He'd done another EKG an hour ago—she was tacky and her blood pressure was still in the cellar, but she was holding her own, and by that he meant she wasn't getting any worse than bad. She had a five-inch scar down the middle of her chest, meaning she'd had open heart surgery, probably some years in the past, judging by how the scar had faded. Still, any history of heart problems under these circumstances was cause for grave concern.

Jack could hear signs of a fluid buildup in her chest cavity, something that could severely compromise both cardiac and respiratory function. Her breathing had steadily worsened to the point he was now considering inserting a chest tube to ease the strain on her heart and lungs. Normally, he would look at X-rays or the results of a CT scan and her medical history before doing anything, but she was slipping away from him.

Needing to do something to avoid watching her die, Jack took a scalpel from his kit and made a small incision in her chest wall. As blood welled beneath his fingertips, he blotted it with sponges and deepened the incision. She didn't move. His diagnosis was spot on—she'd been bleeding into her chest cavity for some time. The simple procedure took what felt like forever to finish. And even then, Jack wasn't certain how much good it was going to do in the long run. Thanks to the storm, there was no way to determine the full extent of the damage done to her ribs or to the inside of the pleural cavity.

By midnight, Jack was past doing anything other than trying to keep his eyes open. It had been a very long day. He'd eaten a bowl of cold cereal for dinner, washed down by more coffee, and had spent the evening reading and watching over his patient. Her skin was warm to the touch, she was breathing easier, her pupils reacted normally to light, but she showed no signs of consciousness.

When Jack settled back into the bedside chair with his book, Binx curled up in his lap, purring, the sound soothing his jangled spirit. He tried to focus on the words in front of him, but he was just so...so... His head nodded, falling toward his chest, and in the space between one breath and the next, he slept.

CHAPTER 3

IS THIS WHAT DYING FEELS LIKE?

"Cold...so cold. Where...how? Tired...Need to sleep. Is this what dying feels like?" As she drifted, she became more aware and the heavy darkness started to lift. Gasping, she opened her eyes for the first time in what felt like forever.

CHAPTER 4

NO ANSWERS

Jack opened his eyes, blinking in the darkened room. The only light came through the partially open door into the living area. Binx stretched, staring up at him, as if wondering why he was awake at four in the morning. Looking at his patient, he couldn't detect much change in her condition apart from her breathing, that seemed stronger and steadier than before. So why was he awake? Just as he leaned back in his chair and started to relax into sleep, the woman in the bed stirred.

Jolted fully awake by the small sound, Jack set Binx gently on the floor and settled one hip on the edge of his bed. Leaning over his patient, he asked, "Hey, can you hear me?" Nothing happened for a few seconds, then she drew another deep breath and turned her head toward his voice. He took her hand, gently squeezing it. "That's it. Open your eyes. How do you feel?"

"Hurt…Hurts!" she stammered weakly, her eyes still closed.

Jack snapped on the bedside lamp and put his hand on her forehead, avoiding the large dressing covering his precise stitches. "It's okay, lie still and try to open your eyes." The woman's eyelids fluttered for a few seconds, then decided to stay open. Her eyes, sapphire blue, rimmed in golden brown, widened as she focused on him. Looking around the room, fear flooded her gaze.

"Who are you?" she whispered hoarsely. Pulling her hand from his, she stammered, "What…what am I doing here? What's happened to me?" She fell back against the pillows, her energy spent.

Jack removed his hand from her head, and leaned close, his eyes fixed on hers. "Don't be afraid. My name is Jack Lockwood. I'm an Ely physician working in partnership with the Boundary Waters Search and Rescue Unit (BWSRU/BWSR). I found you unconscious in my front yard yesterday morning. The reason you're at my home rather than the hospital is the weather. We're in the middle of a blizzard and all the roads are closed so, as much as I'd like to, I can't get you anywhere but here." He smiled, pulled out his hospital identification so she could look at it, and prayed he didn't look too rumpled or scary.

"What…what's wrong with me?" she gasped. Then looking down at herself, she stammered, "What…what happened to my clothes?"

"You've been hurt, but you're going to be fine. I've treated you for a head injury, chest trauma, and frostbite. You're on oxygen to help you breathe. Your clothes had frozen to your skin by the time I got to you. I had to cut them off in order to get you warm. Things will be easier now that I can just ask you what hurts." Hearing the relief in his own voice, Jack smiled faintly.

Jack's smile brought nothing more than a slow easing of the fear in her eyes, but confusion quickly replaced the fear when he asked, "What's your name? And do you have any drug allergies that I should know about?"

Her baffled expression spilled over into tears. She shook her head. "I…I don't know. Why," she grabbed Jack's arm, "why can't I remember?"

After doing his best to calm her, Jack medicated her, then watched her eyes close and her body relax into sleep. There was nothing more he could tell Dan about her identity or what she was doing out in one of the worst storms to impact Northern Minnesota in years with her hands bound.

Standing up, Jack rolled his tense shoulders and glanced outside. Although it was almost daybreak, it was still pitch dark—what Ellie used to call "boo dark"—thanks to the overcast, blowing snow, and moisture-laden air. The heavy, wet snow was coming down faster than ever. According to Dan, everyone was hunkered down in whatever shelter they had, waiting for the storm to pass through. They were predicting in excess of three feet of snow over three to four days and this was only the beginning of day two. Pinching the bridge of his nose between his fingers, Jack took a steadying breath. He and the stranger in his care were in this for the long haul.

CHAPTER 5

A REAL CONVERSATION

This time, waking up didn't hurt so much. Judging by the fuzzy feeling in her head, Dr. Jack Lockwood of Ely, Minnesota, had given her something stronger than aspirin for pain. It was light outside, meaning she'd slept away the darkness.

A black cat with green eyes jumped from the empty bedside chair to the bed and head bonked her arm, purring the entire time as it curled in beside her. "Wow," she said, "you're a friendly baby." She couldn't help it, a smile tugged at her lips as she watched the cat's antics. It felt like mornings at home.

Jack walked through the bedroom door carrying his third mug of coffee for the morning. After sleeping for several hours, showering and having breakfast, he felt human again. Quickly moving to shoo Binx off the bed, he apologized, "I'm sorry about that. Binx! Get down! Not everyone loves you enough to tolerate tuna breath in the morning."

His patient looked up and to Jack's surprise, she had a blush of color in her cheeks and was smiling. "Please, Dr. Lockwood, don't push her away. This is her home, not mine. What's her name? She's beautiful!"

Jack smiled, watching her scratch Binx's ears. "Her name is Binx, she's the seven-year-old queen of the house and she loves being scratched like that."

"So does mine."

Jack was astonished and encouraged by the change he saw in his patient. A smile lit her pale face and she had beautiful eyes. It was obvious she felt better, shared his love for cats, and, most importantly, had remembered something about herself. "It sounds like you've remembered something. You have a cat?"

She nodded. "Yes, I have a charcoal gray Maine Coon mix with blue eyes named Sierra at home." Her eyes met his with a look of remorse. "I'm sorry about losing it last night. I was pretty out of it. My name's Elizabeth—Liz—Talbot. As for drug allergies, there's just one—I'm allergic to penicillin. I live in Grand Marais, so I can't imagine what I was doing all the way over here, walking around in a snowstorm. I'm so sorry for the trouble."

"It's good to meet you, Ms. Talbot," Jack said, "and please don't apologize. I'm glad I'm able to help. Is there someone we should notify that you're safe? Husband? Family?"

"Call me Liz, please. And to answer your question, no, I live alone. My mom lives in Duluth, but she probably has no idea that I've been missing. Unless," confusion clouded her eyes, "I'm sorry, but what day is it? Mom's planning to come up Thanksgiving morning. Is it still before Thanksgiving? I have no idea—I feel like Ebenezer Scrooge walking up on Christmas."

Smiling, Jack reassured her. "It's Tuesday of Thanksgiving week, so your mom isn't due up here for another two days. Besides, they've closed the roads, so she couldn't start north if she tried. However, if you'd like me to contact her, I'm sure I can get through on my two-way radio."

"Thanks, but that's not necessary. I'll call her later on my cell."

Shaking his head, Jack said, "The entire northern tier of the state is without cell or internet service right now, thanks to the storm. Also, you didn't have a cell phone in your possession when I found you—no purse, no ID, no car keys, nothing. At first, I thought you'd been in an accident or your car slid off the road. That would account for your injuries and, possibly a missing wallet or handbag."

"It sounds like you're second guessing yourself," Liz noted. "I don't remember getting here at all, so your scenario sounds plausible to me."

"Liz, I'm confused about a few things, like how you got here and the way I found you. Do you mind if I ask you a couple of questions?"

Sudden fear clouding her expression, Liz nonetheless nodded in assent. "Ask away."

"What's the last thing you remember before waking up here?" Jack asked quietly.

Frowning, Liz stammered, "I remember um...church on Sunday morning. Pastor Derek preached out of Daniel. I remember thinking Nebuchadnezzar was really dense. I mean, if God's hand wrote a message on a wall for me, I'd sure as heck pay attention. So that was yesterday morning, right? I mean if I'm remembering the sermon from yesterday. No...no, it would be the day before yesterday."

"That's right," Jack agreed, bemused by her biblical commentary. "Let's proceed on the assumption that you're remembering the most recent service. It's Tuesday morning now, I found you at about six a.m. yesterday and you remember being in church on Sunday morning. Good. What else do you remember? What did you do after church?"

Closing her eyes, Liz murmured, "I must have gone home. No that's not right. I went out with a friend for coffee, then...then..." Her eyes lit up with triumph. "*Then* I taught a Hardanger class at the North House Folk School[2]. Yes, I started the class Saturday and we finished up on Sunday. That's it, that's what I was doing!" She sat up straight and touched Jack's hand. "Thank you for helping me remember!"

Then, wincing, Liz pressed one hand to the dressing on her head and the other to her rib cage. "Ouch! Remind me not to move like that again."

Jack took his stethoscope from the bedside table. After listening to Liz's heart and her breathing, he looked at her apologetically. "I'm sorry, we should hold off on more questions until later. I'll leave you

---

2 North House Folk School in Grand Marais, Minnesota, is a non-profit educational organization committed to enriching lives and building community through the teaching of traditional northern crafts.

31

alone for a bit, so you can get more rest." He picked up the syringe that had been lying next to the stethoscope. "This will help with the pain. It will also make you a bit sleepy, which is good."

Liz pushed Jack's hand away. "No! I'm fine. I just moved too fast." She must have seen the uncertainty in his eyes because she took his hand and explained, "Dr. Lockwood, I need to know what happened to me. I've lost hours out of my life, I feel like I've been beaten up by someone who's pretty much an expert at beating people up, and just looking at you, I know there's more to all this than what you're telling me. So let's keep going, please."

"Liz, please call me Jack, and I understand what you're saying. What *you* need to understand is that it was a close thing. I nearly lost you yesterday. If you're feeling up to doing this, we can keep going. Just tell me if it gets to be too much."

Jack settled himself back in the chair and continued, "So you taught a class. What time do classes typically end on a Sunday?"

Liz thought for a moment, then answered, "I think the class was scheduled from one to five. After class ends it takes me about a half hour to say my goodbyes and pack up. So it was probably about five-thirty on Sunday afternoon by the time I left for home."

When the furrow between Liz's brows deepened, Jack decided to take a step back to less worrisome ground. "What did you teach and how did it go? Did you have fun?"

Liz smiled. "I always have fun when I teach and this time was really special. It was a parent-child class, one generation getting the next involved in handwork. Everyone in the room had ancestral connections to the Scandinavian countries and since Hardanger embroidery originated in Norway, it was perfect."

Her smile fading, Liz looked troubled. "But what happened to me after class that day or sometime later that night? I remember teaching, I remember everyone packing up and saying goodbye. They asked me about offering an intermediate class in the spring, but Jack," her voice shook, "I don't remember getting home."

Jack leaned closer and took her hand, hoping to anchor her in the present as they talked about the recent past. "Liz, I don't think you got home, or if you did, you didn't stay home. I don't want to frighten you more than you already are, but I don't think you had an accident. Or at least not just an accident. When I found you, your wrists were bound with tape. I think someone took you by force before you got home or from your home, then something happened and you ended up outside, alone, just as the storm really got a foothold on the area. I can't imagine what you went through, dressed like you were with no use of your hands."

Liz just stared at him with her mouth slightly open, saying nothing. After several seconds, Jack got to his feet. "Let's take a break. I'm going to radio Dan Harrison, Ely's chief of police, and update him with what we know. Then I'll bring you something to eat. After that you should rest for a while."

Seeing a look of protest form on her face, Jack held up his hand. "Liz, please, think about how you're feeling right now. I can see that your pain is worse and that you're struggling to stay awake. I know that remembering is important, but, right now, listening to your body is more important. Neither of us are going anywhere, so it's time to take care of you. When you wake up, we'll talk more."

Liz nodded slowly, rubbing her injured temple. "Okay, I guess. I'm not sure I can tell you much more anyway. I'm not hungry, but I'll try to get something down. Mostly I'm cold, scared, and tired. And you're right about the pain."

Her eyes brimming with unshed tears, Liz continued, "Jack, I'm a middle-aged artist and teacher from small town Minnesota. I'm not wealthy, so why would anyone be interested in kidnapping me? Isn't that what we're talking about here?"

Sudden recognition flashed through Jack. Now he understood why Liz had looked vaguely familiar when he first saw her face. "Wait, you're Liz Talbot? The textile artist? *The* Elizabeth Talbot? Your landscapes are carried by galleries all over the state, right?"

Liz seemed bewildered by this turn in the conversation. Wiping her eyes, she acknowledged, "Yes, that's me. You know my work?"

Jack felt a little foolish, he was this woman's physician, not a groupie. Still, he nodded. "Know it, admire it, and have purchased several pieces of it; like the one hanging about a foot above your head. Your Lake Superior scenes are my favorites—they're unique, and the color and texture of the threads and beads mimic the colors and textures in nature."

Blushing, Liz acknowledged his words, "That's one of the nicest compliments I've ever received. Thank you! Have we met before?"

"Yes, once, at a gallery reception in Grand Marais about a year ago. That's why you looked familiar to me, but I didn't know you taught classes at the North House." Jack grinned boyishly. "I'll have to try one."

Liz apologized, "I'm sorry I don't remember meeting you. As for the class, you'd be welcome as my guest." She smiled and touched the dressing on her head. "I already know you're good with a needle and thread. I teach several sessions every season. Mostly different kinds of bead work and contemporary embroidery. Ethnic embroidery is another passion of mine, so I thought I'd try something new with last weekend's class to see if there was any interest."

CHAPTER 6

DANGER WITH SKIN ON

It was after midnight—very early Wednesday morning—and the storm showed no signs of abating. Over three feet of snow had fallen and, if anything, the wind was stronger than before. Jack was exhausted but wide awake. After Liz had eaten a bit of soup and a part of a piece of toast, he'd medicated her and she'd gone to sleep. Now, it was his turn to get some sleep. He'd left Liz and Binx curled up in his bed and stretched out on the living room sofa. Although he was comfortable, he was having a difficult time shutting down.

Closing his eyes, Jack tried to slow his racing thoughts. A mere forty-eight hours before, his schedule for the week had been set. Work, rest, time with friends, and enjoying a Thanksgiving feast with the Harrisons. Liz Talbot had been nothing more to him than a signature on a work of art. Now it was uncertain whether or not he'd be able to leave the house by tomorrow and Liz Talbot lay in his bed, dependent on his expertise to help her recover from injuries she didn't remember getting. Dan had feelers out all over the state, hoping to find a reason for what had happened—something that would explain how a well-respected, well-liked artist ended up miles from home, injured and suffering from exposure.

Thankfully, Liz seemed to be on the mend, but she still found it difficult to move on her own. Earlier in the day, Jack had helped her to the bathroom. After using the facilities and washing up, she'd made it back to bed under her own power—barely. Her EKG trac-

35

ing had returned to normal, and she was no longer on intravenous fluids. Yet Jack still believed she belonged in a hospital, at least until imaging could confirm that she didn't have a skull fracture and show him the extent of damage to her chest and rib cage. He didn't want to remove the chest tube until he could be certain that the bleeding into her pleural cavity had stopped.

The situation was complicated by the increasing closeness he felt to Liz. He was her physician and he needed to remain detached, especially when she was in his home and in his bed. The blurring of boundaries was probably normal given the situation, but it was making him very uncomfortable. No one needed to tell him he was perilously close to lawsuit territory if something went wrong while she was in his care. Yet, every time she smiled at him or he touched her hand, he felt anything but detached. He enjoyed being around her and that made cool professionalism a challenge.

The wind rattled the windowpanes, the sound loud and unsettling in the post-midnight hour. Then Jack thought he heard something move in the bedroom. He sat up, wondering if Liz had gotten out of bed and if she needed help. A few seconds later, Binx came rocketing into the room, sat at his feet and meowed plaintively before bouncing into his lap. Although he'd relaxed a little when he saw the cat, Jack couldn't shake the feeling that something was amiss, especially when Binx jumped back to the floor without settling down. When he tried to pet her, she sidestepped his hand and sat down just out of reach, meowing noisily. Her behavior was the same as on the morning he'd found Liz. Binx was trying to tell him that something was wrong, he was sure of it. He didn't wait any longer. Getting to his feet, he went to check on Liz.

It was dark in the bedroom and when Jack stepped through the door, a blast of cold air hit him in the face. Puzzled, he reached for the light switch, but his hand never connected. He turned when Liz screamed his name but didn't take a step before someone struck him on the forehead—hard—with what felt like the butt end of a gun. Staggering, he battled to stay conscious. Backing into a bookcase, he was still trying to remain upright when a hissing mass of black fur, teeth, and sharp claws hurtled past him. Binx landed, claws flying, on a shadowy intruder holding a struggling Liz. There was a thump as the prowler let go of Liz, grabbed the angry cat and threw her against a wall, then dove through the open French doors that led out to a snow-drifted courtyard.

Jack retrieved his 9mm service weapon from the lock box on the shelf, loaded the magazine and fired two shots through the open doorway. He squinted, trying to see if he'd hit the trespasser, but visibility was so limited and his own vision so compromised by blood in his eyes and dizziness that he couldn't see more than a foot into the night.

A cross between a whine and meow made him look down. Binx was sitting at his feet holding up her right front leg which hung at an abnormal angle. Jack stooped down to pick her up, but she limped under the bed, putting no weight on her injured limb.

Vertigo swept over Jack in waves as he slammed the doors, unable to secure them because of the smashed lock. Stumbling over to a panel on the wall, he flipped another switch. "Why in the name of all that's holy, didn't I arm the alarm systems hours ago?" he wondered fuzzily. It didn't matter, all that mattered now was getting to Liz. He spun around toward the bed and took a single step. That was a mistake. The world went black around him as he crumpled to the floor.

Jack's first thought was that he'd fallen asleep. Slowly he became aware of two things: First of all, he was cold, really cold and second of all, someone was calling his name. Then he figured out that he was flat on his back on the floor. Opening his eyes, he sat up abruptly, regretting that action before he'd finished levering himself into a seated position. Taking the bloody, wet towel that Liz held, he pressed it against the painful, heavily-bleeding lump on his head and concentrated on not throwing up.

"Jack, are you okay? I saw how hard he hit you. You've been out for almost ten minutes." Liz waved at his cell phone, now on the floor beside her. "I tried calling 911 but there's no service."

"Uh, yeah, I know," Jack managed, just before true awareness battered him with memories of the last few minutes before he'd passed out. He realized that the lights were now on in the room and Liz was kneeling beside him. She was pale, but composed, staring at him with worry in her expressive eyes. Throwing up faded in importance. Getting to his knees, Jack dropped the towel and put his arms around Liz. In that moment, he didn't care about lawsuits or professionalism. "Are *you* okay, Liz? Did he hurt you?"

"Nothing serious. I just amassed a few more bruises and he scared the tar out of me. I'm sure it was a he—tall, thin, and strong. I got a glimpse of his face. He had a gun, but it must have jammed when he tried to shoot you. I thought," terror flitted across Liz's face, before she continued, "well, never mind. The shot never happened, and he clobbered you with the gun before grabbing me again. But," she looked confused, "uh, then something happened and the next thing I knew, he let go of me and headed for the door. After he left, I turned on the lights and found you and your gun.

"A few minutes ago, I heard him messing with the doors again. The guy's a coward, all it took were the alarms going off to make him turn tail and run. I managed to get over to the door and fire a shot. I think I hit him in the leg, but he took off on a snowmobile before I could be sure." Liz smiled wanly and held up Jack's pistol. "I have a similar model at home.

"Thankfully, I figured out how to shut off the alarms. But what about you? You're bleeding above your right eye and you're gonna have a bruise that rivals mine." Liz touched Jack's head gently, barely pausing before adding, "Tell me what I should do."

Jack managed a smile and chuckled, "Take a breath." He watched Liz blink in surprise, but the worry in her eyes didn't go away. He needed to touch her in the worst way, to do something to ease the strain in her expression. Caressing her cheek with his fingertips, he murmured, "That's better. Everything's okay, Liz. Thank you for scaring off whoever that was. As for me, my head hurts, but it can't be too bad because I remember what happened."

His smile faded abruptly. "Wait. Binx! Have you seen Binx? She took off under the bed right before I passed out. One of her front legs looked like it had been broken when the guy threw her against the wall."

"Threw her? Against the wall!" Liz exclaimed in a hard voice.

"Yeah. After the guy hit me, Binx landed on him with claws flying, and probably saved us both. The guy let go of you, grabbed Binx and threw her. That gave me time to figure out I wasn't in Kansas anymore and fire off a couple of rounds."

"I should've aimed for his privates," Liz muttered angrily. Then she turned her anxious gaze on Jack. "I haven't seen Binx, but then again I haven't been looking."

Jack needed to radio Dan and let him know what had happened and that they were okay. Before he did that, he needed to check on Binx. He looked under the bed and after a few seconds gently pulled the black cat from her hiding place.

CHAPTER 7

RESCUE

Liz once again rested in Jack's bed where he'd put her, not moving very much because she hurt. She was learning that, like most of the best doctors, he excelled at reading her body language. The problem was, she was every bit as worried about him as he was about her. He'd received a blow to the head that would land most people in the Emergency Room yet he'd once again examined and medicated her, then insisted she rest.

Watching Jack through half-open eyes, Liz tried to figure out exactly what kind of man her rescuer was, apart from determined. She was having trouble pegging his age. He was tall and well built, dressed casually in jeans and a black pullover sweater. She tried not to notice that his body certainly did denim justice, or that his ring finger was bare. His face was largely unlined, his light blue eyes were clear, but numerous silver strands glinted in his brown, wavy hair. He obviously knew his profession and not just the technical side, but the far more nuanced skill of putting his patients at ease so, clearly not a beginner. Late forties? Maybe early fifties?

Liz's eyes widened in surprise and alarm when Jack gave Binx a shot, holding her in his arms afterward. "What are you doing?" she asked. "Was she that badly hurt?"

Jack smiled. "Relax, Liz. I'm just going to set her leg and anesthetizing her is the best thing for both of us, since telling a cat to 'hold still' is generally an exercise in futility."

"But...but you're a people doctor, not a vet." Liz cringed at her statement of the obvious, Jack probably thought she was an idiot, but she was genuinely confused.

This time Jack laughed aloud. "I am indeed. However, I have no idea how long it's going to be before we get out of here and Binx is in a lot of pain because of that leg."

Putting the sleeping cat on a towel on the library table, Jack left the room. He quickly returned with some plaster-impregnated strips of cloth and a basin of warm water. Before long, he'd set the bone and immobilized Binx's injured leg in a cast. Laying the cat gently in Liz's arms, he added, "And as you can see, some skills are transferable. I promise I'll take her to her vet as soon as I can, just to make certain I did right by my girl."

"Show off," Liz teased. Then she gently touched the swollen, oozing bump on Jack's forehead. "What about doctoring yourself, Doctor? That doesn't look so good, in fact, I think you're going to need stitches."

"Not badly enough to put them in myself," Jack replied, shuddering a little. "But to that point, *Dr.* Talbot, excuse me for a moment."

Liz closed her eyes after he left the room and scratched Binx gently. You could tell a lot about someone by the way they treated others. Jack had looked after her and after his cat before dealing with his own discomfort, and, judging by the way he returned her teasing, he didn't take himself too seriously. He was kind, and clearly able to cope with unforeseen circumstances.

God had certainly been working overtime, putting her in Jack's care when she was in danger of dying.

⁓

It was just getting light outside when Jack returned to the room carrying two cups of coffee, the cut on his head sealed with steri-strips. "I got through to Dan and barricaded those doors as best I could. Until the lock's replaced, it's not going to keep anyone out who's determined to get in."

Jack collapsed heavily in the chair by the bed, his gun within easy reach. He gave Liz the coffee with milk he'd brought for her. "Good morning, again." Arching his brow, he added dryly, "Do I know how to show a girl a good time, or what?"

Liz laughed, then put a hand on her rib cage. "Ow! It hurts to laugh."

"Then don't laugh," Jack said, his tone serious, but his smile still firmly in place. He felt strange, almost lightheaded. It had been a bizarre couple of days. Right now all he wanted to do was to relax as much as was possible under the circumstances—bad guys still out there, injured woman still in his bed, cavalry still several miles away and snowbound, a groggy Binx clearly unhappy with him, and his head still pounding in merciless tempo with each beat of his heart.

"That must be why they made you a doctor, you're brilliant!" Liz took his hand. "Jack, truly, you don't look so good. What did Dan say?"

"The same thing he's been saying all along, that he'll get someone out here as soon as he can. The storm system's moving off, so that should be sooner rather than later. He put out a BOLO using your description, but it's pretty generic. Besides, if this guy's after you, he's not going far." Jack put his chin in his hand. "Liz, none of this makes sense, Dan can't find a clue as to why anyone would be after you."

"I think he will when the information flow normalizes," Liz said, "but we don't have to wait, I think I might know what this is about. Last night seems to have unscrambled a few brain cells."

"You've remembered something?" Ignoring the throbbing in his head, Jack sat up straight. "What?"

"I remember leaving the North House on Sunday and stopping for dinner with a friend. After that I headed home," Liz continued, "by that time, the rain had turned to ice. It was dark and pretty late when I got back to the house, and there was a lot of slush on the windshield. I pulled into the garage and had just gotten out of the car when someone grabbed me from behind. Before I could move or scream, they put a funky-smelling cloth over my face. That's all I remember for a while.

"When I came to, I was in the trunk of a moving car—it took me a few minutes to figure that one out. They'd tossed my purse and craft bag in beside me and my wrists were like you found them, taped together. I couldn't hold myself steady and bounced around as the car slid from side to side. That explains all the bruises and why I hurt so much. It was an older model car and it didn't have the egress handle in the trunk that the newer cars have. I tried to get to my cell phone, but I couldn't manage it.

"We must have been traveling for something over an hour, when I felt the car start to skid. It left the road, turned over, landed back on its wheels, and then there was a crash, and everything went black. I don't know how long I was out, but when I came to, my head was bleeding, it hurt to breathe, and I was freezing. The trunk lid had sprung open so I got out of there. The car was pretty much embedded in a big pine tree. There were two dead guys, or so I thought, in the front seat. I didn't stop to check, I just ran. I had no idea where I was, and it was so icy I kept falling. Then I thought I saw some lights back in the woods. I don't remember much more, but I guess that's how I ended up in your front yard."

Jack shook his head; it was a miracle she'd survived. "Liz, I'm so sorry. That's the stuff of nightmares, and it explains how I found you, but it still doesn't answer the why. Why you?"

Taking a deep breath, Liz explained, "Jack, I *am* a small-town artist and teacher, but last August I was in the right place at the wrong time. I was teaching at the Needlework Guild regional seminar in Minneapolis. I'd had dinner downtown and was walking back to my car. It was late, and while the sidewalks were well lit and people were still out and about, there were a lot of shadows. I heard something and looked up just in time to witness a shooting in an alley. I ran into a hotel to get out of sight and called 911. Fast forward a few months, and now I'm both a small-town artist and an eyewitness scheduled to be called in the January murder trial of a rather famous drug-cartel-connected kingpin named Eduard Reynoso."

Silence fell when Liz stopped talking. Jack tried to assimilate all she'd said. Even living and working on the opposite end of the state, he'd heard of the Reynoso case. If what she surmised was happening was indeed happening, this nightmare was far from over for her. He'd worked with the police long enough to know these kinds of predators usually had enough money and power at their command to do any job they wanted done. Afraid for her, he frowned, thinking of something odd. "Why aren't you in some kind of witness protection program or at least under police guard of some kind?"

Liz shrugged. "I thought I'd gotten out of there without being seen, but judging from what's happened, I may have been wrong. That means everyone was wrong—me, the police, the US attorney—everyone. But Jack," Liz took his hand and, curling her fingers around his, she said, "you need to understand that it was my choice to come home last summer. We did talk about protection, security, and the just-in-case scenario at the time, but I live hours from where I'd witnessed the crime and I thought I was safe. And it's been three months, so I don't even know for sure if I'm right about any of this. In any case, after the conference, I didn't think twice about coming home and resuming my life."

"And now?" Jack asked quietly, still holding tightly to her hand.

"I don't know. It's one thing to make decisions for me, but this has spilled over into your life because you helped me. You're hurt," Liz stroked the sleeping Binx, "poor kitty hero Binx is hurt and it's all because of me. I guess once we're able to leave the house we'll have to see if the men who did this are still alive. I want to talk to the police—maybe your colleague Dan—and the US attorney on the Reynoso case. I want to make certain you're safe. You risked your life to save mine, even if you didn't know it at the time."

Both of them jumped when someone started pounding on the front door. For a split-second Jack wondered if a hail of bullets would be next, but then common sense prevailed. Bad guys seldom knocked. Getting up, he took his gun from the night table, handed it to Liz and said, "Just in case these are bad guys with a weird sense of humor, stay here!"

Apparently, following orders, even well-intentioned ones, wasn't among Liz's talents. Slowly getting to her feet, she shook her head. "No way. I'll stay behind you, but you're not going out there alone."

CHAPTER 8

A TIME TO HEAL

By the time Jack settled down to rest again, he was in his own bed. It was once again after midnight—early morning on Thanksgiving Day. Liz was safely ensconced in a room at EBCH, under another doctor's care and police protection. One of the first things Jack had done when he got to the hospital that morning was to ask a colleague to take over Liz's care. After the last four days, he was too close to her to manage the level of clinical detachment ethics demanded.

The X-rays and CT scans done earlier in the day were negative for a skull fracture but had revealed one broken and two cracked ribs on Liz's left side. The bleeding into her chest cavity had stopped so her doctor had removed the chest tube. The rape kit was negative for DNA other than Liz's. After hearing her story, Jack had expected that, but he was still relieved.

Liz had unhappily agreed to spend the night in the hospital after Dan assured her that her cat was safe in her neighbor's care.

A police escort was also a condition of Jack's return to his home. Officer Stan Brings was with Jack for the duration, or at least until they decided on a course of action. Jack knew Stan well, as Jack was the one who'd selected the veteran officer for a coveted slot on one of the BWSR teams. Apart from Stan's qualifications, which were excellent, Jack knew that Stan and his wife Joanne were struggling with money after they'd had to place his parents in an assisted living facility. The on-call search and rescue position paid a premium over and above Stan's normal salary. It also kept a well-qualified officer from leaving the small town in search of better pay. Jack considered Stan a good friend and was glad he was the one Dan had chosen for guard duty.

Officers on snowmobiles had found the scene of the accident Liz had described, a scant mile up County Road 1 from Jack's home. They'd found a male, several days dead, in the driver's seat and evidence that a second person had been in the passenger seat. That person had disappeared, and the storm had obliterated any clues they might have used to track him. Right now, the working theory was that whoever had walked away from the crash was the same person who had broken in on Jack and Liz the night before. Despite a widening search pattern, they'd found no trace of him.

While Jack was undergoing his own diagnostics on the head trauma he'd sustained during the break in, Dan had arranged to have the broken door at Jack's house fixed and new locks installed. When Dan had returned to the hospital that afternoon, he'd fixed Jack with a withering look and muttered something about the next time Jack forgot to arm the alarm systems at the house, he would have something more to worry about than bad guys with jammed pistols.

Unable to rest, Jack sat up and put his head in his hands. Even with Stan in the other room and Binx asleep on the other side of the bed, the house felt empty. Jack hadn't realized just how attracted he was to Liz, until he'd said good night to her several hours earlier. This was no longer about comforting her, helping her to recover, or easing her fear. It had been a long time, but he still recognized the pull of plain old curl-his-toes attraction. She intrigued him—she was funny, smart, close to his own age, and possessed of a creative soul. Jack remembered her gentle manner and touch, yet she hadn't hesitated to take action to protect both of them.

Jack knew virtually nothing about Liz other than her work as an artist, the fact that she had a mother living in Duluth, that she knew how to handle a gun, and that she was single. They hadn't had time to ask the normal questions getting to know one another usually involved, such as "Where did you go to school?" "Where do you live?" "Why northern Minnesota?" and "What kind of pizza do you like?" He had to smile. He'd mentioned that same thought to her before he'd left the hospital and her response had been, "University of Minnesota." "Grand Marais." "Why not?" and "Anything but salty little fishes." So no secrets, well, except for the doozy about being an eyewitness in a drug cartel murder case. Yet calling that a secret wasn't fair to her. They hardly knew each other and she hadn't done it purposefully.

Apart from the close call with Liz's life, what frustrated Jack was that he wanted the woman he was coming to know to be a part of his life for the foreseeable future—an uninjured, unencumbered, not-his-patient version of Liz. Years had gone by since Ellie's death, but apart from a year-long relationship while he was in Denver, there'd been no one serious. He'd dated on occasion, but there'd been no sparks, no real connection with anyone. Then he'd found Liz, a woman who, up until a few hours ago, had been his patient. A woman who was neck deep in the worst kind of trouble. He shook his head in disgust. His timing stunk.

Starting as his cell phone buzzed for the first time in several days, Jack gazed at it for a moment before answering, "Hello."

"Jack, it's Dan, sorry to wake you."

"You didn't. I'm wired and Stan refuses to make me a cup of warm milk with nutmeg sprinkles in it."

Dan chuckled. "Sorry about that. I just wanted to let you know we found the other guy, dead, with a gunshot wound in his leg. He made it as far as Jarvinen's Auto Body on the edge of town. He broke into one of the sheds on the property, then passed out, probably from blood loss. He died of exposure."

Jack breathed freely for what felt like the first time in hours. "That's good news, right? The fact he didn't make it?"

"Well, it wasn't good news for *him*, but yes, that probably means Liz is safe for the moment. The problem is, we have no idea who else knows her identity, her whereabouts, or even what this is all about. Since neither of the guys who died were known associates of Reynoso, we can't just assume they were doing his dirty work." Dan paused, then added, "Jack, be careful with this one."

"You may not be able to assume the obvious, but I can," Jack said acerbically. "And what do you mean by telling me to 'be careful'? I'm not the one at risk here."

"That all depends on how you define 'at risk.' I spent most of the day with the two of you. You care about her." Dan made it a statement, not a question.

"So? I'm her physician, or at least I was until earlier today, I'm *supposed* to care about her. And in a weird reversal of how things generally work, she saved my life. So yeah, you're right, I do care about her. What's the big deal, anyway?" Something in this conversation was making Jack feel oddly defensive.

"You saved her life, too," Dan reminded him, "and that's not what I'm talking about. You care for her in more than a professional or 'I'm grateful' sense. I've known you long enough to read you and all *I'm* saying is be careful. I don't want to see you hurt."

Jack's ire faded. Dan had seen what Jack had missed until about ten minutes ago, at least in its fullness. Rubbing his forehead, Jack responded in a more reasonable tone of voice, "You're right, but I don't think I have much choice. It's been a long time, yet I remember the rudiments well enough to know what I'm feeling. I'm not going to abandon Liz because of what *might* happen to me. I know Reynoso and his cronies will try again. Maybe I can help."

"Or maybe you can get yourself killed," Dan responded flatly.

Silence followed Dan's statement. Neither friend knew what to say. That Dan spoke the truth was not in question. That Jack had made up his mind was also not in question. Finally, Dan relented. "They're releasing Liz from the hospital this afternoon. If you're up to it, I'll let Jerry Simmons, the officer stationed on her room, go when you arrive. Beth and I are expecting you and Liz for Thanksgiving dinner around three. Just so you know we cleared that with her. Given the storm, and uh, other events, she persuaded her mom to stay home. Liz did ask me to ask you if you had another set of sweats she could borrow and if you would please bring any clothing you didn't cut off of her to the hospital with you."

Relief swept over Jack. He hated being at odds with Dan over anything, they were too close both as friends and business partners. He managed a chuckle. I guess I deserve that, and yes, I will. Harrison…" Jack hesitated, trying to find the words.

"I know, Jack. I've got your back, and Liz's too. We'll get through this." Dan acknowledged the unspoken between them.

"Thanks. For everything." Jack ended the call.

CHAPTER 9

───────────────✳───────────────

A THANKSGIVING TO REMEMBER

Thanksgiving with the Harrisons was a thing of beauty. Food, friendship, warm hospitality, and, finally, time to relax in safety. Rather than show up with more of his oversized—for her—casual attire for Liz to wear, Jack had taken the time to stop and buy her a sapphire blue wool dress and the accompanying finery. The color had reminded him of her eyes. He'd called in a favor with a friend who'd opened her store just for him and who'd helped him with the sizes. Liz's response made him happy he'd done it. She looked lovely and if you looked past the bandage on her head and the way she moved, almost normal.

They'd enjoyed most of the evening immensely, at least until Liz broached the subject of going home to Grand Marais. Jack had managed to stay civil until he and Liz said their goodnights to the Harrisons, but the drive back to his place started with an argument and ended in icy silence.

Once inside his house, Jack took Liz's coat without a word. After hanging it in the front closet, he turned his back on her and stalked into the kitchen. She'd clearly lost her mind. More than that she was stubborn and her attitude about all this was making him nuts.

Liz touched his shoulder. "Jack, stop it! If you're going to act like this, I'm going back to the Harrisons until you're ready to stop sulking. They did invite me, you know."

Jack kept his back to Liz. "Fine, go back to their place," he snapped in a perfect imitation of a peeved seven-year-old. "Maybe they can talk some sense into you. Take my coat, it's warmer than yours, and it's a long walk."

Jack felt rather than heard her leave the room. He thought about following her, but he couldn't let their argument go. Yes, she had a right to make her own decisions, but he'd labored for hours to save her life and now she was throwing it away.

Listening for a moment, Jack heard nothing—no movement, no indication that Liz was coming back to try again, nothing. Maybe she was calling the Harrisons right now, asking for a ride back to their place. The thought of involving Dan and Beth in another argument pushed Jack into giving up his passive-aggressive snit in favor of trying to get through to Liz one more time.

Liz wasn't in the kitchen or in the living room. The front door remained tightly closed. Jack walked into the bedroom and found her curled up on one of the recliners in the library area. She was holding Binx and crying softly. Binx was trying to lick the tears from her face and when he appeared, she let out a low, protective growl.

Jack crouched down and brushed Liz's hair away from her face. "I'm sorry for being a jerk. You don't deserve that."

Liz sniffed but didn't look up. "You're right, I don't."

Swallowing the sarcastic rejoinder on the tip of his tongue, Jack said, "I really am sorry. Even the cat knows I was wrong to respond like that, but I still don't understand. Is it me? I've recused myself as your physician, but if…"

A sudden thought crossed Jack's mind, scaring him. Taking Liz's hand, he whispered, "Lord, am I that stupid? Liz, is there someone else?"

Finally lifting her eyes, Liz met his gaze. "Yes, it's you, Jack, and me, but it's not what you seem to be thinking." She squeezed his hand. "You're not stupid and there's no one else. There's been no one serious since Eric died. I feel the same connection between us, and I'd like nothing more than to see if we could have something together. You're smart, kind, and underneath all that doctor armor I think you might have a great sense of humor. So yes, I care for you. That's why

I'm here in the first place rather than at the Harrisons'. That doesn't change the fact that there's still something we need to talk about."

Jack knew Eric was her late husband. From what Liz had said earlier in the day, she'd been a widow for some time. The rest of her last statement made him feel pretty good too, so why was she being so intransigent about this whole thing?

"We were talking about it until, well, until…" Jack didn't know how to finish the sentence.

"Until I disagreed with you about what happens next. Then you shut down," Liz finished his sentence for him.

Forcing himself to stay calm, Jack said, "Look, I know we haven't known each other long, and I've no right to tell you what to do, but what did I suggest that was so wrong? Doesn't it make sense that you stay here until the trial? I have plenty of room and they know where you live. They know you're vulnerable."

"They know where you live too," Liz shot back. Then, lowering her voice, she continued, "Jack, I hate sniping at each other like this. The truth is, we don't know if anyone knows anything since the two guys that came after me are dead.

"Also, you need to understand something. If you can't go to work, you have a fallback position," Liz explained. "You work for the hospital and the Federal government. You have paid time off, paid disability, paid health insurance, a retirement plan, and life insurance. If you aren't able to get to the hospital to do your rounds, someone else does them. If you can't go out on a rescue operation, another physician takes your place.

"I work for a company with one employee—me. Yes, I have money from Eric's life insurance and in my savings, but that's my retirement and safety net. If I don't work, I don't make money, money that I need to pay my bills, maintain my car, and do the upkeep on my home. My clients don't get their commissions and I lose business, I can't send out standing orders and I lose more business. When I'm not home I can't feed or play with my cat, and…"

"I told you we can go get the cat," Jack interrupted.

"And once again, you miss the point of my elegant, long-winded speech. Jack, I can't just sit around here waiting for something to happen while my business goes down the tubes and I ignore my responsibilities." Liz sighed. "As for you, if, and I repeat, *if* the bad guys really know where I am and are out to get me, I don't want you in the line of fire." Liz touched the stitches above his eyebrow. "Helping me has already cost you too much."

"No, Liz, it hasn't," Jack insisted. "It's *you* who's paying the price for doing the right thing. *You're* the one who nearly died, but I think I'm finally starting to understand something. Staying here and putting your life on hold gives them the win. Am I right?"

Liz nodded. "Yes, plus all the other things. I don't want you hurt because of me."

"So you're going back to Grand Marais tomorrow, just as you and Dan discussed?"

"If he can arrange everything, yes. That's what I need to do."

"And that leaves us—us as in you and me—where?"

"I… I guess, for now anyway, it would be better for you to stay away," Liz said miserably.

"And that's okay with you?" Jack pressed.

"What do you mean?" Liz refused to meet his gaze.

Leaning in, Jack forced eye contact with her. "Liz, that gives them the same win that you claim to be unwilling to concede. Don't you see? By allowing them to come between us, you're effectively isolating yourself and giving up on something that could be, something that *is*, important. You know, from bitter experience, that tomorrow is never guaranteed." Jack cupped her chin in his palm, lifted her face and kissed her gently. He barely hesitated before kissing her again, this time more seriously. The touch of her lips moving beneath his felt so right.

Liz touched his cheek gently. "You're not playing fair, Jack, and I can't let you do this."

"You're not 'letting me' do anything," Jack countered. "I'm a big boy and just like you, I've decided what I need to do. What kind of man would I be if I walked away now, when everything inside me is screaming that leaving you is the wrong choice? You've asked me to let you make your own decisions, based upon what you believe to be right. Allow me that same privilege." He put his arms around her and whispered against her hair, "Please, Liz, don't shut me out."

CHAPTER 10

MISUNDERSTANDINGS

Liz plunked down in one of her kitchen chairs and wrapped her hands around a steaming mug of her favorite Earl Grey tea. It was late on Black Friday afternoon and she was home. After petting the cat and calling her mom, she'd taken a shower, grimacing at the reflection of her middle-aged, beat up body in the mirror. The bruises had faded to yellow green, but they were still an ugly reminder of the events of the past week. Jack had seen her body, all of it, at its worst. Maybe that's why, despite his fine words the night before, he hadn't even shown up to say goodbye when Officer Simmons had picked her up earlier that afternoon.

Liz sipped her tea thoughtfully. This was what she wanted, right? To be home, to have Jack out of the line of fire, to return to her normal life. It certainly had been before they'd talked last night, but that was before those sweet, steamy kisses they'd shared and before they'd held each other close. No, they hadn't resolved anything when he got the page from the hospital this morning. Still, she'd expected—what? At least a telephone call before she'd had to leave his place. Tears dripped from her eyes unnoticed as she thought about Jack. She knew so little about him, but she'd been certain of one thing, that he was a good man. So why would a good man say what he'd said to her last night then disappear?

Maybe Jack had changed his mind after they'd resolved the question of her safety. Dan had kept his part of the bargain they'd made. He'd gotten in touch with Brian Stokes, the Cook County sheriff based in Grand Marais. Now Liz had personal police protection in the form of Wanda Hanson, the deputy who'd be sharing her home and life twenty-four hours a day until the trial. Liz hated the idea of taking Wanda away from her family and her normal duties, but this was the least onerous of the options the US attorney had offered her. Besides, Wanda had volunteered. Right now, she was upstairs unpacking in the guest room and Liz was trying to pull herself together before getting to work. Emptiness filled her at the thought. She put her head down on her arms and cried.

A light touch on her shoulder startled Liz back to awareness. She had no idea how long she'd been sitting like that, her tears puddling on the table. Raising her head, she prepared to apologize to Wanda for the drama. But when she opened her eyes, it wasn't Wanda standing there, it was Jack. He crouched down beside her and said quietly, "I'm so sorry."

Thoroughly confused, Liz managed, "What...what are you doing here and why the apology?"

Jack smiled sadly. "Did you write me off that easily? What kind of man do you take me for?"

Gulping, Liz turned away from him. "A smart one."

Jack gently gathered her unresisting form into his arms and settled on the floor, holding her in his lap. "Liz, I know that this morning didn't go as we expected. You know they called me into the hospital. What you don't know is the reason they called me, even though I wasn't on call, and the reason it took so long. They had an emergency come in via *Life-Flight*—a little girl who'd been in a car accident up near Crane Lake. She was bleeding internally from a perforated bowel. Dr. Barstow was on another case, Dr. Birch was on a BWSR run, and the child would have bled out long before reaching another hospital. That's why, even though I wasn't on the schedule, I stayed to operate.

"Liz, I didn't know the particulars before I left for the hospital. If I had, I would have said something to you or asked Dan to delay things, so we could have talked before you left. Since that didn't happen, I made this decision on my own."

Liz wiped tears and snot on her sleeve before she looked up at Jack, not much caring what he thought. "What decision?"

"I'm here."

"I can see that. Where's Wanda?"

"Once I got to town, Sheriff Stokes recalled her from special duty."

That statement caught Liz's attention. "Recalled her? Last I checked, she was upstairs unpacking for an extended babysitting job."

Jack shrugged calmly. "That room's already occupied, so Wanda won't be needed."

Irritated by the faint smile on Jack's face, Liz snapped, "Says who? We have a plan, thanks anyway."

Jack's grin widened. "Wanda won't be needed because you already have your own personal police officer and physician watching over you."

Liz pushed Jack away, angered by his cavalier teasing, especially when she still felt awful. "Where? I don't see a police officer and I thought you'd recused yourself as my physician because of your so-called feelings for me."

Jack rolled his eyes. "Boy, you sure are cranky for someone who's gotten her way about everything. While you do have a point about the physician thing, I work for a combined service, remember?" He pulled one arm away, fished in the back pocket of his jeans and withdrew a leather folder. Flipping it open, he held it up in front of her. "Here, happy?"

Liz glanced at the badge and ID Jack held, but she was still confused and angry. "Ecstatic. So you're a real cop who's a little out of his jurisdiction. How would I know that? You told me you were a doctor, not a doctor plus overachiever. You still haven't told me what's going on or why you're sitting there with that stupid grin on your face. Go away and leave me alone." She tried to stand up, but he held her tightly.

"Liz, I'm not going anywhere." Jack stroked her back soothingly. "I'm so sorry that this morning got fouled up. I'm sorry that you're hurting both inside and outside. I'm especially sorry that we haven't had the time to get to know one another in a more personal way because of ongoing crisis management. If you'll allow me to stay with you, we'll look after each other and spend time getting to know one another."

"No!" Liz said emphatically. "No! You have better things to do than babysit me."

Jack blew out an exasperated breath. "I'm getting really tired of that particular euphemism! Love, no one is babysitting you, and yes, I have other things to do, but *nothing* is more important than what I'm here to do. If you won't let me stay in your guest room, then I'm doomed to live in a sheriff's cruiser at the end of your driveway for the duration, because I volunteered for this, I've taken some personal time from the hospital, and I'm not going anywhere."

"Don't call me that! I'm not your 'love,' I'm not your...your anything." Liz took a shuddering breath and finally looked at him. "Jack, last night, I thought," gulping, she choked, "never mind what I thought, it doesn't matter. You have a home and a job in Ely. Maybe you should just turn around and go back where you belong."

"It does matter, Liz, and I belong right here. Last night I told you I wanted to be with you. That was and is my choice. Please, don't let a medical emergency and a communications glitch come between us. Don't make me choose between you and saving a child's life. Please, let me be here with you and try to trust me, at least a little."

Liz watched as Jack's faint smile abruptly disappeared, replaced by lines of strain in his face. Suddenly she understood what her behavior was saying to him. Sitting up, she hung her head. "I'm sorry, Jack. The only excuse I can offer is that I'm scared. I barely know you and I feel...I feel," she sniffed as more tears dripped from her eyes. "Never mind."

Jack looked at her gravely. "It's been a long time for me too, Liz, and, honestly, this has been a pretty intense ride." He touched her cheek gently. "You're worth it to me. None of it matters though, if you don't feel the same way. Do you want me to leave?"

Breathing deeply, Liz tried to think over the clamor of her fear. Jack sat silent, his arms now at his side, allowing her space. She thought about the last week, about their time together, about the way he'd cared for her—a stranger, about their time with the Harrisons before the arguments, about their conversation the night before, and finally, Liz made a decision. "No."

CHAPTER 11

A TIME TO SHARE

Liz swallowed a mouthful of pizza and said, "Okay, it's your turn."

Jack held up a finger and continued to chew. It was the day after he'd arrived in Grand Marais and he and Liz were on their first official date. They were enjoying lunch at Sven & Ole's pizza[3], a landmark establishment in the Grand Marais community. Just an hour earlier, Liz had sworn that she would die if she didn't get a pizza fix and while he seriously doubted her diagnosis, Jack had to admit the pizza was really good.

Wiping his mouth with his napkin, Jack considered for a moment, then said, "I know about your mom and you told me your father died when you were in your teens. Tell me about the rest of your family—any brothers, sisters, kids?"

"One brother, younger by four years, Todd. He works for the CIA and is based in DC. He and his wife Damson have two teen girls. No sisters and no kids." Liz smiled sadly. "Eric and I wanted to have children, but metabolic syndrome ended that dream for me, for us. How about you? Same question."

---

[3] Sven and Ole's restaurant is located in Grand Marais, Minnesota, but their reputation for great pizza is famous throughout the state. (https://www. svenandoles.com/).

"One brother, Walt, older by a year. He's an electrician in Albuquerque. He and his wife Morgan have three girls and one boy, ranging in age from fifteen to twenty-two. One sister, Vicky, younger by five years. She's an automotive engineer. She and her husband Ted live near Detroit and have two boys, both college age. While I have a lot of fun with my nieces and nephews, I don't have children of my own."

Sipping her iced tea, Liz smiled. "You're blessed to have so many nieces and nephews. I'll bet you're their favorite uncle ever."

"My turn," Jack said. "How long have you lived in Grand Marais?"

"Eight years," Liz replied.

"Can you give me something besides the CliffsNotes version, Liz, or we're going to be here all day."

"Can I help it if you didn't ask an open-ended question?" Liz fired back, a grin on her face. After a few seconds of silence, she relented and elaborated on her answer. "When Eric died eight years ago, we were living in the Minneapolis area. Because of health issues, I'd sold my law practice the year before, so when he passed, I was grieving and at loose ends. I'd never liked the city and I'd grown up in Duluth. After giving it some time, I made the decision to sell our house and move north.

"At first, I planned to move back to Duluth, but then I sold a couple of my embroidery pieces to a gallery here in Grand Marais. They offered to showcase my work and place regular orders for new pieces. There's also a thriving art colony here and the North House Folk School, that specializes in teaching heritage crafts. So instead of Duluth, I moved up here, rented a place for the first year, and finished some proposals for teaching gigs both here and throughout the Midwest. By the time that year was up, I'd fallen in love with the town, so I decided to try to make a go of it as a resident artist in these parts. I bought my house, did a bit of remodeling of the studio spaces, and the rest is history. My turn."

Jack put down his slice of pepperoni-green olive pizza without taking a bite. "Ready."

Liz thought for a long moment before asking, "When did you first know that you wanted to be a doctor?"

"That's easy," Jack said immediately, "as hokey as it sounds, I've always known. At least that's what it seems like. Do you remember a board game that involved pulling plastic organs out of a magnetized board with tweezers?" Seeing Liz nod, he continued, "My parents gave that to me when I was all of five or six years old. I became that game's first world super champion—at least according to my brother and sister—and I never looked back. I majored in biochemistry in college, went to medical school at Johns Hopkins, and did my residencies at the University of Minnesota. My first job was as a trauma surgeon at the Hennepin County Medical Center in downtown Minneapolis."

Her eyes widening, Liz said, "Wow, that sounds intense. What did you do for fun?"

Jack laughed. "Hey, that's two questions," he took Liz's hand, "but I won't make you wait, because you do need to know this part. It wasn't all work. I had a home life and we had a lot of fun, despite my crazy hours."

"We?" Liz asked in a small voice.

Jack nodded. "Yes. My wife Ellie and me. We married just after she finished her Master's in electrical engineering and I graduated from med school. Minneapolis was where her family lived so we were both happy about settling there."

Liz caught her lower lip between her teeth. "Why is it I don't want to hear the end of this story? Especially since I don't really believe that you're with me so that you can be in the running to become the first bigamist in Ely's illustrious history." She took a deep breath and added, "Please tell me Ellie's fine and your marriage ended in an amicable divorce."

Squeezing her hand, Jack smiled sadly. "I'm not going to say 'I wish it had,' because that would have been its own tragedy. Just as we were thinking about starting our family, Ellie died in a car accident. It happened just before our fifth wedding anniversary."

"I'm so sorry, Jack," Liz said compassionately.

"I'm sorry too—sorry that her light was taken out of the world so soon. But that was long ago, and time does heal, you know that as well as I do."

"Yes, I do," Liz responded, "but Eric and I had over twenty years together, time to have experiences and to give me a lot of memories to cherish."

Neither of them said anything for a few seconds, then Liz got up, returning to their table with a takeout box. "We're not leaving our leftovers for the kitchen staff to chow down on or worse yet, to be thrown out. Are you finished? I'm not trying to rush you, but there's a primo dessert ahead of us."

~ ~ ~

"ERGGHHHH!" Jack groaned, flopping face down on the sofa in Liz's living room. "I haven't eaten like that in years. First, you twist my arm into going out for pizza, then, after only eating two of the things, you insist that I finish the bag of 'Mama Olsen's Best Mini-Donuts' that you forced on us. Finally, you top it off by making lamb stew with bread and salad for dinner with homemade pumpkin pie for dessert." He rolled over and pulled her down beside him. "I swear I'll never eat again."

"Quit your kvetching, Dr. Lockwood. You ate at least that much at Thanksgiving and I couldn't let all those fixings for the pie go to waste, could I? It's not my fault that Thanksgiving with Mom didn't go off as planned." Liz looked at him sheepishly. "I'm sorry if it was too much. If it's any consolation, I'm really full too."

"You know I'm teasing you, right?" Jack sat up, his eyes searching her face.

"Yes, I do." Liz touched Jack's cheek gently. "Thank you for today. I know that we've talked through a lot of intensely personal stuff. There's a huge part of me wondering why you're still around. You saved my life and got hurt while trying to protect me. I repaid you by arguing about coming home and trying to send you away when you showed up here. Now we've been dredging up the past all day long just so I can get to know you better. I'm…"

61

Jack shook his head. "Please, Liz, don't apologize. I know we've been going about things a little backward thanks to circumstance, but I wouldn't trade a moment of today. In fact, I wouldn't trade most of the last week except the part where you almost died and the wondering about Eduard Reynoso part. I feel more alive than I've felt in years." Leaning forward, he kissed her slowly, deeply, the sparks flying between them stealing his breath.

When they pulled apart, Liz touched her lips, her eyes wide. "Wow."

Jack put his arms around her, drawing her back against him. "My sentiment exactly."

Jack learned something else new about Liz later that night. He'd just gotten out of the shower when he heard singing from her room. He stopped by the open door. She was sitting cross-legged on her bed, dressed in a white tee shirt, gray cardigan, and gray flannel pajama bottoms with kitties on them. Sierra and Binx had curled up beside her, making Jack glad he'd brought Binx with him. Liz had her eyes closed as she played her guitar and sang.

Jesus I am resting, resting
In the joy of what Thou art.
I am finding out the greatness
Of Thy loving heart.

Thou hast bid me gaze upon Thee
And Thy beauty fills my soul.
For by Thy transforming power
Thou hast made me whole.

Simply trusting Thee, Lord Jesus
I behold Thee as Thou art.
And Thy love so pure, so changeless
Satisfies my heart.

Ever lift Thy face upon me
As I work and wait for Thee.
Resting 'neath Thy smile Lord Jesus
Earth's dark shadows flee.

Brightness of my Father's glory,
Sunshine of my Father's face,
Keep me ever trusting, resting
Fill me with Thy grace.[ii]

As Liz played the final cords, Jack knocked. "May I come in?"

"Of course. Do you need something? Another blanket, more towels," Liz's eyes twinkled, "maybe another pot of coffee?"

Jack sat down on the bed next to her. "No, thank you. Believe it or not, I've had my fill of coffee for the day and I'm quite comfortable. Your house is very you—quirky, fun, and easy on the eyes. I just wanted to tell you how much I enjoyed your music. You have a lovely voice and that sounded like a favorite song."

"Thank you." Liz blushed. "I often sing that song before bed because it's only in Christ that I can truly rest, especially when, well," she looked at Jack, her expressive eyes speaking volumes, "when things are confusing, painful, or are just plain changing. Please don't take that wrong, okay?"

Jack wrapped his arms around her. "I won't, Liz. I feel much the same about the way things are right now." He grinned, trying to coax a smile. "Believe it or not, I'm not big on change, but being with you is worth it."

Liz kissed Jack, then rested her head on his shoulder. "Thank you. I feel the same way about being with you."

CHAPTER 12

A DECLARATION OF WAR

"Jack, for the love of heaven, will you quit daydreaming and focus? I need to fly the aircraft, which means that you need to watch the terrain for our lost campers."

Jack started guiltily at Dan's words and picked up the binoculars that were hanging on a strap around his neck. "Sorry. I don't like leaving Liz."

Snorting derisively, Dan replied, "What do you mean, leaving her? It's not like she's alone, Beth's with her at our place and our fearless probie, Jerry Simmons, is staying with both of them until we get back. Which," he tapped the binoculars and frowned, just enough to communicate his message, "we will never do, unless you concentrate more on search and rescue and less on hormones."

Dan put the helicopter into a steep climb to move on to the next search grid, missing Jack's reply. It was probably just as well. When things quieted down—a relative term in a helicopter—Jack managed a more civil response. "You know this isn't about hormones. I'm concerned, that's all. We haven't heard or seen anything that suggests Reynoso or anyone else is still after Liz. It's been three weeks; the trial starts in under a month, and nothing. Doesn't that seem a bit odd to you, Mr. Chief of Police?"

"Not necessarily. We were never certain if Reynoso was involved in what happened to Liz. It could have been the two that died orchestrated the whole thing, hoping to ransom her and her testimony off to the highest bidder—Reynoso, the US Attorney's Office, or a rival cartel. We simply don't know for certain and maybe we got lucky."

"Got lucky? Would you be willing to bet Beth's life on that kind of rubbish? How would two yokels from Northern Minnesota know about Reynoso, the trial, or that Liz was even involved?"

"News travels, Jack, you know that. Look, Liz is under guard 24-7. Let's just do this—help some lost folks out of a tight spot—then we can go home and you can see for yourself that Liz is fine. Another month and the trial will be history and you guys can get on with your lives."

It wasn't until after the rescued campers were safe at the hospital and Dan and Jack were in Dan's official four by four on their way back to the house, that Dan returned to the subject of Liz and Jack. "Apart from being a bit jumpy that Reynoso hasn't reared his ugly head, how are things?"

"Fine." Jack tried to keep a straight face, knowing that answer would nowhere near satisfy Dan's curiosity, but not above eliciting a little payback for that "hormones" crack. "How are things with you and Beth?"

"Jack," Dan grumbled, "you've been at Liz's for over three weeks now and you two certainly seem, uh, cozy. Do I take it there's good news?"

Relenting, Jack grinned. "It's been good. Better than good. Dan, she's an amazing woman—smart, talented, and funny. We've spent a lot of time backtracking, getting to know one another. Did you know she was a lawyer, as in a lawyer admitted to the Federal bar? She's argued before the US Supreme Court and her team won."

Dan looked surprised. "I thought she was an artist."

Jack made a face and explained, "She *is* an artist; she *was* a religious liberty lawyer. She moved up here from Minneapolis after her husband died and has made a life doing what she loves. That's more than can be said of most of us."

Dan arched an eyebrow. "You resigning on me? Or thinking about it."

"Relax," Jack said quietly, "you know I believe in what we're doing up here. I just think it took an awful lot of courage for Liz to make a mid-life change of direction like that."

"I never doubted Liz had courage," Dan acknowledged. "Neither of you would be here if you didn't share that particular character trait. I...What the..."

They'd just turned into Dan's driveway, when an explosion shook the air. Smoke and flames erupted from the house, shattering the living room window. Slamming the truck into park, Dan and Jack sprinted for the house. Jack ran around the back and forced open the door into the kitchen. Covering his mouth and nose with his jacket sleeve, he searched the room. "Beth? Liz? Jerry?" he gasped, coughing as the smoke scorched his lungs.

"Jack, in here!" Dan rasped from the living room. When he got to his friend, Jack saw Dan pick up a choking Beth in a fireman's carry and head for the door. A still-bleeding Jerry and a semi-conscious Liz were lying motionless at Jack's feet. Fighting to stay conscious as both the smoke and heat increased in intensity, Jack felt for a pulse on Jerry's throat and found none. Liz coughed weakly, her eyelids fluttering, so he picked her up, struggling to his feet with her over his shoulder. They'd almost made it to the front door when the entryway ceiling gave way burying the two of them in flaming rubble.

⌒⌒

"Jack."

From far away, Jack became vaguely aware that someone was calling his name. He knew he needed to answer, but he was so tired.

"Jack, honey, please wake up."

Jack's eyelids snapped open, responding to the worry he heard in Liz's voice. He focused on her face. Her skin was chalk white behind a covering of ash and soot. He was lying flat on a narrow gurney, an oxygen cannula in his nose. His back and head hurt. He blinked, trying to figure out what had happened.

When Dan walked into the curtained off room, it all came back. "Dan, Liz, are you—is everyone—okay?" Jack croaked, his throat stinging.

Dan sat down beside Liz and patted Jack's arm. "Take it easy, buddy. Beth and Liz swallowed some smoke and received some minor burns, but they're both going to be fine. You swallowed a lot of smoke, got a little singed, mostly a few burns on your back, and now have a second lump on your head that rivals the one you got in your last misadventure."

"You?" Jack eyed his friend.

Dan waved his hand in dismissal. "I'm fine. Nothing fell on me and I didn't have the exposure you all did."

"Jerry?" Jack frowned; the soft-spoken officer was becoming a good friend.

Dan shook his head, a sad expression on his face. "DOA."

"What happened? The house?"

"Pretty much totaled," Dan muttered ruefully. "We're not certain what caused the explosion. The fire inspector is going through the rubble, but he won't have complete access until they make sure what's left standing is stable."

Dan put a hand on Liz's shoulder. "Neither Beth nor Liz witnessed what happened. They were both in the kitchen when something detonated in the living room. They found Jerry who, judging from his injuries, must have been at ground zero. Before they could help him or get out of there, they passed out from smoke inhalation."

Dan rested his head in his hand, looking morose. "Had we not gotten home when we did…" He let the sentence hang. They all knew how lucky they'd been.

❧

Hours passed before the four of them were back at Jack's home. There was no question that Dan and Beth had a place with Jack for as long as they needed it. Still it was unnerving to think of how close they'd all come. No one felt like eating, or even talking. Over the Harrisons' protests, Jack insisted they use the master suite.

Rather than returning to Grand Marais at this time of night and before they had any answers, Jack and Liz camped out on the sofa bed in Jack's study, neither of them feeling up to climbing the stairs to the loft with its real beds. Wearily, Jack grabbed a set of linens from the closet. By the time they made up the bed, neither of them had enough energy left to do anything but collapse into the sheets, fully clothed.

Jack put his arms around Liz, trying to quiet his uneasy spirit. Were it not for the fast action of the Ely fire department and their proximity to the front door when the ceiling had fallen, he and Liz would be dead. And Liz would never have known what was in his heart. Jack brushed her cheek with his fingertips and whispered, "Are you awake?"

Liz opened her eyes. "Yes. Despite the hospital pumping me full of meds, I'm kinda wired. How about you?"

Jack nodded and agreed, "The same. I don't know if I could move more than a foot in any direction, but sleep is a long way off. Liz, I need to tell you something. It was a close call today and this just can't wait." Kissing her deeply, Jack whispered, "This last month has been crazy, but you should know that I'm in love with you. If you're not ready to hear that, I understand. I just needed to say it."

Liz smiled and cupped his face in her hand. "Jack, honey, I know when we met, I agree about the crazy part, and I love you too."

Jack raised his head from the pillow, a slow smile appearing on his face. "Yeah?"

"Yeah." Liz eyes twinkled.

"Well, that's just about the best news ever. You're sure? This isn't just the drugs talking?" Jack teased.

Liz yawned then pulled Jack down until they were nose-to-nose. "Very sure. When I don't reek of smoke and have a bit more energy, I'll prove it to you."

"Message received and understood." Drawing Liz into the curve of his body, Jack brushed her temple with a soft kiss. "This is nice. Try to rest now." He couldn't help repeating the words singing in his spirit, "I love you."

Jack got out of bed, pulled on his robe, and started down the stairs in Liz's home. They'd been back in Grand Marais for two days and Christmas was almost upon them. Dan and Beth were now with her family to celebrate the holidays, after which they would return to a rental property in Ely while they rebuilt their home.

Jack walked into the kitchen and noticed something strange. Every day for the over three weeks he'd been here, he'd come down-stairs to find the light on over the stove and a pot of coffee waiting for him. Usually, Liz was there too, a smile on her face, waiting to give him a good morning hug and kiss. Beginning the day in that way had become a ritual with them, one that filled his heart with joy. Today the room was dark and silent. He loaded the coffee maker and turned it on to brew, then went in search of her. He wasn't worried, at least not as such, but he missed her. It was odd for her to sleep past 7:30 a.m. and he wanted to make certain she was okay.

Liz wasn't in her studio where Jack had expected to find her. The second floor was quiet, but her bedroom door was open, so he stopped and looked into the room. She was still in bed. He was just about to go back downstairs and let her sleep when she moaned and turned over. Even in the dim early morning light, he could see pain etched in her expression. Forgetting respect for her private space, he moved quickly and sat down on the bed beside her. "What's wrong, love?"

Liz turned so she was face up and touched his hand. "Jack, I'm fine. I had a bad night, that's all." A strange look crossed her face. She put a hand over her mouth, scooted around him to stand up, and ran from the room. Seconds later, he heard the sound of retch-ing. Getting up, he found the bathroom door slightly ajar. Kneeling beside her, Jack rubbed her back. After a few minutes, she lifted her head and braced her forearms on the stool. He handed her a cold, wet towel. "Here, this might help."

Liz took the towel he held, sat back on her bottom, and wiped her face. Smoothing her hair back, Jack said, "This doesn't look like just a bad night. I'd say it was the meal we had at the restaurant last evening, but I ate the same thing. You don't have a fever, so that prob-ably eliminates the flu."

Getting to her feet, Liz flushed the toilet, washed up, then brushed her teeth. Pressing the wet towel to her forehead, she returned to the bedroom, beckoning to Jack to follow her. After she laid down, Liz patted the bed beside her and waited until he sat before saying, "Jack, honey, you didn't have to help me throw up." A ghost of a smile crossed her face. "I'm pretty good at doing that all by myself. After I went to bed last night, my shoulders and my hips started to bother me, which is pretty typical fibromyalgia nonsense. I didn't get much sleep and woke up with a migraine. I hate it when that happens because if the pain gets ahead of me, there's not a lot I can do except stay quiet in a dark room and, of course, be within running distance of the bathroom. I'll be okay, I'm used to this so don't worry."

Although he was familiar with her health history, Jack was still worried. The force of her vomiting had broken blood vessels around her eyes to the point that, if it happened again, she'd be sporting two shiners. "You can't be telling me that this is normal for you?"

"When I wake up with a migraine, it is."

"What medication are you on for the migraines?"

"I used to be on a prescription drug but because it acted by constricting blood vessels my cardiologist nixed it. I take an over-the-counter migraine formula with aspirin, acetaminophen and caffeine in it, at least when my stomach will handle it."

"That's it?"

"Well that, along with an ice pack, a dark room, and rest." Liz must have seen the disapproval in Jack's expression because she held up her hands. "Hey, don't get mad at me. My doctors all know what I'm doing." She closed her eyes and sighed, "Could we argue about this another time? I feel pretty awful right now."

Jack put his fingertips on Liz's temples and started a gentle massage. "Liz, I'm not arguing, I'm trying to understand. I'm certainly not upset with you. How does this feel?"

"Mmm, good, thanks."

After a few minutes, Jack got to his feet and said, "I'll be right back." When he returned to Liz's room, he sat down beside her and put an ice pack on her forehead. "There," taking her hand, he asked, "is there anything else you need?"

"Yes, but you're going to think I'm a floozy if I ask," Liz said quietly.

Jack couldn't help chuckling. "Makes me wonder what you're going to ask. But ask away and I promise not to think anything without your permission."

Liz's faint smile returned. "I'm freezing and I can't seem to get warm. Would you, um, hold me for a little while? I promise not to impugn your virtue or barf on you."

Jack didn't stop moving until he held Liz in his arms. Pulling the covers up around them, he said, "I swear I'm not thinking floozy here. The truth is, I don't really want to leave you alone right now. This may be something you're used to, but it concerns me. Can we talk a bit later about what having fibro and chronic migraine means in your world? I promise to listen well."

CHAPTER 13

A CHRISTMAS GIFT

"Let's sing this beautiful carol together as we close our service," Liz invited the congregation. She picked up her guitar and softly strummed a few chords.

Silent night, holy night
All is calm, all is bright
'Round yon virgin Mother and Child
Holy infant so tender and mild
Sleep in heavenly peace
Sleep in heavenly peace

Silent night, holy night!
Shepherds quake at the sight!
Glories stream from heaven afar;
Heavenly hosts sing Alleluia!
Christ the Savior is born!
Christ the Savior is born!

Silent night, holy night
Son of God, love's pure light
Radiant beams from Thy holy face
With the dawn of redeeming grace
Jesus, Lord at Thy birth
Jesus, Lord at Thy birth.[iii]

The darkened church was silent as Liz's voice died away and she played the final notes. Jack swallowed around the lump in his throat as he watched her walk off the platform toward him. It had been many years since he'd found himself in church on Christmas Eve, and listening to Liz sing had touched him deeply. Yet tonight, being here with her in her small home church in Grand Marais, he was having trouble believing that he'd told her the truth when she'd asked if he believed in God. At the time, he'd said "yes" without much thinking about it.

That was the problem, Jack had never much thought about it—not since losing Ellie. Even then, she'd been the religious one in their marriage. She was the one who'd made certain they'd gone to church as a couple whenever his schedule allowed, she was the one who'd participated in and led Bible studies, and she'd even been the one to lead prayers in their home. When she died, he took comfort in the fact that she believed and that if the Bible was trustworthy, she was with her Lord and not really dead.

Since then, Jack had gone back to not thinking much about God. When Liz had asked, his answer had come easy, yes, he believed in God but what he'd really meant was that he'd lived a good life, saving peoples' lives by the dozens, and he was even moral far beyond the standards of the day. He lived his faith and he didn't need others, especially the kind of hypocrites often found in the pulpit, shoving anything down his throat. If there was a god, Jack had always believed he was in a good place despite his aversion to organized religion.

But the God that Liz, and Ellie before her, believed in was different. Like Ellie, Liz's faith was in God with a capital "G." Far more than staid religiosity, her faith was in a God Who made a daily difference in her life, a God she sought out regularly in prayer, no matter her life's circumstances, and a God who knew that Liz, Ellie and yes, Jack, were all sinful beings—an assumption he found disturbing in the extreme—who needed a Savior. That also bothered Jack—this man, Jesus Christ, whose birth they were celebrating tonight—did Jack owe him? No, he'd never really thought about it, but here he was, sitting in church on Christmas Eve with the woman he loved, feeling like a fraud.

Liz slid into the pew beside him and Jack leaned over and whispered in her ear, "That was beautiful, and you were perfect."

Flushing scarlet, Liz squeezed his hand. "Thank you, Jack. Merry Christmas!"

~⌒~

Jack stood alone in the hours just before dawn, dressed in sweats, wrapped in a blanket, and sipping a cup of coffee. Sleep had eluded him on this holiest night of the year, and he'd come up here, to the deck outside Liz's attic studio, to think. His life had changed so much in the space of just over a month and he wasn't completely comfortable in his skin right now. Still, he knew beyond a doubt that he and Liz belonged together, and the best thing was, she knew it too.

Yet this Christmas, happy as it should have been, fell under a shadow of threat. A shadow that had impacted those he loved most in life. The Harrisons' home was in ruins, laid waste by an arsonist with a firebomb. Jerry Simmons was dead and both Jack and Liz bore scars from their encounters with those who wanted to silence her and who were still at large. How was he supposed to find peace or joy under these circumstances? That was part of the problem, Jack realized guiltily, he was feeling joy—subdued joy perhaps—but joy nonetheless.

"Hey, I thought I heard you get up. Are you okay, hon?" Liz stood beside him, in slippers, yoga pants, a long-sleeved t-shirt, draped in a knitted shawl of her own design against the cold.

Jack put his arm around her shoulders, sharing the blanket and his warmth and nodded. "I'm fine, just thinking, that's all."

"Good thoughts or worried thoughts?"

"Honestly, a little of both." Jack kissed the top of Liz's head. "Something about Christmas encourages a bit of introspection, don't you think?"

Liz nodded. "Yes, introspection, gratitude, celebration, all of it, but something else is on your mind. Is it the Harrisons?"

Jack tried to put his jumbled thoughts into words. "It's tough to lose your home anytime, but now? Right before Christmas? Their first home together and their first Christmas married? Yeah, I'm thinking about them, hoping that they can find some joy today, some sense of home while they're with her parents. I'm so grateful that they're both okay, but I know it has to be hard. I also feel for Jerry's parents, coping with their first Christmas without their son. And I'm worried about you. I'm afraid my rescue attempt did more harm than good. I know your back and ribs are still really painful."

"Jack don't go there," Liz warned. "You tried to carry me out of a burning building and despite what you seem to be saying, you saved my life, again. And you're still in pain from what you did for us that day. The fire inspector's report said that had you not made it to the front entrance carrying me, they wouldn't have gotten to either of us in time."

Liz raised herself on her toes and kissed Jack on the cheek. "None of this is your fault and in my saner moments I know it's not my fault either. If I'm to believe you and Dan, the fault lies squarely with Eduard Reynoso. I love you and you *are* my hero."

Turning to face Liz, Jack pulled her into his arms and kissed her. "I love you, too, so much." He smiled against her lips and whispered, "That's part of the problem. In the midst of all this mayhem, I'm thoroughly, ridiculously, crazy happy thanks to you."

Liz giggled. "Me too, thanks to you, only I wasn't going to confess. But you know what? I don't think Dan and Beth will mind. They love you too much. As for me, apart from my Savior, you're the most wonderful Christmas gift of all."

Jack looked down at her and knew that he'd never have a better opening than this. Dropping to one knee, he pulled a small box from the pocket of his sweatpants—it hadn't been out of his possession since he'd left Scott Harmon's jewelry studio yesterday morning. Liz's eyes went wide as he took her hand and said, "I was going to wow you with the perfect setting, or at least with breakfast in bed, but right now my heart is so full of love for you, I can't wait." Flipping open the box lid, Jack took the platinum and diamond eternity band from its satin bed and slipped it onto the third finger of her left hand. "Elizabeth Joy Talbot, you are my joy. I know it's only been a short eternity since we met, but I'm certain of two things: I love you and my life will never again be complete without you by my side. Will you marry me?"

CHAPTER 14

A COVENANT PROMISE

"Are you sure about this, honey?" Liz's seventy-nine-year-old mother took her hand. "You hardly know Jack."

"I know when we met, Mom. I was the one dying from exposure when Jack came along, remember?" Liz took a deep breath and retreated from her snarky response. "Look, I know this is unusual, but you gave him your permission to ask me to marry him—something I was unaware of until he told me on the way down here today—so you must think he's okay. I'm old enough to know what love feels like and to separate it from infatuation or some kind of weird 'Stockholm Syndrome' thing stemming from when we were stranded together. He's a wonderful man, a fine physician, and I can't envision my life without him anymore. Can you please just be happy for us?"

Liz sat back, for the moment wanting to be anywhere else but where she was on this Christmas afternoon. About an hour ago, Jack had retreated to the guest room to take a nap. After being up most of the night, driving to Duluth and having Christmas dinner with Nancy, her mom, he was beat. Liz also knew that he'd wanted to give her and her mom some time alone together before they opened gifts.

"Honey, I *am* happy for you and I couldn't have wished for a better man for my only daughter than Jack seems to be." Nancy squeezed Liz's hand soothingly. "Still, you two haven't had much time to get to know each other and you're getting married so quickly. I just want to make sure you're doing the right thing for both of you."

"I'm as certain of this as I've been of anything in my life, Mom," Liz asserted, "and waiting to get married seems a bit silly for two people of our age. In fact, getting married on New Year's Day was my idea, not Jack's. I love him and I just want to be with him."

"And I want to be with Liz." Jack's words broke into their conversation as he came into the room and sat down beside Liz. Looking at his fiancée sheepishly, he apologized, "I'm sorry, I couldn't sleep, but I guess I should have given you two a little more time alone together."

Reaching across the table Jack took Nancy's hand and met her gaze. "Nancy, I love your daughter and I give you my word that I will devote the rest of my life to keeping her safe, happy, and healthy. I want nothing more than to call you and Liz my family."

"What about *your* family, Jack?" Nancy asked levelly. "How do they feel about your upcoming marriage?"

"My brother and sister think it's wonderful—we called them both on the way down here. They and their families will be there to share our day. My mom died about six years ago."

"And your father?"

"Dad left mom and us kids when I was thirteen." Jack's eyes were sad. "We don't speak much anymore. I tried calling him this morning but got his service. I did leave a message." The pain in Jack's expression deepened. "He typically doesn't answer calls until he screens them, even calls from us kids."

"I'm sorry, Jack," Nancy said, "life's too short for that kind of nonsense. I'll pray for healing between you and your father as I pray for you and Liz, with all my heart. And in the meanwhile," smiling, Nancy took Liz's hand again to form a circle, "welcome to the family, dear son. Let's ask God to bless this miracle of new love."

By the time Nancy finished praying, Jack had tears in his eyes. Her words had touched him deeply. It was as though someone had given him a glimpse into the throne room of God himself. A door had opened somewhere in his spirit and he wasn't sure where to go from here, but he was certain that he was on a transcendent journey that would take him along unexplored paths. Jack squeezed her hand gently and whispered, "Thank you."

～～～

"Engaged? As in getting married?" Dan blew out his breath and stared at Jack. "I leave for a week and the universe tilts on its axis. Married?"

Jack nodded. He and Dan sat at Jack's dining room table, waiting for the women to get back from Duluth. "Yes, married, as in five days from now—a bride and a groom, a preacher and a church. Liz's pastor is going to marry us on New Year's Day at eleven in the morning. I know things are crazy busy for you and Beth right now, but will you consider celebrating that day with us? The wedding will be very small, just family and a few friends, but it won't be complete without the two of you by our sides."

Jack noticed his best friend still hadn't closed his mouth. "Harrison, are you paralyzed from the neck up or what? Will you and Beth be our witnesses?"

Dan's mouth finally closed with an audible snap. "You...You're serious, aren't you?"

Jack growled in exasperation. "Yes, I'm serious! Come on, join the party. This news can't have been that unexpected."

Dan held out his hand. "Wow, buddy, congratulations." When Jack took his proffered hand, Dan pulled him into a hug, slapping him hard on the back.

Pulling away after several seconds, Jack grinned. "So that's a yes?"

"Of course it's a yes, brother. As if Beth and I would be anyplace else. I just can't believe that after all these years single, you popped the question so soon." Concern flashed across Dan's face. "Um, you two haven't known each other for very long and the crazies are still out there. You sure about this?"

"Yes, I'm sure," Jack replied. "Do you remember that first night in the middle of nowhere Montana years ago? I was standing on the side of the highway, where the bus had dropped me. After flying into

Billings, I'd been traveling for hours; it was two in the morning and I was waiting for my ride to Don's place. I was thinking of someone in a car, you know? After an hour of standing there, cold, lost, and tired, I'd just about decided to thumb a ride back to civilization when you started buzzing me in that helicopter of yours. I thought you were crazier than a rooster on meth, but I knew we'd be life-long friends by the time we landed at the clinic. It's like that, only on steroids."

Dan blinked. "I haven't heard a speech like that out of you in… in…come to think of it, I've *never* heard a speech like that out of you. I…"

They both looked up as Liz and Beth came through the door, their arms loaded with packages. "Whoa," Dan exclaimed, "what did you two do, buy out the county?"

Beth shed her coat on a dining room chair, plunked herself in Dan's lap, put her arms around him, and kissed him soundly before answering, "We did just what you expected us to do when you left us in Duluth this morning with our wallets and the rental car. We shopped all the after Christmas sales we could find. And Lord knows, DH, that we need just about everything. Including some wedding attire."

Beth looked around him at Jack. "You did tell him, didn't you?"

Jack nodded. "Yeah, I told him, but while the porch light's on, I'm not sure anyone's home."

Liz tucked the hand-made quilt she'd given Jack for Christmas around her shoulders and settled back happily against the leather cushions of the sofa in his living room. She watched the fire snapping in the wood stove and relaxed.

Sitting down beside her, Jack handed her a cup of tea, putting the pot on the coffee table. "Sorry, all I have in the house are bags, but it's Earl Grey, and I hope I got it right—tea with milk and a little sugar." He rolled his eyes. "All those cups of coffee I gave you only to find out that you're a tea drinker."

Liz carefully took the mug of tea and set it on a coaster on the end table. "Jack, honey, thank you for the tea and don't give the coffee versus tea thing a thought. I drink and enjoy both. Actually, drinking coffee is pretty much a requirement for anyone living up here. It's just that when I have a choice, I prefer tea, that's all. And bags are fine. Thank you for being considerate enough to stock up on some for when we're here."

Squeezing Liz's hand, Jack asked, "To that point, love, I've been meaning to ask, why did you want to drive over here again? We're getting married the day after tomorrow in Grand Marais. Starting tomorrow, our families will be arriving in Grand Marais. Your pastor wants to meet with us tomorrow afternoon in Grand Marais. So why are we in Ely? I meant to ask you earlier, but we got into that discussion about crime in the Boundary Waters and I never got the chance." He put his arm around her shoulders. "Not that I'm complaining, but I'm curious."

Liz snuggled close to Jack. "We're here because I love you, I wanted some time alone with you, and I wanted to see more of this beautiful house of yours. Besides," she grinned, "this way no one knows where to find us, right?"

Jack unclipped the pager[4] from his belt and set it on the table. "Well, no one except the gods governing on-call physicians. So far, it's been quiet, so here's hoping. And they all think I have an hour and a half drive back here, so we'll have a little time even if I do get called into the hospital."

Laughing, Liz shook her head. "As if you'd wait to go help folks who need you. Still, it's a nice thought and if you have to go in, that's fine. I've gotten used to sharing you with," she pointed to the pager, "the evil black box."

Liz took a sip of her tea. "Since we might be interrupted, why don't you kiss me then take me on that tour you've been promising for weeks."

---

[4] Do doctors and hospitals still use pagers in this day and age of cell phones and texts? The answer is yes. Here is one article that discusses the reasons why: https://slate.com/technology/2016/02/why-do-doctors-still-use-pagers.html.

Grinning, Jack took her in his arms and kissed her, the crackle of attraction between them almost audible. "How about if we skip the tour and I just kiss you again? The house isn't that big and it will wait."

Pulling away, Liz objected, "You promised me a long time ago that you'd show me the rest of the place. All I really saw were the first-floor spaces. Not that I'm complaining, those parts of the house are spectacular, I mean who has a library, an honest-to-goodness library, in their master suite?"

Jack shrugged. "Me. So I enjoy reading, what's the big deal?"

"It's a big deal because we're going to have to buy a couple more shelving units. I also love to read and plan to augment your collection with mine. Now," Liz stood up and held out her hand to Jack, "let's commence to touring so we can get back to kissing."

Later, as they cuddled on the loveseat in the library and enjoyed the crackling fire, Liz finished her now lukewarm tea and said, "Wow, I didn't realize you'd built this place. I love everything about it, but I especially love that it came from," she laid a hand over Jack's heart, "here. Do you remember when we were talking about where we'd live and pretty much decided that we'd split our time between Grand Marais and here?"

"Yes. I remember. What about it?" Jack asked curiously.

"I think that solution would put a lot of stress on you. You're the one geographically tied to a location. It's not great when you get paged and you can't get to the hospital or the BWSR staging area for over an hour. Both of us know that."

"Everyone's agreed to work with it," Jack pointed out. "Besides, they can send a chopper after me if it's urgent."

Liz shook her head. "Honey, when someone needs a trauma surgeon, or when folks are lost in the wilderness, or even when bad guys are trying to hide in that same wilderness, it's *always* urgent. Besides, flying a helicopter all over creation to find you isn't a good use of Dan's time or the BWSRU's resources."

"Okay. So what do we do? And why are we talking about this now? There's time after we get married to decide where we're going to live." Nuzzling her ear, Jack finished his thought, "It's late and I say let's just enjoy being with each other."

"In a minute. You asked why we came up here." Taking his hands, Liz looked at him seriously. "I want us to live here full time, Jack. I can manage in the loft or the upper floor of the garage or even in here. For the most part my art doesn't require a lot of space or a dedicated place to work."

"Liz, you remodeled your home so that you had a studio and it's perfect for you."

"That was when my art was the primary thing in my life, Jack. Now I have you. I can easily drive over to Grand Marais to do meet-and-greets or to teach. Beyond my supplies, which I can store in the unfinished part of the loft—the US mail, a computer, and a tele-phone are the only things I need. You, on the other hand, need to be close to where you work. Peoples' lives depend on it."

Seeing Jack open his mouth to object, Liz kissed him, effectively smothering his protest. "Hush now. My house is just a house, but your house is a work of your heart and I want to be here with you. It's perfect for us. Unless for some reason you don't want to live here full time."

Relief in his expression, Jack kissed the top of Liz's head. "Love, thank you. The truth is that, house aside, I was concerned about how the distance thing would work. I was even considering resigning from EBCH and seeing if the Grand Marais hospital might need an on-call surgeon." He turned her in his arms so she faced him. "Are you sure?"

Liz caressed his cheek. "Yes, I'm sure. It will probably take a while to get my place ready to put on the market and we definitely want to do that in the summer or early fall, not the winter. After the wedding, we can move my stuff up here as we have time. That will make showing my house easier come next summer." She cuddled close to him and murmured, "I love you and I love it here."

The house was quiet, it was very late and Liz and Jack sat cuddled together on the sofa in her living room. It was the first time they'd been alone since their drive back from Ely that morning. Since then they'd met with Liz's pastor, greeted their families, performed introductions, and gotten everybody settled at Liz's house or in a lakeside block of hotel rooms. Liz's family—her mother, brother, and sister-in-law—were staying with her while Jack's brother, sister, and their families had the block of rooms in town. Jack's father hadn't bothered to respond to the wedding invitation and, to Liz's chagrin, that didn't seem to bother Jack very much.

Looking down at Liz, Jack asked quietly, "Are you having any second thoughts, love? This has all happened pretty fast and I want you to know I'll wait as long as it takes."

Liz kissed Jack's cheek. "No, no second thoughts apart from the Reynoso thing. I just hope you won't regret it."

Pressing Liz closer, Jack kissed her tenderly. "What I'd regret is never again seeing your smile over our morning coffee, never knowing what it's like to make love with you, and never having the chance to build a life together. I won't let Reynoso have those things. Besides, he'll be out of our lives in about three weeks' time. So no second thoughts here either."

Long minutes passed in silence. Jack held Liz close, his chin on the top of her head. When the mantel clock chimed 2:00 a.m., he reluctantly moved and kissed her on the forehead. "I love you, Liz, but it's time for me to walk you upstairs then come back down here and spend my last night single sleeping alone on your sofa."

"I can stay here with you—I want to," Liz objected.

"I know and I want you here," Jack looked at Liz seriously. "Still, it's probably best to put a little space between us, because right now I'm having trouble remembering there's only one ring on your finger. We decided when I first came down here to stay that we would wait."

Liz stared at Jack. "Are you saying…"

Jack's eyes twinkled in the dim light. "Yes, I'm saying that, and apart from anything else, I don't want your mother or your brother to walk in on our first time together. Given your brother's connections, I'd probably end up practicing medicine in Greenland." Kissing Liz with a passion that left them both breathless, he came up for air with a crooked grin. "Understand me now?"

Liz got to her feet and held out her hand to help him up. "Point taken and just so you know I'm feeling the same way."

When they got upstairs to her room, Liz hugged Jack close. "Why don't you take the bed? I'm pretty wide-awake and the couch will be fine."

Holding her tightly against him, Jack whispered, "Good night, Elizabeth. Sleep well in that big, lonely bed of yours, because tomorrow night, you're going to have company in there and you won't be getting much sleep."

~⌇~

"Do you, Jackson Paul Lockwood take Elizabeth Joy Hanley Talbot to be your wife? To love her, honor her, and keep her, forsaking all others, all the days of your life?"

Jack's hands tightened around Liz's hands. "I do."

"And do you, Elizabeth Joy Hanley Talbot take Jackson Paul Lockwood to be your husband? To love him, honor him, and keep him, forsaking all others, all the days of your life?"

Liz looked at Jack, a joyful expression on her face. "I do."

Reverend Derek Coleman smiled at the couple in front of him and finished, "Then by the power vested in me by God and the state of Minnesota I pronounce you husband and wife. What God has joined together, let no man put asunder."

~⌇~

Lifting Liz into his arms, Jack carried her across the threshold of her home. Two meows welcomed them, singing out a chorus of congratulations, or maybe they just wanted treats, he couldn't be certain, and he didn't really care. He and Liz were alone together at last and now belonged to each other in the sight of God and man. This day had been perfect, or as close to perfect as he was going to get in this life. He stood still, holding her tightly to his body, feeling her heart beat against his chest. Stroking her hair, he whispered, "Thank you."

Jack could feel his wife's surprise as she asked, "For what?"

"For this wonderful day, for marrying me, and for trusting me enough to help us find a way through together." Kissing her, Jack took her hand and together they climbed the stairs to what was now their room.

CHAPTER 15

INTO THE WOODS

"Yes, Mom, I told him." Liz looked up as Jack walked in the door and rolled her eyes. "Really. He knows about that too. It's okay. I just wanted to let you know that Jack got a call and we're in Ely. I gotta go, Mom, he just walked in the door. Love you, bye."

Jack finished talking to Gus Walters, closed the door behind the officer, and raised an eyebrow at Liz. "He knows what, pray tell?"

Liz shook her head sadly. "She was going through a laundry list of things I might have forgotten to tell you before the wedding."

Smiling faintly, Jack sat down in one of the dining room chairs and pulled his wife into his lap, much to the chagrin of both cats who'd intended to claim the same space. Ignoring their outraged meows, Jack teased Liz, "Come on, tell your doctor all about it. What juicy details have you forgotten to tell me?"

"You recused yourself as my doctor, remember?"

"Fine, then as your husband, I believe it's within my purview to ask the same question. What's your mom worried about me knowing, or not knowing, as the case may be?"

Liz scowled. "I wish the details were juicy. She was wondering if I'd told you about the migraines, the fibro, the heart issues—pretty much about my entire sordid health history. Then she was worried because she didn't know if I remembered the finer points of what it was like to clean or cook for two. She pointed out that it's been a while since I had anyone to take care of, and she doesn't really think I've been doing such a great job of caring for myself."

Up until that moment, Jack had been teasing, enjoying the shared fun of the moment. Now he realized that Liz didn't find this at all funny. In fact, it sounded like the conversation with her mom had turned into a laundry list of his wife's shortcomings. Hugging Liz close to his heart, Jack said quietly, "I'm sorry. When we see her next, I'll be certain to let her know that I've been privy to your health history since just before Thanksgiving, and I'll most certainly disabuse her of any notion of spousal neglect."

Jack looked at her seriously, "Liz, I love you. That won't change because of your health or anything in your past, and it certainly won't change because of something your mother thinks. I know I'm a blessed man. As for the part about cooking and cleaning, we'll do what we've been doing, share the work and enjoy the benefits. Speaking of cooking," he sniffed happily, "something smells awfully good. What's for dinner?"

Cuddling closer to Jack, Liz answered, "A couple of steaks, cheddar cheese potatoes, a salad, and a really good bottle of Sangiovese to wash it all down. I also made brownies, just in case we feel like dessert. I'm waiting to start the filets until we're ready to eat."

Jack looked at her quizzically. "That's sounds fabulous and I'm starved, but what's the occasion?"

Pushing away from Jack, Liz swatted him playfully. "Really? For your information it's our one-week anniversary. How could you forget?"

Slapping his forehead, Jack groaned, "Our one-week anniversary and I've already screwed up." He hugged Liz close again. "Thank you for such a wonderful homecoming. It was a rough day and I was going to suggest we go out, but what you've planned sounds like heaven."

Liz looked at Jack with concern in her eyes. "I know you and Dan were called out again today. Did something happen to one of you?"

Jack hurried to reassure her, "Dan and I are both fine. We were looking for a young couple who'd gone cross-country skiing early yesterday and never made it back. We found them but were pretty much too late to do anything other than recover their bodies. One was dead on the scene and the other died on the way to the hospital. There was nothing I could do except hold the wife's hand as she passed."

"I'm so sorry." Liz held Jack close but didn't say anything more. Her warmth and empathy were enough to soothe his ragged spirit. After a few minutes, he kissed her and said, "I'm okay, really. Let's put those steaks on and commence to celebrating!

Hours later, they lay in their bed relaxing in the wake of their loving and watching the fire. Jack nuzzled Liz's neck. "This has been a perfect evening." Brushing her cheek with gentle fingers, he said quietly, "You have such beautiful eyes. I could get lost in them."

Liz smiled. "Thank you." Sliding her hand over his chest, she said, "I feel the same way about pretty much all of you. People are going to think I'm a cougar when they see us together—which, actually, I am, so that's okay."

Jack pressed her palm to his lips. "Being a year older than me hardly qualifies you for cougarhood. Besides, darlin'," winking at her, he pulled her into his arms, "you..."

Jack sat up when the lights in the room went out. A split second later, the property alarm started shrieking. Looking outside, he realized that the outdoor lights were still off, meaning that someone had tampered with the system. He didn't see anything or anyone, but that meant little. He turned to his wife and said tersely, "Get dressed, Liz, and hurry."

Following his own advice, Jack dressed, pocketed a flashlight, his emergency kit, and his gun along with an extra magazine, then pulled outerwear for both of them from the closet. This time when he looked outside, he could see several shadowy forms converging on their front door. Rather than go out the French doors in their bedroom, the logical route of egress, Jack led Liz into the master bathroom, and they climbed through the window.

Crouching behind a large pine at the edge of their cleared property, Jack watched as the men forced open the front door of the house and spread out. He could see their shadowy forms moving throughout the first floor, thanks to the glow of the fire. They must have been wearing some sort of night-vision equipment, because they performed a very efficient search in near darkness. Jack saw at least four others around the garage.

Taking Liz's hand, Jack led her into the woods, trying to keep to packed snow or exposed earth to avoid leaving footprints. They went on this way for over an hour, as he worked to keep his bearings in the star-lit darkness.

Finally, Jack pulled Liz down beside him on an exposed granite boulder. "Let's rest for a minute," he whispered, his lips against her ear.

Liz nodded, then she asked Jack, "What about Binx and Sierra?"

Admiration for Liz flooded through Jack. His wife was tired and afraid, yet her first thought had been for the two fur children who shared their home. Squeezing her hand, he whispered again, "It'll be okay. They're smarter than these guys, remember the last time?"

Liz smiled faintly, but then her face fell. "Binx is still in a cast. How will she get away?"

"Sierra won't leave her and Binx's leg is almost healed. She moves pretty well even with the cast. Besides, you know how good those two are at hiding in the dark.

"Can you keep moving?" Jack eyed his wife with concern. Just yesterday, Liz had spent much of the day in bed, suffering through a fibro flare, but tonight she seemed to be moving more easily. Whether that was due to the new meds she was on, or exercising more, or a change in diet, he wasn't sure, but he was hopeful for a better future for her. A better future that depended on them escaping their pursuers tonight.

"Yes, I'm fine. Why don't you just call Dan?" Liz asked as she got to her feet.

Jack showed her his cell. "No bars, reception has been erratic tonight. But we're getting close to town and…"

Two slugs plowed through the air between them. Jack grabbed Liz's hand and, keeping low, they ran for the trees and cover. For what seemed like hours, but in reality was less than thirty minutes, they dodged bullets, searchlights, and men wearing goggles. Much to Jack's chagrin, the search drove the two of them away from town and into the BWCA. Thankfully the moon was in its crescent phase and close to setting, so darkness was on their side, at least when it came to avoiding assailants who weren't wearing night vision equipment.

Sunrise was only an hour or so away and Jack needed to find them shelter before daybreak. He vaguely remembered a lake just ahead and on the far side of that lake there was a granite outcropping with several caves. The going became rough as they headed into the heavier underbrush along the shore. They'd almost circled the lake when Liz crumpled, falling face-first into the snow. Turning her face up, Jack paused only long enough to make certain she was breathing, then put her over his shoulder and ran on.

Jack eventually found the cave he'd been searching for in the semi-darkness. Squeezing through the narrow entrance, he cautiously turned on his flashlight, praying that they wouldn't find themselves face to face with a sleepy bear or a cougar. To his relief, they were alone.

Swinging Liz from his shoulder, Jack paled when he got his first good look at her. Her face was pasty white and her pulse almost nonexistent. He rapidly pulled the parka from her body and found what he'd feared. She was bleeding from a shoulder wound. Had she received immediate treatment, it would have been no big deal, but she'd been losing blood for some time. One of the bullets he thought they'd dodged had found its mark. He had to stop the bleeding, or very soon he was going to be a widower for the second time in his life. How could an evening that started with such promise have gone so far wrong?

CHAPTER 16

SHADOWLANDS

"He's still not answering," Dan said to his wife. It was just after daybreak and Dan had been calling Jack for the last hour to tell him to stay home. It had been a quiet night and there were no calls awaiting the team's attention, but Jack wasn't answering, and neither was Liz.

"Try the radio," Beth suggested.

"I did." Dan frowned, something in all this was giving him a raging gut ache. "Something's wrong."

A scant thirty minutes later, Dan stood in the middle of Jack and Liz's living room, his fears confirmed. Intruders had trashed the place. Snow, scratches, and soggy ashes covered the cherry hardwood floors. Jack and Liz had disappeared. Trying to think past his worry, Dan examined the footprints outside the house. From the look of things, at least eight pairs of boots had been tramping over the property and inside the house.

"Chief Harrison," Officer Stan Brings interrupted Dan's thoughts.

"Stan, did you find something?" Dan asked with some trepidation.

"Yes, sir, no sign of Jack or Liz or," Stan cleared his throat, "um, bodies, sir. No blood either. But we found these two hiding in the top of the closet." Motioning to the man behind him, Stan stepped aside. Officer Gus Walters stood there, holding two confused looking cats.

Dan took his first deep breath of the morning. That they'd found the cats unharmed would be the first bit of good news he could share with his friends, that the house was still standing would be the second. It was clear they'd gotten out, but it was also clear, from the lack of communication from them, that they'd not reached town and safety. Jack was an expert in outdoor tracking and survival, so he and Liz might be hard to find. Straightening his shoulders, Dan thought, "Well, I'm an expert too. We're coming, guys. Hold on."

The morning wore on as Dan and the team worked to follow an elusive trail. Sometimes there were no signs for several miles at a stretch—a testimony to Jack's expertise. Fortunately, the dogs always managed to pick up the scent. They were now almost eight miles from the house and coming up on Little Gabbro Lake. At first, Dan didn't see anything that would suggest that Jack and Liz had come this way, but suddenly the dogs let out a chorus of yelps and excited barks.

Following them, they found the place where Liz had collapsed and for the first time since finding the Lockwoods' home empty hours before, Dan felt a renewed chill of fear. Blood spatter showed dark red on the pristine white of the snow. Jack's footprints leading away from the area were deeper, indicating that he was now carrying Liz. "Jack, Liz," Dan shouted, cupping his mouth with his hands, "it's Dan. Where are you?"

Silence was his only answer, but the dogs were hot after a scent, almost outdistancing their handlers. "Here," Stan shouted after a short time, "Chief, we've got them. Hurry!"

When Dan squeezed into the cave, his fear turned to ice. Jack bent over Liz's unmoving body, his arms at his side, his face gray with grief and exhaustion.

"Sir," Stan whispered in Dan's ear, "we found him doing CPR on Liz, but I couldn't find a pulse. She's gone."

Anger like he'd never known blind-sided Dan. "No," he said softly, "no, no, no, no!" With every word his voice got louder until finally, kneeling beside Liz, he resumed CPR, oblivious even to Jack.

Dan worked on her for what seemed like forever, but in fact, was just minutes.

Gus had his fingertips on Liz's carotid artery. Suddenly he looked up, "Chief, I've got a pulse!"

❧

Dan quietly opened the door to Liz's hospital room in the Intensive Care Unit at Duluth's St. Luke's Hospital. He didn't want to wake Jack if he'd gone to sleep, but, as Dan surmised, his friend was awake, his eyes fixed on his wife's face.

The trip back to EBCH and then the second airlift into Duluth had been some of the worst hours of Dan's life. On the way into Ely, Jack sat huddled beneath blankets, unmoving, saying nothing, even when Liz's heart stopped while in flight. The physician on the team, Zachary Birch, managed to resuscitate her.

At EBCH, they'd been able to get Liz on whole blood and stabilize her enough to chance transferring her to the nearest regional trauma center. During the trip to Duluth aboard *Life-Flight*, Jack had thanked Dan, but then had withdrawn into silence again. Even now, Jack looked up when Dan walked into the room, but said nothing.

Sitting down beside his friend, Dan squeezed Jack's shoulder. "How is she?"

Jack said nothing, so Dan tried again. "Jack, talk to me. How's Liz doing?"

This time Jack's eyes met Dan's, he said nothing, but shook his head.

Dan swallowed his fear. Liz was on a ventilator, but her heart was still beating. This time he took Jack's hand, squeezing hard. "Don't you dare give up on her."

Saying nothing, Jack went back to staring at Liz's face. Tears trickled from his eyes, but nothing Dan did or said elicited a response. Gently squeezing Jack's shoulder again, Dan finally said, "I'll be here when you need me, but right now, I'm going bastard hunting."

❧

At some level, Jack knew when Dan left. He felt badly for not responding to his friend, but he didn't know what to say. It was Jack's own fault that Liz was dying. Had he been looking out for her as he should have been, he would have noticed that she was slowly bleeding to death as they ran through the woods. After all his fine words, he'd failed to keep a single promise he'd made to her.

Jack hadn't slept in over forty hours. Perhaps if he'd been able to get some rest, he would have been better able to see that he'd kept Liz alive long enough to get her help. Perhaps he would have realized the wisdom of drawing strength and comfort from friends and family. But exhausted and grief stricken, Jack retreated further into himself. Ignoring the tray with breakfast and coffee they'd brought in, he waited, expecting each beat of Liz's heart to be her last.

"Trust Me."

Jumping to his feet, Jack looked around. There was no one in the room except for him and his dying wife. He was hearing things. Collapsing back into the bedside chair, he resumed his death watch.

"Trust Me."

"Who's there?" Jack yelled heatedly. There was no answer. He was certain he'd just taken his first step toward insanity. Nonetheless, he tried again, more quietly, "What do you want?" His only answer was the hiss of the vent and the beep of the heart monitor.

Leaning over Liz, Jack's tears flowed freely as he confessed, "I'm sorry, love, I don't know how to save you."

"She is Mine before the beginning of time."

This time Jack felt the voice inside, or rather sensed it. Abruptly, he knew that he'd spoken the truth. Liz's life was out of his hands, but what did that mean? His wife believed that God determined the times of her life. Could that be? Could it be that God was waiting for something from him? Having nothing to lose, he whispered, "Is that you, God? Liz's God? If You're really here, Liz needs You, not me. Please, help her."

CHAPTER 17

A LOSS LIKE NO OTHER

Dan knew the next five steps would require every ounce of strength he possessed. Squaring his shoulders, he moved to the lectern at the front of the small room. Cameras of all kinds whirred, clicked, and flashed. Why they wanted to take his picture, Dan would never understand. The press release was what they'd all come to hear—they were like vultures gathering.

Clearing his throat, Dan began, "Good morning. I'm going to read from a prepared statement. Because this is an active investigation, I won't be taking questions from you fine folks. Today we lost one of our own. Elizabeth Talbot Lockwood, the artist, died of injuries sustained Tuesday when armed intruders broke into the Ely home she shared with her husband, Dr. Jack Lockwood. As many of you know, Jack and Liz had been married for less than two weeks. Jack's requested and we've granted an extended leave of absence from the Boundary Waters Search and Rescue Unit. Following Liz's memorial service tomorrow, Jack will be leaving the area to spend time with family. He and I ask that you respect their privacy in this painful time. The FBI, the Ely police department, and law enforcement entities throughout the state are committed to bringing those who killed Elizabeth to justice. Thank you."

Despite Dan's earlier statement, there was a chorus of "just one question, Chief" as he walked off the platform. He ignored them completely, concentrating on keeping it together until he reached the shelter of his office. He didn't even acknowledge Stan, who stood guard in front of his door.

Jack sat in front of Dan's desk. "Is it done?" he asked sadly.

Dan looked around then nodded. "In a few hours, most everyone in the area will know of Liz's passing. I asked them to give you privacy. I hope you don't have to cope with an onslaught of, well, of anything. Jack, I know this goes without saying, but I'm so sorry. I can't begin to imagine how difficult this is for you. If there's anything I can do…"

Jack nodded mutely, then got to his feet. "Thank you for handling the press release." He took a shuddering breath. "I have to go. I'm meeting with Liz's pastor to plan her service." Without another word, Jack turned on his heel and left.

Dan shook his head, knowing that Jack was dangerously close to collapse. How much could a man take? His calm was extraordinary under the circumstances and Dan could only pray that time would do its healing work before his friend imploded.

Jack stood alone in front of the church, facing the small urn, his head bowed. He took a breath, then another, trying to force himself to turn around and walk away. There was a group of their friends waiting in the front of the church to offer their consolation, support, and love. The sad thing was he didn't want to talk with them, all he wanted was to be alone. He needed time and space to get his head together, time to think about what had transpired in the hospital room that awful morning, time to remember the joy, time to convince himself that life was still worth living. Most of all, he needed to get away from here.

The last few days had been like walking through a bog in the dense fog. Nothing seemed solid or real, and all he could do was go through the motions—playing some kind of macabre part in a nightmarish story. Jack knew that if he could get through the next few hours, he and his sister would drive to Duluth and be on a flight for Detroit before nightfall. That thought alone gave him the strength to turn his back on the dead and move toward the living. He hoped he would find some peace in the journey before him.

～〜〜

"Jack, we're home."

Jack woke with a start and looked around. He'd always loved visiting Vicky and Ted, their two college-aged boys, two dogs, and three cats. Their home in suburban Detroit was in a continual state of joyful chaos. Although Vicky was five years younger than Jack, they'd always been close. That's why he'd chosen her to make this journey with him. A part of him wished he could stay more than a night, but there was something he had to do. Something that couldn't wait.

Climbing out of the taxi, Jack paid the fare, and grabbed their luggage. Once inside the house, he hugged his nephews, greeted Ted, and collapsed into a chair. Looking up at his sister and her husband, Jack said, "Thank you both. I don't know what I'd do without you."

～〜〜

A little more than twelve hours later, Jack stood at the foot of a fifty-story condominium building in downtown Chicago, feeling small and insignificant. That was probably the point. The "Magnificent Mile," they called it. It shouted to the world that it was a mecca of conspicuous consumption. He greeted the doorman, explained his business and who he'd come to see. Sixty seconds later, a private elevator deposited him on the penthouse level. Bracing himself, he knocked at the imposing door in front of him. A tall, handsome, older man with a longish mane of white hair answered. Jack stood silent for a moment, then put out his hand. "Hello, Dad."

After shaking his father's hand, Jack walked into the condo. Then the awkward silence he'd expected filled the space between them. Normally, this was when Jack would retreat, outside or to his assigned room, anywhere away from his father. He couldn't do that today, there were important things that he needed to say.

"Nice place," Jack winced. Of all the words he hadn't planned to start with, an inane complement that was not at all heartfelt was pretty much at the top of the list.

To Jack's surprise, his dad smiled, looking pleased. "Thanks. I got a great price on it. The couple was underwater on their mortgage and jumped at my first below market bid." He rocked back on his heels. "Yep, timing is everything."

Jack took a deep breath to avoid saying something stupid like "way to take advantage of another's misfortune, pops. Score one for you." No, starting an argument wasn't what Jack had come for, so he simply nodded and said, "Well, it's nice, and I know you love this area. Are you feeling okay?" Jack's dad was seventy-seven and had tangled with prostate cancer the year before.

Slapping himself on the chest, the older man quipped, "Never better, but I understand you've had a rough time recently."

Jack realized that this was what passed for empathy in Lloyd Beckett's world. So once again he nodded. "That's putting it mildly but, yeah, a rough time. Dad," Jack took a deep breath; this wasn't going to be easy, "I know you didn't have to do this, so, thank you."

"You're still my son, even though you took your mother's name. Never understood that, but I suppose it was her idea—her final way of getting back at me." It was obvious that this was an old argument that gnawed at Lloyd when they were apart and flared to life whenever they were together.

Jack refused to let his dad draw him into the familiar quarrel. "Whatever your reasons, I'm grateful for your help."

The older man nodded in assent then asked, "Are you still planning to go through with this?"

"Yes, Dad. It's for the best."

"I suppose you want to get on with it then." Lloyd turned to walk down the hall.

"Please." Jack shrugged out of his coat, hung it in the front closet and followed his father.

Opening the last door on the right side of the long hallway, Lloyd stood aside so Jack could enter. Then, without saying a word, he backed out of the room, closing the door behind him.

Once he was gone, Jack began to shake. What if…if…

"Hey, it's my doctor." A familiar voice came from the recliner across the room. "I've missed you so much!"

Her soft greeting broke the ice and Jack crossed the large room in three long strides. Another breath and he had Liz in his arms. Before he could say anything, his calm shattered. He buried his face in her hair and sobbed.

"So do you and Dan think it worked?" Liz asked her husband.

It was dusk outside, the sounds of the city at rush hour muted by the height. It had taken time, but Jack had calmed enough to fall asleep in his wife's arms. Now, several hours later, he felt human again. He nodded. "You're officially dead. The only ones who know otherwise are the US Attorney, FBI agent Bornell, Dan, the medical examiner, Pastor Coleman, our immediate families, and your doctor at St. Luke's."

"Dan didn't tell Beth?" Liz sounded surprised.

Jack shook his head. "The fewer people who know, the better. Dan's had to be really careful around the station, because no one there knows."

Liz covered his hand with her own. "This must have been an awful week for you."

"What gave it away?" Jack smiled crookedly. "I'm sorry about losing it before. This whole week—the hospital, the memorial, all the people with platitudes—it was just about what I deserved after failing you so badly."

"Jack, where is this coming from?" Liz backed away and sat up. She was pale and a sling cradled her left arm, but otherwise she looked just like she had when he'd made love to her on their one-week anniversary, now just over a week in the past—gloriously alive.

"Where is it coming from?" Jack repeated cynically. "I just spent a week pretending you were dead, only I didn't have to do all that much pretending. Actually, you did die—twice in fact—once in the helicopter on the way into Ely. Zach brought you back that time.

And once in the cave, earlier on. Dan was the one doing CPR then while I sat and stared at a rock."

"Jack Lockwood, that's not what happened, and you know it! I know it too because Dan told me the real version of this story. You were giving me CPR when the team found us and had it not been for Stan pulling you away from me, you wouldn't have stopped. Please tell me what's going on inside your head. This isn't you."

"Maybe it's the new me. The physician who woke up one morning and couldn't even save his own wife. I…Ow!" Jack flinched when Liz pinched his forearm. "What's up with the spousal abuse?"

"Because you're wallowing in self-pity and I want to know why!" Liz exclaimed. "We're sitting here together, both of us reasonably healthy, with our lives ahead of us. You should be thankful, but instead, you insist on taking this flawed trip down memory lane. I could list all the reasons we're alive because of you, but you know them as well as I do. Something else is going on. So give!"

Jack studied his hands, acutely uncomfortable. Liz was right. Under the circumstances, he was being grossly unfair to himself and exceedingly ungrateful. There was more to this than his tendency to hold himself to a higher standard than others around him. There was even more to it than Liz's close call, Eduard Reynoso, or the role Jack had played over the last week.

Lifting his head enough to look at Liz, Jack saw her eyes fill with concern. Of all the things he didn't want to do, causing her distress was at the top of the list. Resting his head on her good shoulder, he muttered, "Love, it's weird."

Liz patted his knee comfortingly. "So it's weird. What about our relationship hasn't been weird? Please, talk to me."

Jack shrugged his shoulders. "I don't even know if I can put all of it into words, but I'll try. You may not know this about me, but I can be a bit controlling, particularly when it comes to medicine." He grinned, to show Liz he knew he was making the understatement of the century. "I have a lot of confidence in my abilities."

"As you should, honey," Liz encouraged, "you're one of the most gifted people I know."

"You've borrowed my rose-colored glasses but thank you." Jack recaptured the thread of his story. "Anyway, that trait helps me make life-saving decisions quickly, but it can also make me overconfident—it did make me overconfident that night in the woods. I thought I had everything under control until you collapsed. Someone shot you, you nearly bled out, and I missed it all."

Jack cupped Liz's cheek in his palm. "You didn't say anything, and I think I understand why, but any physician worth his salt would have seen the signs. Liz, we stopped twice to rest, and I still missed your symptoms. After I got us settled in the cave, it seemed that nothing I did worked. I couldn't stop the bleeding from your shoulder, at least not completely. I couldn't even light a fire for warmth because I couldn't leave you alone to collect wood."

Liz opened her mouth, but Jack shushed her, "Please, love, let me finish. Otherwise I'll never get through this."

Liz nodded her okay.

"When your heart stopped, I could hear the voices of the team outside, but I couldn't move because that would have meant interrupting CPR. I yelled, but we still lost valuable time while they searched for the right opening in the rock. Then Stan came in, felt your neck for a pulse and told me you were gone. That was something else I'd missed. I was certain you were responding.

"Needless to say, my world came crashing in. Your life was in my hands that night and I failed you. Even when Dan brought you back, I couldn't quite accept that you were alive. The rest of the time between our rescue and the next day in Duluth feels not quite real. Except for one thing."

A single tear slid down Liz's cheek. "What's that?" she asked shakily.

"After Dan left your hospital room that morning, you and I were alone again, I expected every heartbeat to be your last. In fact, I didn't eat breakfast, because I was certain you'd die and I would miss it because I was buttering my toast or something stupid like that." Jack cringed, his reasoning sounded ludicrous, even to him. "So I sat there and waited for you to die. Then someone started talking to me.

Liz, I swear there was no one in that room but you and me. Yet I was and am certain I heard a voice say, 'Trust Me.'"

Liz's eyes widened, but she didn't say a word.

Seeing her look, Jack shrugged. "Yeah, I pretty much thought I was going crazy too. So after a few minutes, I went back to my watching and waiting. Then it happened again. This time I was certain that someone was behind me, but we were still alone in a glass-walled room.

"The third time I felt, rather than heard the words. 'She is mine before the beginning of time' rang through my spirit like someone had shouted them into my ear." Seeing Liz frown, Jack squeezed her hand. "I know how crazy this all sounds, but I'm telling you the truth. I heard those exact words, weird time sense and all.

"It wasn't until a few minutes later that I connected the dots. I realized that it was God talking. Not the insipid, convenient God that I'd grown comfortable with, but *your* God, Ellie's God—God with consequences. I realized that in the face of that kind of power, my abilities were insignificant. I couldn't give life where there was no life, and I couldn't take life when God decides that life should continue. In that moment, I had a blinding flash of insight—I was nothing without God. I prayed, Liz. I begged God to save you. I fell on my knees, pleading with Him, offering my life in exchange for yours, whatever He wanted. To my surprise, He didn't ask me for anything, at least not that I could discern.

"Then, unlikely as it sounds, I fell asleep. The next thing I knew, your doctor shoved me out of the way so he could remove the endo-trach tube in your throat, because you were breathing on your own. By noon, you were awake and talking. By nightfall, we'd made the decision to fake your death in the hopes that disappearing would keep you safe. I called Dad and the rest you know."

Liz looked at Jack, her heart in her eyes. "Forgive me, honey, but having an encounter with God and the fact that I survived a nasty experience are both positive things, so why are you so negative?"

"Because since that morning when I was hearing voices, I've heard nothing. I've felt nothing." Jack's face showed his uncertainty. "I don't know what I've done wrong, but God's abandoned me."

CHAPTER 18

CLOSING IN

"Do you still think God's abandoned us?" Liz asked. They were in police headquarters in Duluth, Minnesota, behind the reflective glass in Interrogation. They'd flown in from Chicago that morning in a private jet. The US attorney wasn't taking any more chances with Liz's life. Everything seemed to indicate that their subterfuge had worked. The trial had started, and Liz was less than a week away from her scheduled testimony.

"I never said that God abandoned *us*, I said that He abandoned *me*. Now I don't know what to think. You're alive, Dan and Beth are alive, and we're all safe, even the cats, so God answered every one of my prayers. Yet I still don't know what He wants from me in return." Jack rubbed his forehead. "I'll get it figured out."

As Liz opened her mouth to respond, Dan walked into the room, his face grim. "Hey, glad to see you made it." He looked at Jack curiously. "How are things with dear old dad?"

"About the same." Jack rapidly changed the subject. "So we got a call early this morning from the US attorney, packed our bags, traveled up here in style, and we still don't know why. What's going on?"

"What's going on is this." Dan flipped a switch and the one-way mirror brightened into transparency, revealing a room on the far side. A man sat at a table. He was clearly uncomfortable; his wrists were manacled together, and he kept looking around like a caged animal.

Looking at Dan inquiringly, Jack asked, "Who's that?"

"That, my friend, is Al Heikkinen, a long-time resident of Hovland, Minnesota. We found this guy's fingerprints all over the inside of your house after the break-in. Is there any legitimate reason this man would have been in your home in the recent past?"

Jack shook his head, then looked at Liz. "I don't recognize him, do you?"

Liz shook her head. "I've never seen him before. Where'd you find him?"

"Having his own little party in his car," Dan answered. "He was weaving down Highway 53, just north of Duluth, smoking a joint and drinking a beer. He was way too hinky for someone busted on a simple DUI. It wasn't until AFIS[5] found the fingerprint match that things began to make sense. He got really nervous when he saw that I was here in Duluth. I guess the word's out that I'm looking hard for this group and don't plan to be very particular about due process." Dan smiled grimly and Liz looked a little worried.

"Um, so why exactly are Jack and I here?" Liz asked nervously.

Dan smirked. "I just thought you'd like to join our little party."

Liz bit her lip. "Um, Dan, that thing about due process. I'm still a licensed attorney, even though I don't practice, and that makes me an officer of the court. You're not going to hurt him or do anything stupid, right?"

Dan looked at Jack. "Come on, buddy, tell your wife what a prince I am."

Jack eyed Dan skeptically. "No. I think I'm with her. You're definitely acting a bit strange, even for you. This is not a question, it's a statement. You're not going to hurt that guy. Agreed?"

Dan looked from one of them to the other. "You two are taking all the fun out of this. Fine, I asked you here on the off chance you might have recognized Al. Since you don't, the fingerprint match will do. Now do either of you have a problem if I'm not terribly polite?"

Jack smiled. "Can we watch?"

---

[5] The Automated Fingerprint Identification System (AFIS) is an identification method that uses digital imaging technology to obtain, store, and analyze fingerprint data. AFIS was created by the FBI for use in criminal cases.

Dan turned to go. "Help yourself, but don't go far. No one's supposed to know you're here."

As it turned out, there wasn't that much to see. Al was so terrified by Dan's presence that he'd waived his right to counsel and started talking before Dan even sat down. That was good. The fact that he was a third-party underling hired by a flunky and was at the bottom of the food chain in this group was not so good. They did find out that "the boss" believed that Liz was dead, but Al couldn't say with any certainty that "the boss" and Eduard Reynoso were the same person.

Their instructions that night had been to kill both Jack and Liz, but after hunting for them all night then hearing the dogs, the invaders scattered without reporting back to the man who'd hired and outfitted them. Al didn't know who that was. He was only there because his friend Matt couldn't make it and promised to share the money with Al if Al would take his place. Since they'd failed to kill the Lockwoods, no money had been forthcoming and Matt was in the wind.

Dan was rubbing his forehead when he walked back into the small room where Liz and Jack waited. "Sorry guys, that was a bust. The only thing you didn't hear was Al trying to catch a plea deal by telling me that there's an inside guy in our department that the boss pays very well. I think Al's been watching too many cop shows. I know our guys and there's not a one of them I don't trust with my life or yours."

"Dan," Jack began, "I..."

The door opened before Jack could shield Liz from prying eyes. Recognizing the interloper, Jack calmly greeted him, "Hey Stan. I didn't know you'd made the trip down with Dan."

Dan looked irritated. "What are you doing in here, Brings? You're supposed to be going through Heikkinen's file."

Stan had the most curious combination of astonishment and anxiety on his face as he faced Dan. "Uh, sir, Captain Tusakey wants to see you. Liz...I...I thought..." The veteran officer gave up and just stood there with his mouth open.

Liz smiled. "Hi, Stan. Sorry to have surprised you like this. What can I say except rumors of my death have been greatly exaggerated?"

Still looking flummoxed, Stan said, "I'm glad to know that, Liz, I'm glad. You too, Jack."

Dan got in Stan's face. "Nobody, I repeat, nobody hears anything from you about this, because if they do, getting canned will be the least of your worries. I will draw and quarter you myself if I hear so much as a whisper that Liz is anything but dead. Am I clear?"

"Yes, sir. Perfectly, sir." Then Stan smiled faintly. "Glad you're okay, Liz. I'm outta here."

Dan rolled his eyes when the officer left. "This case will be the death of me yet. Since we got here, it's been difficult to keep Brings busy on department business. Now he's wandering the halls acting as an errand boy for Tusakey. I was going to make the trip by myself, but Stan volunteered to come along because he was off for the next few days, he said he needed the overtime, and I'm a pushover. Anyway, it's decision time. You guys want to go back to Chicago for the duration, or shall I arrange for a safe house here?"

Shrugging, Jack turned to Liz. "We're less than a week away, the trial has started. I say let's stay here. Moving from place to place carries with it its own risk. What do you think?"

Liz sighed. "Whatever you and Dan think best is fine with me. All I want is for this to be over, so I can reclaim my life. I don't know if my business will ever recover, because all my customers think I'm dead."

Jack held Liz close, trying not to let his frustration with the situation transmit itself through his touch. Kissing her temple, he whispered, "I know, love. I want this to be over too. We have a honeymoon to take and a life together to create." He looked up at Dan. "We'll stay here in Duluth if they've got a place and enough manpower. Before we leave, do you have a minute?"

CHAPTER 19

THE FACE OF BETRAYAL

An hour later, Liz and Jack were heading to a safe house under Stan's protection. He'd volunteered for guard duty, pointing out that there was no more paperwork for him to do. Dan had agreed. Slowing, Stan eased the car into an almost invisible drive in Duluth's steep central hillside area. A short while later, they'd settled into a two-bedroom apartment that for all its seediness commanded a breath-taking view of the harbor. Jack and Liz relaxed on the sofa, coffee cups in hand. Stan sat in a chair across from them, a glass of water by his side. Jack yawned and stretched, they'd left Chicago early and it had already been a long day. It was cool in the apartment, so he put his arm around Liz.

"Sorry about the accommodations, guys. They don't have too many options for visiting VIPs," Stan apologized.

"VIPs? Stan, you know us better than that," Jack objected. "Both Liz and I would far rather be home, doing our jobs. We sure appreciate your willingness to watch over us."

"Oh, that's no problem. Especially," Stan pulled his service automatic and pointed it directly at Liz, "seeing as how you're about to make me very rich."

Jack sat up straight. "Stan? Why? We've been friends for a long time."

Stan's expression hovered between anger and unhappiness. "I know, Jack. It's been over two years. I owe you a lot, but it's also been

107

two years of schlepping along in your wake, following your orders or Chief Harrison's, and working every bit as hard as the two of you for a fraction of the pay. I just couldn't afford to do that anymore."

Jack sat very still and replied, "Stan, I don't understand. I've always considered you and Joanne friends. Please tell me Liz was really gone that morning you found us in the cave. Was she really dead or was the CPR doing its job?"

Stan looked even more unhappy. "You're the doctor, Jack, figure it out. I thought the job was done once I got you off of her, then Harrison ruined everything." He waved the gun at Liz. "Still Liz's dying act had me convinced and Reynoso too. Now I have to go through it all again, in order to keep up my side of the bargain. Can you imagine the look on Eduard's face if Liz had actually shown up in court?"

"Stan, I can still do that," Liz said calmly. "I'd be happy to forget about all this and just go about my business in the courtroom."

"I'm sorry, Liz, but I've got a family to support and bills to pay."

Liz frowned. "You don't think I have those same things?"

Stan moved over and sat down beside her. "No, I don't Liz. You're a fancy artist and you married Jack, so I don't think you know anything at all about money trouble, trying to keep food on the table, and wondering how to pay the bills." Stan glanced at the clock on the wall. "Thankfully that'll all be over as soon as they get here. I'll make sure it's fast and painless for you and Jack. Neither of you deserve this and I know that."

"You do know there's a reward, a significant reward, offered for any information about the attack on our home." Jack reminded Stan, sliding forward on the couch cushion as he did so.

Shaking his head sadly, Stan said, "It's too little, too late, Jack. I need the kind of money I'm about to come into just to keep my two kids in college, my parents where they are, and pay the mortgage. Besides, if I back out now, my family's as good as dead. You know Reynoso."

"Stan, you can't possibly be this stupid. Unless you do something to help us now, none of us are going to walk out of here alive. Reynoso's goons will just kill us and then kill you. That way Liz doesn't testify, plus your drug lord pal ties up a loose end *and* gets to keep all his money. He's used to using people caught in bad situations." Jack leaned in a little closer and said, "Liz and I might get killed because she cares about doing the right thing, but you'll end up just as dead. Who'll take care of your family then?"

"No! That can't happen!" Stan stood up and swung wildly at Jack with the gun. That gave Jack the opening he was looking for. He grabbed Stan's arm and pulled him down, putting all his body weight behind the move. Liz dove for the other end of the sofa, trying to give her husband room to maneuver. The gun discharged at the same time as Jack's fist cracked against Stan's jaw, sending the officer sliding to the floor unconscious. After kicking the gun away from Stan, Jack got to his feet, holding his side.

<hr />

"We've got to stop meeting like this," Liz said as she plopped her hip down on the edge of the gurney where Jack rested. "What's with you going all James Bond on Stan, anyway? You knew Dan was right outside, listening to every word."

"It was taking too much time to talk Stan into being the hero, besides," Jack groaned and sat up, swinging his legs over the other side of the gurney, "I get tired of everyone assuming I'm not a real cop. I worked too hard for that badge. So I thought about what Dan would do."

"Did I hear my name?" Dan stuck his head into the curtained off ER cubical. "I certainly didn't teach you how to get shot while disarming a suspect." Dan patted Liz's hand soothingly and said to Jack, "Doc says you're fine. It's just a crease. I'm sorry to say no one showed up at the safe house after you left. Word must have gotten out that we'd fingered Stan for our mole. Jack, that was nice work, by the way. I would have bet he was one of the good ones. What made you so sure he was hinky?"

"In the cave, when I was working on Liz, I was certain that her heart was responding and that I was detecting spontaneous respirations," Jack replied. "Stan practically leveled me to get me away from her and he barely touched her neck before announcing she was dead. It takes practice to find a carotid pulse that fast—practice he didn't have. I was pretty out of it, but the fact that you brought her back so quickly suggests I'm right. Did you get everything you needed from Stan? I hope he'll cooperate."

"Yeah. He started in on a deal as soon as he woke up," Dan said. "By the way, that was a nice haymaker. Is every bone in your hand broken?"

Jack held up his right hand, wrapped in an ice pack and a towel. "Not broken, just sore and it was a stupid thing for a surgeon to do." Getting to his feet slowly, Jack put his arm around his wife. "Come on, it's been a long day and I can't feel good about what happened here. Let's go home."

Dan held up his hand, "Not so fast. You," he pointed at Liz, "still have a trial to testify at in about four days. What would you both say to lying low in the nicest room the Northland Inn has to offer? With room service and a friendly, loyal guard outside your door who has orders not to disturb you unless called, but to quietly dispose of any bad guys?" Dan arched an eyebrow. "Well?"

Jack looked at Liz, Liz looked at Jack. Finally, Liz said, "I guess we'd be safer if I stayed dead for a couple more days. I've heard that the Northland has steam baths and nice big tubs, king beds with lots of pillows. And," she eyed her husband demurely, "we did have to postpone our honeymoon."

Jack smiled, his expression lightening a little. "Say no more." He fixed Dan with what Dan called his doctor look. "On expense account, everything?"

Dan nodded. "It's the least we can do. After all, you both got shot."

Jack pressed his side and winced. "He's right and it hurts." Eyeing Dan, he pushed, "Room overlooking the lake?"

Dan was now the one who looked pained, but he nodded. "Is there any other kind for wounded warriors?"

"No per diem restrictions, since we have to order in," Jack added.

"Jack!" Dan growled.

Reaching for his shirt, Jack shook Dan's hand. "I believe we have an accord, but as soon as Liz finishes telling the jury her tale, we get to go home, and Liz gets to make a miraculous recovery. Deal?"

This time Dan happily shook Jack's hand. "Deal."

CHAPTER 20

A DIVINE APPOINTMENT

"Come on." Using his key, Dan opened the door to the Lockwoods' home, helping his limping friend inside. Although he was in dry clothing, Jack's hair was damp and even more wavy than usual. Both of them collapsed tiredly onto dining room chairs. "You okay?" Dan asked.

Jack nodded. "Still a little soggy, but fine. Who would have thought that there'd be soft ice on Snowbank Lake at the end of February?"

"It's been a strange winter, weather-wise," Dan noted, "we get the blizzard of the century in November and almost two weeks of forty degrees and sunshine in February. At least you got to the guy."

"Yeah," Jack sounded disgruntled, "we would have been fine had his snowmobile not decided to go for a swim."

"No, you would have been fine if the idiot hadn't decided to jump in after the thing and drag you with him." Dan looked at his friend's face and said seriously, "You're not kidding me, right? You're okay? Your wife will kill me if something happens to you just as things are getting back to normal." He looked around curiously. "Speaking of your wife, where is she?"

"*I'm* fine," Jack said sourly, "thank you for your concern. The lights were on upstairs when we pulled up, so at a guess Liz is putting in some studio time and is probably plugged into her music."

"You guys get the loft project finished already?" Dan sounded surprised.

Jack nodded. "For now. At least Liz has a dedicated place to work. We'll do the skylights, her wet studio, and build the guest-house out back come summer. The contractor did a great job, thank you for the recommendation."

Throwing back the blanket that was still over his shoulders, Jack got to his feet and stretched. He looked at Dan significantly. "Don't you have your own wife to get home to?"

Dan took a round metal tin from his pocket. "Why yes, I do, but I have to deliver this to Liz before I go. It's some of Beth's choco-late-orange shortbread cookies for you guys to share."

Jack held out his hand. "I'll take it."

Dan pulled the tin away from Jack's outstretched fingers. "No way, Beth made me promise to give it to Liz, and I'm more afraid of her than I am of you." He eyed Jack suspiciously. "I don't think she trusts you to do the sharing part, buddy."

Jack gave in and they climbed the stairs together. They could hear Liz singing softly from the newly constructed room at one end of the hall. Tilting his head, Jack stopped and smiled. "I love hearing her sing. It means she's happy."

Dan blew a razz-berry. "Gah! Dude, you got it bad."

~ ⁓ ~

"He's right, I do have it bad," Jack thought late that night. Liz was already asleep, and it was time he joined her. Relaxed and happy, he crawled into bed. Life was finally starting to normalize for them, and they found themselves settling into the routines of work and play.

The pain and drama of their first few months together were fad-ing into memory, especially since the jury had returned a life without parole verdict and incarcerated Eduard Reynoso in a maximum-secu-rity facility far away from where they slept.

The joy Jack felt being married to Liz was so intense that he wanted nothing more than to go on for years, sharing life with her, their families, friends, and meaningful work.

By the next morning, Jack needed to amend that statement. He wanted nothing more than to go on for years, sharing life with Liz, their families, friends, and meaningful work—and to quit coughing. He'd awakened that morning feeling like he'd gone three rounds with someone a lot bigger than him. He was coughing, running a fever of 102 degrees, and his head was so congested he felt like it was going to explode.

Every time Liz came anywhere near him, Jack shooed her away. But when he was alone, he brooded, wondering why everyone had deserted him. He was miserable.

"How are you feeling, hon?" Liz stuck her head into the bedroom. "Any better?"

"Do I look like I'm feeling better?" Jack asked grumpily.

"No," Liz answered calmly, "you don't sound much like it either. I brought you some lunch." She stepped through the door and Jack saw she carried a tray with a steaming bowl, a glass of what looked like cranberry juice, and a coffee mug.

Jack quickly rolled over, so he was facing away from her. "Just set it on the dresser and go away. You don't want to catch this. Be sure to wash your hands after you leave."

Liz continued around the bed and set the tray on the nightstand. Stroking his temple, where Jack's brown hair was feathered with silver, she said, "I know this is going to make you even grumpier, but I don't want to go away. We need to take your temperature again, you need to take some more medication, you need to have some of my fabulous homemade chicken soup, and my heart needs to take care of you, because I love you. Besides, I had my flu shot."

Jack sat up, sudden remorse clouding his face at Liz's words. Putting his arms around her, he croaked, "I'm sorry for being grumpy. I want you here, I'm just worried about you. I had a flu shot too, but this bug doesn't seem to be playing by the rules."

Liz eyed him saucily. "Well falling into Snowbank probably didn't help."

"Dan told you?" Even with his voice reduced to a whisper, Jack managed to convey his outrage. "He promised to keep his big mouth shut. Besides, I didn't fall in, I..."

Giggling, Liz stuck a thermometer into Jack's mouth. "That's what you get for keeping secrets."

———

By dinnertime, Jack hadn't improved, in fact, he was a bit worse. He'd managed to keep lunch down, but his fever was up a half a degree and he had a painful sore throat. Liz knew it was bad when she'd asked him about calling Dorrene Rock, their family physician, and Jack had simply nodded.

———

"Liz?" Dorrene called from the bedroom.

Liz walked back into the room she'd vacated fifteen minutes before to give Jack and their physician privacy. "What's up, other than the fact I have a sick husband?"

Dorrene gave her a half smile as she stood up. "Well, you're right about that, you do have a sick husband. He's got an upper respiratory infection that's already more than halfway to pneumonia. I suggested putting him in the hospital and my ears are still ringing."

Slapping a package of designer antibiotics into Liz's hand, Dorrene said, "Here. Make sure he takes these—as directed and until they're gone. I also left a bottle of codeine spiked cough syrup on the nightstand. If his fever goes above 103 degrees or he has trouble breathing, call the paramedics. Don't let him pull that 'I'm a doctor' crap on you."

"I'll be sure he cooperates," Liz assured the younger woman.

"Hello! I can hear you both," Jack growled from the bed. "I'm sick, not deaf."

Dorrene turned. "Then see that you behave. Stay in bed, no work, no going out on calls," she paused and snickered, "and no more falling into icy water in the middle of winter."

"I didn't fall in," Jack grumbled. "I was dragged in by the ankle, by a guy who was trying to save his snowmobile from drowning."

Dorrene held up her hand. "Whatever, just get better. Your life-saving technique needs work."

Clearly disgruntled, Jack flopped over on his side, turning his back on both of them.

Liz saw Dorrene to the door. "Thanks for coming out. I hope you and Chip will come for dinner after Jack recovers."

"An experience to be savored," Dorrene said, "and we'd be delighted. Let me know when and what we can bring. Call me if you need me to send in the troops."

"You awake?" Liz called quietly.

"Yes." Jack flopped over to face her.

Sitting down on the bed beside him, Liz caressed Jack's forehead. "Have you gotten any sleep?"

"That depends. What time is it? Did Dorrene leave?"

"It's close to eight and Dorrene left about an hour ago. Since you clearly wanted some time to yourself, I cleaned up the kitchen and sent out some invoices."

Jack smiled faintly. "That sounds like good news, must mean you still have some customers left."

"Uh-huh. Not everyone forgot about me, but I think I disappointed a few of my more mercenary customers when I came back to life. Generally, when an artist dies, his or her work escalates in value."

"Well, they can just wait, because I like my artist alive and feisty," Jack squeezed Liz's hand, "and no, I haven't slept much. I think I'm going to take some of that cough syrup. I hate the stuff, but every time I get comfortable, I start to cough."

Liz measured out a dose of the cherry red liquid, watched as Jack took the medicine, then held his hand until he fell asleep. Even then, she didn't leave his side. He'd watched over her so many times in the months they'd been together and now it was her turn.

Closing her eyes, Liz prayed for the man she loved. It was one of Heaven's most awesome privileges—to talk to the Almighty in peace and privacy and to know that He listened to every word, filtering them through His great heart.

Liz sensed that Jack had a divine appointment to keep. She now prayed that God would use this enforced quiet time to draw Jack to Him.

Liz had tried to talk to Jack about what had happened that morning in her hospital room, but something had always interrupted them—all manner of chaos, betrayal, and the time they'd spent with Jack's father. She almost groaned out loud, the Reverend Doctor Lloyd Beckett was a piece of work. Even after the trial, in the days immediately following her testimony in January, Jack studiously avoided talking about God or his experience on that morning.

Awake again, Jack groaned, tossing in the bed. Leaning forward, Liz asked, "Hey, hon, what can I do?"

Emerging from the sheets, Jack sat up and put his head in his hands. "Nothing," he snapped, "I'm not due for meds yet. I just can't get comfortable." He eyed Liz and asked in a softer tone, "Why are you still up?"

"It's not that late," Liz said soothingly. "It's just after eleven."

"I was hoping it was closer to morning." Jack sounded discouraged.

Hugging her husband close, Liz winced at the feel of his fever hot skin. "Is there anything that would make you feel better?"

Jack nodded. "Sing for me."

"What?" Liz wasn't certain she'd heard him right.

"Sing for me. Please."

Getting to her feet, Liz grabbed her guitar. Settling into the chair again, she looked at Jack. "I'll sing if you lay down and rest, okay?"

To her surprise, Jack complied without argument, putting his head down on his pillow. "There, I'm ready."

Picking up her guitar, Liz strummed a few chords and began to sing.

Amazing grace how sweet the sound
That saved a wretch like me.
I once was lost but now am found
Was blind but now I see.

'Twas grace that taught my heart to fear
And grace my fears relieved.
How precious did that grace appear
The hour I first believed.

Through many dangers toils and snares
I have already come.
'Tis grace hath brought me safe thus far
And grace will lead me home.

When we've been there ten thousand years
Bright shining as the sun.
We've no less days to sing God's praise
Than when we first begun.[iv]

Jack was silent as Liz finished the song. She thought he'd gone to sleep when he asked, "Why did you pick that song?"

Liz shrugged. "I guess because I love it. It's familiar and it feels like a benediction on the day."

"I don't like it," Jack complained.

Liz shook her head in derision. "I'm sorry, but who doesn't like 'Amazing Grace'? I'll sing something else, but why don't you like it? I think it's beautiful."

"You're not some wretch who needs saving. You're one of the kindest, most loving people I know. That song makes you sound like someone you're not."

Liz never ceased to be amazed by how the Almighty opened doors. She prayed silently that God would give her the words. "I am exactly who that song suggests, Jack."

"No, you're not," Jack insisted, "and you don't need a God Who condemns you to a life-long guilt trip. Nobody's perfect."

"God is." Liz spoke softly. "His Son, Jesus, is."

"Putting the question of perfection aside for a moment, what gives God the right to condemn you for being human? It's not like you're out there doing bad things, it's not like you're immoral, you're a good, loving, hard-working person." After a moment of silence, Liz heard Jack add in a ragged whisper, "And so am I."

Setting her guitar on the floor, Liz crawled into bed and put her arms around Jack. "Good by who's standard, honey? You and me, maybe we are good people as judged by the world. We try not to hurt others, but even then, we don't always succeed, right? Stan was a case in point."

Jack frowned and tried to turn over, but Liz held him close. "Don't pull away, Jack, you've been running from this long enough. Let me ask you something. What do you consider good? How many failures does good allow? How many friends can I hurt with a care-less word delivered at the wrong time, before I'm not a good person? How many times can I get unfairly frustrated with those who love me, before I'm not a good person? How many times can I skate by, doing a half-way job at something, before I'm not a good person?"

Looking at her disbelievingly, Jack said, "Who quantifies that kind of thing, Liz? The point is, we try to be good, right?"

Liz could tell Jack wanted her to leave, or at least to be quiet, but she wasn't giving up. "Answer the question, Jack. One time? Two? Five? And is that one, two or five times a day, a week, a month, or a year? Would five goof-ups, for lack of better words, in a year be enough to make you good? Good enough to face God down?

"Yes," Jack answered, "I think five sins—as you'd call them—a year would be great. This world would be a much better place if we could all keep to that standard."

"Who's standard?"

Jack looked at Liz with a puzzled gaze. "What do you mean?"

"Who's standard of good are we using? Yours? Mine? Your father's? The Pope's? Al-Qaeda's?" Liz raised her hand to Jack's face, stroking his skin gently. "God is the only answer that makes sense. The Holy God of the Bible. The God who can't abide the presence of even one sin.

"I love you with all my heart, Jack, but my love pales in comparison to God's love. He is the God who loves You so much that He called you into existence. He loves you so much that He wrote a book to tell you all about Him. And He loves you so much that He sent his holy, perfect Son to die for you—to redeem you. In that single act, He's the God who resolved the issue of sin once, for all."

Tears shimmered in Liz's eyes as she continued, "Please, think back to those moments in my hospital room. What did He ask of you?"

"To trust Him," Jack whispered, his eyes fixed on Liz.

"That's all He asks of any of us, just that we trust Him. He loves you like a..."

Jack turned away. "Like a father?" His voice was bitter. "That's not saying much. My father, the charismatic senior pastor at one of Chicago's mega-churches, deserted my mother, my brother, my sister, and me years ago. He walked away with a twenty-five-year-old convert who he divorced a year later. A man who's still a minister, forgiven and supported by his church. Yet in reality, he's still a man whose only true gods are money and fame."

Liz cupped Jack's face with her hands, forcing him to look at her. "I was going to say that God loves you as a son—as a member of His household, and that can never be taken from you. Unlike your father, God will never walk away from you. He will never disappoint you. And He will always be there for you."

Liz paused, then asked, "Remember what you told me about your blinding flash of insight that morning in the hospital?"

"That I was nothing in the face of that kind of power."

"And yet, you are *everything* to God and you cost Him everything. No, you're not perfect, but the God of the Universe loves you and paid for you with His most precious currency. He's the same God who carried Ellie safely to His side, the same God who helped you save my life, He will be the same God who carries us through whatever lies ahead, and finally, He will be the same God we will glorify in Eternity together. All you have to do is accept Him."

Jack reached out and took Liz's hand. "Show me, please."

PART 2

THE BLESSINGS
OF A YEAR

CHAPTER 21

A GIFT OF THE HEART

Liz looked up as her husband of almost a year shimmied into the room, tying his robe shut as he swayed in time to a melody he was humming quietly. The effect was sexy and fun. Her bemused expression turned to a gasp when Jack pulled her to her feet, whirled her around the room, and sang to her, "*Good morning, wife. Good morning, sun, how are your skies above? Gee it's great to be alive and in love.*"[v] After plopping her back into her chair, he kissed her soundly. "Good morning, wife!"

Her eyes wide, Liz managed, "Well, good morning to you too. What's with channeling Dean Martin? And uh, it's 'good morning, *life.*'"

"Everyone's a critic." Jack shrugged. "I just feel great today, that's all. By the way, Merry Christmas, my bride."

"Merry Christmas, dear husband," Liz responded. Seeing this side of Jack was a rare and unusual treat. She assumed that his serious demeanor was natural for someone who routinely had the lives of others in his hands. Sighing happily, she took his hand. "How does it feel having Christmas Day all to ourselves? Well not exactly all to ourselves. It's going to be fun to treat Dan and Beth to relaxation for a change. Since they finished the house, it seems like we're always scrounging meals at their place."

"I don't think they'd have it any other way, but you're right, I'm glad they're coming here for the next few days. What a great way to inaugurate the guest house. I've got the tenderloin trimmed and ready for later and the cross-country skis and snowshoes primed so we don't all gain a ton between now and New Year's." Jack grinned broadly.

"I have never, in all my born days, seen anyone get so excited about exercise," Liz muttered. "Anyway, I can't believe you guys didn't draw a shift between now and New Year's. What's up with that, anyway?"

"It's called vacation. And after the summer and fall the search and rescue teams had, it's overdue." Jack took a deep breath. "Although, I do have to confess something."

Liz frowned. "Uh-oh. What's up?"

"I'm on call at the hospital tomorrow. With Andi, one of the other trauma surgeons sick, they needed a stand-by in case Zach gets called out on a BWSR run." Jack glanced at Liz. "I hope that's okay. It just means I need to stay within pager range."

Leaning over, Liz rested her head on his shoulder. "My hero. Of course, it's okay. If you have to go in, then I'll be forced to eat your share of the goodies Beth is bringing." Reaching down, she pulled a gift from the seat of the chair next to her. "Merry Christmas."

Jack took the gaily wrapped present from Liz and looked at her quizzically. "I thought we were going to do this after breakfast. Can you wait for me to open this, while I go get your gifts?"

Liz stopped him from getting up with a gesture of her hand. "Hey, park it, will you? It's still really early and I'm not hungry yet. This is something for us to share. Afterward, we'll rustle up some grub, call and wish our families Merry Christmas, open the rest of our gifts, and then get ready for our guests. Sound good?"

Jack nodded. "That sounds great. So you want me to do the honors?" At Liz's nod, he slit the wrapping paper carefully with his pocketknife, neatly folding the paper once it was off the package. That way he could reuse it. Liz just rolled her eyes. Pulling the top off the box, he lifted an album from the bed of tissue paper. Its cover was a work of art—Liz's art. Needlework and beads glistened, transforming the hand-painted fabric into a beautiful depiction of their home in Ely. Opening the book, he found a title page with the words *"Our First Year"* and their wedding date inscribed in his wife's fine script.

Looking up with a curious gaze, Jack asked, "So is this a photo album?"

Liz nodded. "In a way, there are photos and stories and other treasures. Shall we?" She leaned over and flipped to the first page.

CHAPTER 22

THE BEGINNING OF
A LOVE STORY

Liz had chosen her favorite of their wedding photos to begin their trip through the past year. It was of Jack, wearing a black suit and dark green tie and of her in a simple full-length dress, the same color as his tie. She'd made the white-on-white Hardanger collar and cuffs years before to teach at a national seminar, never imagining she'd wear them at her wedding. Dan and Beth stood at their sides, each of them holding a cat, Dan with Sierra and Beth with Binx. What Liz loved most about this photo was the expression on Jack's face. He looked utterly joyful.

Jack smiled, his expression much the same as on that day. "If I remember correctly, this wasn't exactly the beginning of our love story." He shook his head in mock sorrow. "I tried so hard, Liz, I really tried."

Liz was confused. "Tried what?"

"You've no idea. There I was, a confirmed bachelor, a physician, and, worst of all, I was *your* physician. Yet I was having these very un-physician-like feelings every time we were in the same room which, if you recall, was most of our first four days together. It really hit me when you went all Annie Oakley on me the night of the break-in. There I was, completely out of it on the floor. When I finally came to, I found you, my patient, holding a smoking gun and defending poor, defenseless me. You hardly looked rattled as you gave me the details of what I'd missed. As soon as I put my arms around you that night, there was no going back. I tried to convince myself that it was just the situation and that love didn't grow that quickly between two people, especially two people who didn't know each other. None of it worked. I was in love with you by Thanksgiving."

Taking a sip of her tea, Liz calmly challenged him. "No way. You were so mad at me that Thanksgiving, I thought you were going to make me walk back to the Harrisons' place."

"Why do you think I lost it like that?" Jack asked. "I finally decide to love again and the woman I'd fallen for had clearly lost her mind. All I wanted to do was keep you safe in my cave and all you wanted to do was leave."

"Safe in your cave, huh?" Liz arched her brow. "So that was your idea of loving me?"

Jack had the good grace to look embarrassed. "Well, yeah, in my own cavemanesque sorta way. Anyway, it all worked out. You finally 'caved' into my charms."

Liz kissed him, slowly and deeply, until the album slipped from his hand and thumped on the table. "Actually, honey, I 'caved' into your kiss."

"Uh, okay," Jack choked. He pulled Liz closer. "What's say we take this set of memories into the other room?"

Liz pulled away reluctantly. "I'd like nothing better and I'm sorry for teasing you, but this," she tapped the album, "is important to me too. If we don't do this now, I don't know when we'll get back to it, since it's not for public consumption, even if the public is just Dan and Beth. Is that okay?"

Jack winked at Liz. "Just as long as you promise we can get back to that other 'not for public consumption activity' later." He picked up the book and turned the page. "What's next?"

CHAPTER 23

PEACEFUL PLAY

"Need you ask?" Liz smiled broadly at the tryptic of photos at the top of the page. "These were the most perfect two weeks of my life. After all, what could be better than a two-week cruise in the tropics in early February when you live in northern Minnesota? Well, a two-week cruise in the tropics in early February when you live in northern Minnesota and are on your honeymoon was way better."

"Agreed." Jack grinned.

The first photo was of Liz in a turquoise bathing suit, sound asleep on a chaise in the sun. Their cabin had a private balcony and they'd spent many peaceful hours out there, enjoying the ocean breezes and idyllic views.

The second photo was a formal shot taken of the two of them before their dinner seating one evening. Liz wore a classic short-sleeved LBD with beading of her own design and execution on the bodice. Jack coordinated perfectly in a black linen, double-breasted suit with a cherry red tie. They'd had so much fun that night. After dinner they'd walked the promenade deck several times, enjoying the balmy temperature and the starlight. Not ready for the evening to end, they'd gone dancing and had closed down the venue before returning to their cabin in the wee hours. Then they'd continued their dance in private. Liz woke late the next morning energized and happy, ready for what the day would bring, or so she'd thought.

Liz touched the final photo and grinned at Jack. "I still can't believe you talked me into this." She remembered her apprehension as they'd strapped her into the sling chair on the launchpad. Billed as the world's highest zipline, they were at the uppermost point on the Dutch side of St. Martin and the view was breathtaking. Liz would have been content to simply look around and catch a ride back down the mountain on a tourist jitney, but Jack insisted that ziplines were perfectly safe and that she'd never forget the experience.

Liz made a face. "Well, honey, you got that right, I'll never forget the experience. I never want to repeat the experience, but I'll never forget it."

Jack elbowed her gently. "Come on, admit it, you had fun and didn't get even one little ouchie."

"Does emotional trauma count?" Liz asked playfully.

Nuzzling her neck, Jack murmured, "Not even a little fun?"

Liz gave in, laughing. "Okay, okay, I was scared stiff, but I have to admit it was pretty awesome. In fact, our honeymoon is full of my favorite times ever!" Gently pushing Jack's head away from her neck, she added, "I think we'd best move on before the honeymoon memories get the better of us."

Jack straightened, a resigned look on his face. "As you wish." He reached out and turned the page.

CHAPTER 24

A CELEBRATION OF ETERNITY

Jack smiled. "I thought this was going to be our Valentine's Day midnight ski followed by getting warm, but this is so much more appropriate. This is the culmination of the most important decision of my life and our life together."

Liz touched the photo, wishing it could talk and share the immense nature of that day. Pastor Steve Lynch stood with her husband in the baptismal pool on the side platform of their new church in Ely. Jack was dripping wet, but the smile on his face spoke of eternity. Beneath the photo she'd penned the words *Amazing Grace.*"

"Have I mentioned how much I love that song?" Jack asked Liz. "Or how much I love you for the gift you gave me."

Liz smiled. "It wasn't me giving the gift, Jack."

"The gift I'm talking about is staying with me until I was ready to find my way to God on my own. You never gave up, yet you never pushed," Jack paused, "well, hardly ever. You did kinda take advantage of a sick man, but I'm literally, eternally grateful." He caressed Liz's cheek with a gentle finger. "I know my love for you will last eternity and a day."

"Well, that was a sweet thing to say," Liz's eyes misted with tears, "not to mention, totally sappy. We need to move on before I have to clean the floor." She turned the page.

CHAPTER 25

SOME SILLINESS

Copies of two scanned photos filled the top quarter of the page. The first showed a young couple at what looked like a wedding, doing a polka. The photo froze in time their twirling bodies, flying hair, and arms and legs at odd angles. It captured the fun of the dance perfectly. The second picture couldn't have been more dissimilar. A stylish, middle-aged couple were waltzing at what looked like a competition. Their elegant coordinated clothing and perfect pose conveyed the idea that they'd danced together for years.

Below those scanned photos were two others, pictures of alcoholic drinks. The first was of a colorful Tequila Sunrise, served in a mason jar and the second of a ruby red wine, served in the perfect goblet.

Jack was mildly horrified. "This isn't what I think it is, right?" Seeing Liz's mischievous smile, he groaned, "I didn't even think you two were listening to us that night. It was just guy talk."

They'd been at Gus Walter's bachelor party last April. Beth and Liz had dropped into the station to convey their congratulations. Gus was the youngest officer on the force, in his early twenties, and the guys were razzing him about his age, his girl, and the wedding night. Jack completely forgot about their audience.

Later in the evening, Gus got brave enough to say something along the lines of at least he was young enough to enjoy the wedding night. He fixed his eyes on Dan and Jack, both of whom were

131

recently married men in their fifties. Whistles and cat calls erupted, the friends around the table recognizing a challenge when given.

Dan looked at Jack, his eyebrow raised, "You wanna explain it to the kid, or shall I?"

Jack sipped his coffee—he was on call—and volunteered, "I'll take this one."

"Son," Jack put an arm around Gus's shoulder, "you don't know what you're missing, and you won't until you have a few more decades on you. I'm speaking from experience, having done both the young love thing and the middle-aged love thing. Loving at your age, well, it's like a...a," he looked at the ceiling as if for inspiration, "it's like a polka." Jack eyed Gus doubtfully. "You do know what a polka is, right?"

Gus nodded. "Yes, sir, I do."

Jack nodded back. "Good. Where was I?"

"Polka, sir," Gus snickered.

"Oh yeah," Jack continued, "young love is like a polka. Arms and legs flying, jumping around like you've got fire ants in your britches—well, if you had britches on, anyway."

Jack looked at Dan appraisingly. "As I recall, complete removal of one's clothing wasn't always necessary, so the fire ant analogy is sound. Do you concur?"

Dan nodded. "Absolutely, fire ants."

"So yeah, you probably got us older folks on the stamina thing," Jack conceded as he turned back to Gus. "Although the next time you want to try climbing Oz, that 5.13b monster down at Palisade Head, I'll take you on.

"However, I digress, back to loving. Now middle-aged love is like a waltz. A flawless waltz, when the partners are perfectly in tune with one another. It's not about how *fast* you dance, but about how *well* you dance. Loving is about finesse, about spending an hour perfecting a kiss. It's about expressing your love for the woman in your arms with each touch, and it's about the woman in your arms expressing her love for you in the same way."

Jack's mouth twitched as he tried to hold back a smile. "It pains me to say that, youth and stamina notwithstanding, you have years to go before you'll understand just how spectacular that kind of loving can be and why everything else pales in comparison."

Jack's appreciative audience lifted their glasses and thumped their hands on the table.

Not one to let Jack have all the fun, Dan broke into the conversation. Slapping Jack on the back, he raised his coffee cup—he was also on call—and pontificated, "Well said, my brother, well said."

Dan looked at Gus. "To put all those fancy words into a language you might better understand, young love is like a Tequila Sunrise. Colorful, crazy, and potent, but you feel like a truck hit you the next morning. Middle-aged love is like an expensive glass of wine. Vintage and...uh...well...uh, those vintage women are fine!" He turned and winked at Beth, who blushed scarlet.

"And that's when I figured out you were both still there." Jack had just finished reading all Liz's fine print and was ready to rip the page out of the album.

Liz laid her hand over Jack's. "Don't you dare. That's one of my favorite memories."

Jack stared at her, puzzled in the extreme. "Why? I was just, well, a little crazy that night."

"That's why it's one of my favorite memories, just because you were a little crazy and you were having fun. After all we went through at the end of last year, just seeing you like that made me ridiculously happy."

Understanding swept over Jack. He felt the same way every time he heard Liz sing. All desire to remove the story from Liz's lexicon vanished. It was part of their history.

Putting his arm around his wife, Jack turned the page.

CHAPTER 26

IN SICKNESS...

This page puzzled Jack, not because he couldn't place it in time, but because of the drawing at the top of the page. It had been a night in the late spring when Liz developed a migraine that was so bad, they'd gone into the Emergency Room. The drawing was of him bending over Liz as she rested on a gurney. The artist had depicted them both with their eyes closed, and Jack held Liz's hand pressed to his heart.

Jack looked at Liz questioningly, "Who drew this?"

"Maggie did, after she got off shift," Liz answered. "She was so touched by the way you cared for me, that she sketched this from memory."

Jack shook his head sadly. "That's not how I felt that night. You were in so much pain I thought about starting a morphine drip at home, but that would have been unwise, not to mention unethical. There's a reason why medical ethics forbid family members to treat other family members, except in emergency situations. Still, I was close to calling your condition an emergency that night."

"Jack, you shoulder too much blame—blame that isn't yours to carry," Liz asserted. "My migraines are not your fault. When you got home from work, you did everything you could think of—including ice packs, meds, and massage—all of which had been somewhat effective in the past. When none of it helped, you drove me to the hospital after midnight. After they started the drip and I went to sleep, you sat with me and, if this drawing is accurate, you prayed for me." She squeezed his hand. "I'm a blessed woman."

Jack kissed Liz gently. "And I'm a blessed man, but I hate when you're in pain. Since we married, I've done a lot of research on both chronic migraine syndrome and fibromyalgia and the interaction between the two. I'm infuriated by what I've found."

Pulling away, Jack looked at Liz seriously. "I understand that both migraines and fibro involve the brain and central nervous system and those are two things that researchers are a long way from understanding completely. Yet there's more than a lack of understanding to all this.

"Fibro, in particular, has long been known as a 'women's syndrome.' For years, the medical establishment wouldn't even call it a disease. Early on, medical journals explained the symptoms away by saying that women were 'frail' and 'got the vapors' easily. That might be forgiven, but the problem extends into the here and now. Up until just a few years ago, fibromyalgia had no diagnostic code, giving insurance companies carte blanc to refuse to cover needed medications or doctor visits.

"How in the world can we as a medical community justify that? This is a disease that effects about ten million people in the US alone. I'll tell you how we justify it—80 percent of the diagnosed cases are in women. That means the money isn't there for research, for big pharma, for…"

"Jack honey, stop it." Liz started to laugh. "You're preaching to the choir here, but getting you hyped up about medical politics isn't why I included this memory. I'm so grateful to have a husband who happens to be a physician and who cares enough for me to stay current on research on disorders that aren't in his field. That's the point of including this drawing and the memories it engenders. It's about your love for me, and your willingness to leave your medical science behind when it's not working to seek out Jehovah Rapha—our Master Physician. When I look at this drawing, I see one physician talking to another, and I see the depth of your love for me." Liz's eyes shone. "Thank you so much."

Jack lost his breath as he always did when she looked at him that way. Swallowing hard, he said, "You're welcome, Liz. Loving you is the greatest joy of my life. I'm sorry that I climbed on my soapbox, but," he caressed her cheek, "how long will men have to watch the women they love suffer chronic, debilitating pain because the best thing that limited medical research can offer them is a handful of opiates? That's not an answer, that's just another health issue they'll have to address down the road."

Liz hugged Jack close. "I love you, but this is supposed to be a happy time, so why don't we move on?" She turned another page, moving their story forward.

CHAPTER 27

SHARED ADVENTURES

"I don't know how you talk me into these crazy things. I've told you at least a million times—give or take—that I'm afraid of heights," Liz said. "So where do you keep taking me when you feel the need for an adventure? To the top or bottom of the highest place around, where you then propose we jump off, climb down, climb up, free dive, base jump, or some other such craziness. I mean, Jack, I'm older than you are, and you know I have a heart condition."

Jack rolled his eyes. "And you only admit to either of those things when you're trying to get out of doing something that will broaden your horizons. Besides," he pointed to the photo with a car-abiner fastened to the page below it, "that rock face you're climbing is just a baby-rock face. It certainly wasn't the highest place around. More to the point, I had you secure on belay the entire time. Even if you'd slipped, which you didn't, nothing would have happened to you."

"Wrong!" Liz pointed to the photo again, this time to her knee and a small rubbed raw patch on it. "I was injured that day."

Jack snorted. "Oh, I forgot, the boo-boo on your knee. Do you, by chance, remember how that happened?"

"All I know is that my knee was perfectly healthy when we left the house that day," Liz said teasingly.

"Let me enlighten you, dear wife. You 'falled down' on the side-walk just outside Dairy Barn. Why were we at Dairy Barn you may ask? Because you insisted that if I insisted we burn calories that day, then I had to buy you some calories to burn. So yes, you sustained an injury, but it wasn't rock-climbing that was the culprit, but rather milk-shake hunting."

"Details, details," Liz waved her hand airily, "all I know is that I came home missing skin." She grinned. "Still it was worth it to be first-aided by you."

"All kidding aside, Liz, you did really well on that climb. You're a natural," Jack said.

Liz made a face. "A natural rock climber who's afraid of heights? I don't think so."

"Let me ask you this, what did you think of rappelling?"

Liz's face lit up. "Now *that* was fun and didn't require reams of instruction. 'Drop the heaviest part of you first'—that's a technique I can wrap my head around. Besides, working with gravity is always easier!"

Jack couldn't do anything but laugh. Then he asked, "What about our adventure at Palisade?"

"You mean *your* adventure and I was terrified just watching you and Gus climb that cliff. You're both crazy." Liz squeezed his hand. "I have to admit, I was extremely impressed, especially once you were both safe up top. You're a very gifted man, not to mention athletic, but just thinking about your antics that day gives me the shivers."

Liz turned the page.

CHAPTER 28

AN ARTIST'S GIFT SHARED

"And speaking of being extremely gifted," Jack kissed Liz on the end of the nose.

"Well," Liz studied the photos and teased, "I'm not sure I'd say extremely gifted, but you did a pretty good job."

"That's because I had a great teacher." The photos of him in class and of his finished piece were proof that Jack had taken a plunge into his wife's world after they returned from their climbing lessons. He'd been a student in the 'Beaded Lakeshores' class Liz had taught at the North House last July. For twelve hours that weekend, he'd plied needle and thread in an artistic rather than medical context and, to his surprise, he'd had a lot of fun. "Just so you know, I was talking about you being extremely gifted, not me."

Jack looked Liz in the eyes. "I had no idea how technically difficult bead embroidery was to execute. Learning all the stitches, getting the beads to do what you want them to do, and then combining the two to create a recognizable landscape isn't easy. Yet you made it seem doable to a bunch of rank amateurs. I know my landscape turned out better than I ever thought possible and I think most of the others in the class felt the same about their projects. That's the mark of a great teacher, Liz."

Liz blushed. "I had a terrific class that weekend and I'm glad you had a good time. But what I do is nothing compared to what you do."

Jack cupped her chin in his palm. "Don't ever say that! What you do is simply different than what I do. What would this world be like without art? Liz, you talk about God being the Master Physician, and I agree with you, but God is also the Master Artist. His great heart beats with yours when you create beauty with your hands, using the gifts He gave you. When I watch you work what amazes me the most, is that you make it look easy. The pieces of yours that I purchased before we met mean so much more to me now, because I can visualize you working on each of them, weaving your beautiful spirit into each thread."

Liz's cheeks went from pink to scarlet. "Wow, um, thanks. I don't know what to say."

"I do," Rubbing her cheek with his, Jack continued, "you help me and so many others see the beauty in the ordinary when you share your work as an artist and a teacher. I look forward to my next lesson with you, whether that's at the North House or here at home, but before I embarrass you further, let me do this."

Jack turned to the next page.

CHAPTER 29

CHANGES

"No, no, no, no, I don't eat it no more..." Liz sang softly as she studied the page in front of her. Instead of a photo, she'd attached the ubiquitous yellow wrapper from one of her favorite fast food sandwiches to the top of the page.

Spearing Jack with a gaze, Liz said, "I was so mad at you."

Jack chuckled. "I know you were, but I'm not sorry."

"I'm not sorry, either," Liz confessed. "I feel better than I have in a long time, but that was the closest I've come to regret marrying you so quickly. I knew you were kind of a health nut, but I didn't expect you to force me to become one too. I liked my diet."

Groaning, Jack shook his head. "How can someone who's such a good cook develop a love affair with fast food?"

"Remember that someone was a busy someone who lived alone, worked hard, and coped with several chronic health issues that made her awfully tired sometimes," Liz defended herself. "Fast food was easy. Besides, my mother warned you that I didn't do a very good job of taking care of myself, remember?"

Pulling a face, Jack took her hand. "Love, let's leave your mom out of this, please. I know it's hard, I was single for a long time and I know cooking for one stinks. But your eating habits back then and your medical history were on a collision course of the grandest sort. I'm sorry I got a bit overbearing, but your diet terrified me."

"A bit overbearing?" Liz choked. "You threw out everything in *my* house that wasn't lean meat, vegetables, healthy oils, or starches that met with your approval. All my chocolate, which, by the way, is healthy, my chips, my home-baked cookies, the leftovers from our evenings out, everything! Then we went grocery shopping and, in that irritating, condescending way of yours, you explained why I should buy what *you* were putting in the cart. Besides, I cooked real food when we were together."

"As I believe I've mentioned already, you're a terrific cook," Jack said soothingly, "but when I wasn't around, what you ate was scary. I didn't mean to be irritating or condescending, but we were newly engaged and I was so in love with you that I couldn't imagine life without you. That was the only way I knew to shock you into thinking about what you ate." He hugged Liz close. "Apart from my poor behavior, eating healthy's not so bad, is it?"

Liz shook her head. "It took some getting used to, but no, it isn't. To be fair, we do go off the wagon now and again, especially where Beth's goodies are concerned." She leaned into Jack. "You were right. I didn't think much about what I ate as long as I didn't gain weight. The fibro made it hard to exercise, so I probably *was* a ticking bomb. Honestly, I understand your motivation, but your bedside manner could have used some work. All high and mighty," she grinned and pointed out, "after all, you didn't have to give up coffee."

"Now, that would have been cruel and unusual," Jack admitted. "Besides, like chocolate, coffee does have some health benefits, at least according to current research. I thought we reached a fair arrangement. I keep my coffee and you keep your chocolate."

"Which you indulge in every now and again."

"I'm only human, my love," Jack teased, "and, just to be fair, I share my coffee."

They sat for a moment, their arms around each other. For all her bluster, Liz was grateful that Jack had taken action. She not only felt better, but the symptoms of her fibro had eased with the change in her diet, allowing her more activity and fewer days in bed. Like

Jack, she wanted to spend years enjoying the wonderful relationship they shared.

Turning the page, Liz smiled, thinking back to pay-back time for Jack. She'd not done anything purposefully. Then again, it might have been worth the loss of all her snacks to see him truly confounded.

CHAPTER 30

OOPS, DID I FORGET TO MENTION THAT?

"Hey, Liz," Jack shouted from the porch.

Liz stepped outside. "What's up?"

"I'm going to chop wood out behind the garage. I just wanted you to know where I disappeared to." Jack smiled at her. "Want to go out for dinner when I finish?"

Liz almost missed his question because she was busy enjoying the view. Jack had been working outside all afternoon and he'd stripped down to his jeans, socks, and work boots on this hot summer day. She forced herself to pay attention and answered, "That would be fun. Just you and me or shall I invite the Harrisons?"

Coming over to the door, Jack kissed her soundly. "I want some time alone with my bride. Is that okay?"

Liz flushed, her thoughts veering toward the X-rated. "Um, yes, that's great." She kissed Jack back. "Please be careful, you're all sweaty and you're going to be swinging an ax. I'd like to enjoy an evening with my husband that doesn't involve the Emergency Room."

Jack winked at her. "Have a little faith, love. I want to enjoy this evening as much as you do. Think about where you'd like to go tonight." Patting her on the behind, he jogged off across the yard.

The doorbell rang, startling Liz. She was working on her newest project and had lost track of time. Glancing at the clock, she was surprised that over an hour had passed since she'd retreated to her studio. When the doorbell rang again, she headed downstairs, assuming that her husband was still out in the back forty. The doorbell rang a third time, "I'm coming," Liz shouted, wishing that whoever it was would take it easy on the poor, defenseless doorbell.

Liz opened the door and her irritation disappeared. Opening the screen door, she threw herself into the arms of the man standing there.

Jack was just coming back to the house when he looked up and found his wife in the arms of her—late husband? How was that even possible unless Liz, well, unless she'd lied to him? Could it be that she was divorced, rather than widowed? It wouldn't have mattered all that much, except why would she lie? And why would she look so happy to see her ex?

Jack kept walking, feeling angrier and more hurt with every step. It took a while but they finally noticed him, pulling apart as he climbed the steps. He looked from one of them to the other then muttered, "Hello Eric. You look mighty healthy for a dead guy."

There were a few moments of silence until Liz processed what Jack had said and figured out why he looked so miffed. Then she laughed and took Jack's hand, drawing him closer. "Oh, honey, this isn't what you think. Didn't I ever tell you that Eric was a twin?" Grinning when Jack shook his head, Liz apologized, "Oops, that was my bad. Jack, this is Eric's twin brother, Ray Talbot. Ray, this is my husband, Jack Lockwood.

"Ray lives in Germany with his wife Maria. They have two adult children, Fritz and Max. Ray's back in the States to help his mom pack up, sell her house in Two Harbors, and move to a senior community in Duluth. My mom told him where we live, and he came up to surprise us."

Jack cleared his throat and put out his hand, "Um, well, it certainly is that. It's good to meet you, Ray. I apologize for my rather unfortunate assumption."

⁓

"You had to include this." Jack speared his wife with an irritated glance. "I was so embarrassed, but what was I supposed to think? The guy looked exactly like the photos you showed me of Eric."

Liz patted him on the back. "Oh, Jack honey, I'm sorry for not saying anything, but I hadn't seen Ray since Eric's funeral and it didn't really cross my mind to give my new husband a lesson in my late husband's genealogy. But the look on your face," she giggled, "was priceless."

Seeing Jack's frown, Liz turned the page, knowing that the next set of memories would soothe his ruffled feathers.

CHAPTER 31

LESSONS WELL LEARNED

Jack studied the photos in front of him. The memories they brought to mind were among his most treasured. The first was of a loaded canoe, with Liz smiling and holding her paddle aloft; the second was of one of their campsites deep in the BWCA; the third was of Liz on a portage, carrying a load, the sky behind her dark and threatening; and the fourth was at their take-out point, the culmination of an adventure with an unexpected twist.

Looking at his wife fondly, Jack said, "I wondered if this was going to make it into our memory book. I know that you were a little uncertain about spending a week in September off grid with yours truly."

"Actually, the 'yours truly' part didn't worry me at all." Liz poked Jack in the chest with a gentle finger. "If I was going to do something like that, there's no one else I would trust to be my co-adventurer."

"Look how that turned out," Jack muttered sourly.

"It turned out fine, maybe not how either of us would have scripted it, but at least you know I took all those lessons of yours to heart. Besides, we had a great time up until those last few days, right?"

'Great time' was an understatement as far as Jack was concerned. He'd been eager to share his world with Liz. They'd planned carefully, Jack showing Liz how to read the topo maps[6] and indoctrinating her into the world of rods[7], designated campsites, latrines, and bear safety. As they'd traveled, he'd taught her the finer points of orienteering and wilderness survival. He'd even fixed one entire meal from fish they'd caught and edibles found along their chosen route, still plentiful on that early autumn day.

The near-perfect days passed, each one finding Liz more comfortable with her surroundings. Putting his chin on Liz's shoulder, Jack nodded. "Yes, we did, and I hope we can do it again next fall, all except for that last part."

"Didn't like having to be rescued by your wife, huh? Bad for your reputation…" Liz yelped as Jack nipped the skin of her neck. "What was that for?" She looked at him, mock outrage in her eyes.

"I had no problem at all with you rescuing me but having to be rescued…" Jack made a face, remembering the day their trip had taken an unforeseen turn. They'd been on the return part of the trip, heading back to civilization. They'd awakened that morning in one of Jack's favorite campsites. Their plan had been to linger longer, maybe stay another night, but the perfect weather had turned nasty. Black thunderheads rumbled in the distance and in the space of an hour the temperature dropped twenty degrees. The storm hit more quickly than Jack had anticipated, lightening dropping out of the clouds while they were still mid-lake.

Jack and Liz quickly paddled toward the nearest land, beaching the canoe amidst weeds and swampy ground. Rather than jumping into the muck, they stayed where they were and he pulled a tarp from the pack, draping it over them. Yellow scrub willow branches

---

[6] A topographic map uses elevation contour lines to show the shape of the Earth's surface. Elevation contours are imaginary lines connecting points having the same elevation on the surface of the land above or below a reference surface, which is usually sea level. These maps also show many other kinds of geographic features, including roads, railroads, rivers, streams, lakes, boundaries, place or feature names, mountains—and in the BWCA—designated campsites.

[7] Portages—overland trails connecting bodies of water—are measured in rods, one rod corresponding to 16.5 feet. There are 320 rods per mile. To convert portages into miles, multiply the number of rods by .0031.

overhanging the water gave them some protection from the rain and, in the event of a nearby lightning strike, the Kevlar canoe was not a conductor. More to the point, they were no longer the highest object in the surrounding landscape. They'd waited like that for over an hour, until the rain finally let up. Then, pushing away from where they'd taken shelter, they paddled until they found the designated landing.

Jack thought their misadventure was over. The clouds still threatened, but he and Liz were off the water. They were safe for the moment, or so he'd thought. It was just after he'd taken the photo of Liz on the portage that the wind picked up, increasing in intensity until it was strong enough to bend young aspen saplings parallel to the ground. After stowing the canoe and packs under an uprooted tree, Jack led Liz, shielding her with his body, along the trail. In these conditions, they were safer on the open lake shore, just a half-mile ahead.

They'd almost made it when a large aspen at the side of the trail cracked at its base, catching both of them beneath its branches as it crashed to the ground. Liz was the first one to recover, finding Jack just coming around, his head bruised by whatever had hit him. A tree limb, now laying off to one side, was the likely culprit. Although the wind had died down and the storm was moving off, their adventure was far from over. The moment Jack tried to stand, excruciating pain shot through his ankle. Although they'd determined it was nothing more than a bad sprain, Jack couldn't walk—could barely stand—without support.

It had been Liz who'd managed to get both of them and their belongings back to the take-out point. She'd found Jack a walking stick, done the portages, and set up camps, while he helped the best he could, by cooking, paddling, and navigating. Liz was slow, but rock steady and in the end, those final days had been fun in their own way. The student had now become the leader and Jack saw the fruit of his instruction realized. He wouldn't have chosen the circumstances, but, looking back, he wouldn't trade a minute of that trip.

"Actually, having to be rescued wasn't that bad, *especially* since it was you doing the rescuing." Jack smiled, remembering, "You saved my sorry hide and I still had fun."

"Yeah, ordering me around." Liz's grin matched his own. Squeezing Jack's hand, she finished, "I hated that you were in pain, but it's kinda cool knowing that I can actually do something like that without dumping us in the lake, destroying the packs, or getting lost in the woods. Thank you for being such a good teacher."

Jack took a deep breath. Liz was looking at him like that again, with love in her eyes. He'd never expected to see that look again in his lifetime, but she was here, and they were reliving wonderful memories from their first year married. He realized that, impossible as it seemed, he loved her more today than when he'd said, 'I do.' Swallowing around the lump in his throat, he whispered, 'No, thank *you*.'"

Taking his hand from Liz's shoulder, Jack turned the page.

CHAPTER 32

THE GIFT OF ANOTHER YEAR

"Happy birthday to yous, Happy birthday to yous! And many mooooorrrreeee…" If Liz closed her eyes, she could still hear Dan and Beth's big—albeit slightly off key—finish to the familiar song. The page in front of her had a half-burned birthday candle attached below a photo of the four of them, wearing silly hats, and standing behind a birthday cake alight with candles. "I can't believe Dan and Beth surprised us like that. 'You don't have to bring anything, it's just a simple dinner,' Beth told me. A simple dinner, bah! Between the art colony, the hospital, and the police department half of several towns were there, even a couple of the Federal guys showed up." Liz wrinkled her nose at Jack. "Remind me never to trust those two again!"

Jack grinned. "At least when we're due for another set of birthdays."

Jack and Liz hadn't realized until just before they were married that their birthdays were two weeks apart in October. Even then, they hadn't suspected a thing when Dan and Beth invited them over in early October to see the new house and have dinner. After all, the Harrisons' hospitality was legendary. Wrapping his arms around Liz's waist, Jack laughed quietly. "That evening sure was fun, wasn't it?"

"It was." Giving up on her pretended outrage, Liz smiled. "I haven't celebrated a birthday like that in years. Gag gifts and all. And that cake—yum! You do remember that cake, don't you? I've never seen your affection for healthy food disappear so fast. How many pieces did you have, anyway?"

Jack definitely recalled that cake, with its base of Beth's dark chocolate layers, blackberry filling made with last season's wild blackberries and her blackberry cream cheese frosting. "One less than I wanted to have, thank you very much. It was amazing. I couldn't believe that some of the folks there asked for ice cream. What a perversion of perfection."

"Beth gave me the recipe," Liz whispered in Jack's ear. "So if we pick some blackberries next summer, we'll have our own party."

"That will be wonderful, but the best part of that day came after we got home. Remember?" Jack nudged her.

How could Liz forget? The next photo showed her hard at work in her wet studio, felting the fabric for her next project. She'd attached a swatch of that fabric below the photo. She remembered walking with Jack through the door of their home hours later, still reeling from the unexpected surprise that the Harrisons had managed to pull off. Spending the evening with so many friends had left Liz's heart glowing and replete with joy. She couldn't imagine being any happier than she was at that moment.

She was wrong. Thanks to Jack, there was another surprise awaiting her. After walking upstairs together, he'd asked Liz to close her eyes. After she complied, he led her down a newly finished hallway to the right of the stairs, opened the door, flipped on the light, and whispered, "Happy Birthday."

Unbeknownst to Liz, Jack and the contractor had finished her wet studio while she'd been out of town, teaching at the American Beading Guild's national seminar, the week before. Everything in the room was just as they'd planned, from the large stainless farm sink, to the customized storage units, to her work area, complete with comfortable seating for her and any visitors. Off of the main room, there was a teaching area with a large table and eight chairs. The task lighting was just as she'd specified and when she looked up, she could see skylights above her. It was dark outside now, but the northern light they'd bring in would bathe the room in a soft, natural glow year around.

Jack's gift had touched her deeply, but, at the time, Liz had been a bit confused. "It's wonderful, Jack, but I thought we'd decided to wait on this build out until the house in Grand Marais sold?"

"Nope," Jack had responded adamantly, "*you* decided. *I* decided that you needed to be able to work and teach here, now rather than later. Besides, according to the Realtor, your house won't be on the market for long."

The Realtor had been correct. Liz's house in Grand Marais was on the market for the space of three hours, another artist jumping at the chance to buy a place remodeled by an artist for an artist.

In the end, all Liz could do was throw her arms around Jack. Impossible as it seemed, she loved him more at that moment than when she'd said "I do."

Nuzzling Jack's neck, Liz responded, "Of course I remember. You are the most incredibly caring man. I love my workspaces and I love you so much more. Are you ready to move on? We're almost done, then we'll have breakfast."

At Jack's nod, Liz turned the page.

CHAPTER 33

AN ADDITION TO THE FAMILY

"What a Thanksgiving it turned out to be," Jack remarked as he looked at the photo and touched the small swatches of fur attached to the page. "I never thought we'd be eating leftovers for Thanksgiving dinner."

Liz smiled. "It was worth it, though, wasn't it?"

Jack's heart warmed at the memories as he glanced at the chair where their cats were sleeping in the sun. "Yes, it was. Some of it was sad, but we witnessed a miracle that night." He touched the photo fondly. The tiny ginger kitten resting in the palm of his hand didn't know the miracle of his birth, all he wanted was to eat, sleep, and stay warm.

Jack and Liz had been preparing their contributions for the Harrisons' Thanksgiving feast. Liz spooned her homemade orange-cranberry relish into a crystal bowl, and Jack's sweet potato casserole was just out of the oven. Everything looked and smelled wonderful and they were almost ready to leave the house when whoosh—Binx went flying through the kitchen with Sierra in close pursuit. Neither Jack nor Liz thought anything about it until the two cats started chittering, that was the only word that came to mind for the sound they were making. It was downright weird. The two of them followed the noise and found the cats batting at the window in the study. Thankfully, Jack thought their behavior strange enough to check outside.

"Liz," Jack called a few minutes later. "Please come here and bring a towel. Quick."

An unfamiliar cat had crawled up on the porch, taking refuge behind the wood box. Jack could hear its faint whines when he walked outside. Following the quiet sounds of distress, he found a female tabby. She was bleeding from numerous lacerations and her left rear leg hung by only a thread of skin and muscle—almost amputated by whatever had attacked her—Jack supposed a fox. He cradled the dying cat in his arms, hoping to give some comfort. With a start, he realized she was in labor. Checking the place where she'd rested, he found a newborn kitten laying in the snow. When Liz arrived with the towel, they carried the mother and baby into the kitchen. The kitten died without drawing a breath.

Jack did his best to care for the mom, who, against all odds was still breathing, trying to give her babies life. The second kitten didn't survive the mother's trauma, living only a few short minutes after birth. Immediately after it was born, Jack placed the still moving kit next to its mother's face, hoping that the smell and movement of the baby would help both mother and child. Sadly, the mother didn't move and the baby died.

Just a few minutes later, the mother cat drew her last breath. Jack had to blink away a sudden glaze of tears. Liz just stood there stroking her fur. "Poor mama, you tried so hard. Jack," Liz looked up suddenly, "I just felt something move. Is it possible there's another kitten in there?"

Jack ran for his bag, and, taking a scalpel, he carefully made an incision in the mother's abdomen. Before he could tie off the still-seeping blood vessels, a tiny head poked out of the opening. Moving as quickly as he could, he pulled the baby free, cut the umbilical cord, and wrapped the small form in a towel. Liz grabbed the heating pad from the hall closet and laid the still moving bundle on its warm surface, stroking the baby's fur as she toweled it clean and dry.

Needless to say, they never made it to the Harrisons' house that evening, but instead became experts in the care and feeding of a newborn kitten. Jack had called their vet who, animal lover that she was, made a holiday house call. Before she left their place, the Lockwoods had a heating pad designed for kittens, kitten formula, a syringe feeding setup, and instructions on how to care for the wee addition to their family. The vet also told them they were the proud parents of a baby boy.

After she left, they introduced Sierra and Binx to the as yet unnamed kitten, expecting some fireworks. Instead, both cats immediately took to the role of surrogate parents, cleaning the kitten and keeping him warm. Jack and Liz fed the baby, helped it go to the bathroom, and named it. 'Lazarus' became the newest addition to their family that day—their Thanksgiving miracle.

Liz leaned over, hugging Jack close. "You were amazing that night. I couldn't believe how calm you were, not being a vet and all. That kitten is a part of our family, thanks to you."

"And mama kitty," Jack reminded her. "We can't forget her or her fight to save her babies."

Looking at Liz, Jack asked, "What's next?"

"That's all for now." Liz closed the album. "I'll finish it with some photos from the next few days. Do you like it?"

Kissing his wife warmly, Jack said, "I love it and I mean that in the deepest sense of the word. I couldn't have asked for a more beautiful or more meaningful gift. Just reliving these times with you has been such an incredible way to start Christmas day."

CHAPTER 34

A CHRISTMAS BREAK

"Merry Christmas, Dr. Lockwood."

Jack looked up to see one of the emergency room RNs stepping into his office. "Merry Christmas to you and the boys, Carol. I hope you had a good celebration."

Carol nodded. "It was great, thank you. Um, I just wanted to let you know that Team 2 is inbound with casualties." She shook her head unhappily. "I wish folks who can't be bothered with safety would stay out of the BWCA, especially in the winter."

Jack got to his feet. "Did they say anything about the nature or extent of the injuries?"

Carol shook her head. "No, just that we have three inbound and that all the injured are stable." She turned to leave. "I'll see you in receiving."

Jack washed his hands then followed her out of the door. It was bad enough that he'd had to leave Liz, Dan, and Beth on one of the most perfect cross-country skiing days they'd had so far this season. The sun was out, it was above zero and the snow was perfect. They'd been having a great time when his pager went off. Since then, he'd operated on a man who'd tangled with the business end of a snow-blower, set the leg of another man who'd decided that today was the day to take his Christmas lights off the roof, even though it was just the day after Christmas, and now, this. He, too, got frustrated when people did reckless things, especially when in unfamiliar territory far from help. Still, that's why he was here.

By the time Jack got to receiving, the helicopter was just landing. He waited until the rotors slowed, then ran up to the bay doors, opening them from the outside. After the team lifted a gurney to the ground, Jack bent over the patient, not waiting for a report from those inside the chopper. He gasped. Dan Harrison lay in front of him, unconscious. Not looking up, Jack snapped, "What happened and where are the women he was with?"

"Right here." Liz jumped down beside Jack, with Beth close on her heels. "And we're fine, so be nice."

Jack hugged both of them, before turning back to Dr. Zachary Birch, the physician on Team 2. "I'm sorry for the attitude, Zach. What happened out there?"

"Dan got caught in some unstable snow and rock out near Basswood Lake. It started sliding down the slope to the lake and he went with it. He's been conscious on and off, has a fractured wrist and a dislocated shoulder, both right side, a laceration on the back of his head that'll need stitches once its cleaned up, and, when he comes to, you're probably going to have to medicate him for sheer cussedness." Zach rolled his eyes. "You should have seen the trouble we had getting him to stay put on the stretcher."

Jack grinned. "I can imagine." His smile fading, Jack looked at Zach seriously and said, "Dan's a very good friend, do you think you can stay with me on this one? Just in case?"

Nodding, Zack followed Jack into one of the ER treatment rooms. "Happy to, but don't worry, he's going to be fine. Just a little recovery time and he'll be the rescuer again, rather than the rescuee."

~~~~

Beth and Liz sat in the quiet waiting room. Liz squeezed her friend's hand. "Don't worry, you heard what Zach said, Dan's going to be fine."

"That's not what's worrying me," Beth groaned. "It's that 'recovery time' thing that Zach talked about that's worrying me. I don't know how to keep Dan down, even when he's under medical orders to stay put. You saw him after the team arrived. He had a bee in his bonnet about the slide and I thought they were going to have to sedate him just to get him on the chopper."

"Jack will get through to him. You know that," Liz reassured Beth.

Beth made a face. "Jack's the same way, *you* know that. Those two will probably engineer a breakout from bedrest for Dan."

Liz grinned. "Now there's a picture. Hey," she turned worried eyes on her friend, "I know you can't be as calm about this as you seem. The slide carried you a long way down the slope too, and you were the one who actually found Dan unconscious. Talk to me."

"I'm fine, at least sorta fine. I'm used to living with the possibility that something bad could happen to Dan. I mean when your husband's not only the co-leader of the Boundary Waters Search and Rescue Unit but also the chief of police, it's always a possibility. But not when we're out having fun. You know what I mean?"

Liz nodded her head. "It's like our trip into the BWCA last fall when Jack got hurt and I had to get us back to civilization. Dan's injuries are worse than Jack's were, but trying to keep Jack still long enough to figure out that he'd sprained his ankle, not broken it, was a challenge." She looked up with a wry smile. "That's what we get for marrying these alpha types."

Beth looked at Liz and asked curiously, "You know, I thought Jack was crazy intense even compared to Dan and when you two got together, I wondered if you'd be able to handle that, but here you are giving me lessons in coping with my own Type A husband. How do you do it?"

Liz shrugged. "I guess it helps that I'm Type A, too, and can be stubborn when I need to be stubborn. But honestly, I've come to realize that Jack's at his most intense when people's lives are at stake, especially when it's those he loves who are at risk. That's why I think Jack's cussedness, as Zach called it, will trump Dan's cussedness. Especially when Jack tells him to think about what that stubborn behavior is doing to you." Seeing the look on Beth's face, Liz grinned. "Those Type A alpha males aren't above using a little emotional blackmail when needed. Neither is this Type A artist, which is how I got Jack to sit back, sit still long enough to diagnose himself, and then accept the fact that his woman was rescuing him."

"Giving away marital secrets now, are you, wife?" Jack, in blue surgical scrubs and a white coat bearing his name, sat down in the chair beside Liz and kissed her. "That's fine as long as you share any payment you receive for practicing psychology without a license with me."

Jack leaned forward and took Beth's hands. "Beth, honey, Dan's going to be fine. He's bruised, has a fractured wrist and a separated shoulder which I put to right. The head trauma, along with the pain meds are what kept him out of it for a while, but the films were negative for bleeds or fractures. I don't think there's a concussion either, since he remembers everything that happened. He's hard-headed, sore, and cranky, but he's okay."

"Can I see him, Jack?" Beth asked.

"See him and spend the night with him, if you'd like. As soon as Dan's settled in a room, someone will come for you. I'll release him tomorrow morning. I just want to make certain that I'm right about the concussion. He's a little groggy from the meds, but seeing you is what he needs most."

Jack frowned and asked, "Just answer one question for me, is everything okay with you? Zach said you refused to be examined and I don't want to be the one explaining to your husband how we missed something where you're concerned."

"I didn't refuse, exactly, I just wanted Zach to concentrate on Dan." Beth patted Jack's knee. "Jack, I'm fine. I took a shorter ride down the slope so I may have a few bruises, but nothing serious."

"I know you want to see Dan right now, but will you let me have a look for myself when we bring you both back to the house tomorrow?" Jack asked.

"What?" Beth looked confused.

"We still have a house party to finish and this way I can keep an eye on all three of you. You can either drive home on Friday as planned, or if you prefer, we'll take you home. If that's okay with you."

"Truthfully," Beth blinked back tears, "I can't think of anything I'd like better. Thank you!"

⁓

"Jack, I'm telling you that snow was stable. The rock face behind the snow was stable," Dan insisted. "We'd just settled down for a rest and some sandwiches when rocks and snow started shifting around us. I shoved Beth and Liz out of the way, but," he made a face, "I tripped over the pack and went down."

The two of them were in Jack's living room, sipping steaming mugs of cider and talking. "So the granite bedrock just started shifting on its own?" Jack arched an incredulous brow.

"Yeah, it did, and I know how unlikely that sounds. In fact, it sounds impossible. It *is* impossible unless that face was somehow disturbed before we got there."

"Dan, are you saying that someone caused that slide on purpose? To what end?"

Dan looked up, his expression suddenly weary. "I've no idea, Jack. All I know is that last year Reynoso's biggest advantage when he went after Liz, was that nobody, including me, really believed that he was gunning for her. What happened two days ago was deliberate. I don't know who, or why, but something is going on."

Seeing the doubt in Jack's expression, Dan continued, "Look, cause of the slide aside, you know me pretty well. You left the woman you love in my care. Why would you trust me like that?"

"Because you know that area better than I do, and because I know you'd never take a chance with..." Jack looked up in sudden comprehension. "Harrison, I'm sorry. Did you see or hear anything unusual?"

Dan shook his head. "Not a thing, not at the time anyway. We heard what we thought was a sonic boom earlier. We saw the jet trails and just assumed."

"Explosives? Targeted at you," Jack looked puzzled, "or a rifle shot, maybe poachers who set you up?"

The following day, a trip to the scene resolved the question. Up slope, away from where the picnickers had rested, there were definite signs that a small explosion had set off the rockslide. No one knew if the wrongdoer had purposefully targeted Dan, Beth, and Liz or if there was another explanation.

CHAPTER 35

QUESTIONS OF ETERNAL IMPORT

"What do you think?" Liz put the album she'd created on the table in front of Jack and opened it to the penultimate page.

Jack smiled. At the top of the page Liz had attached a hand-embroidered felt Christmas tree, a stitched question mark, and three photos. The first was of the four of them ready to head out on their cross-country ski adventure on the day after Christmas. The second was of Jack and Dan taken later that same day, just after they'd settled Dan in his hospital room for his overnight stay. Zach had snapped the photo when Jack was bending over Dan, claiming his right to be the first to sign the fiberglass cast on Dan's wrist. The third was of the four of them later in the week, lounging around the Christmas tree in the Lockwoods' home. They all appeared relaxed and happy and, as usual, both Harrisons had a cat in their lap. Jack held Lazarus, but the kitten was a blur—not able to stay still for the time needed to take the photo—and Liz held her guitar.

Beneath the photos and the memorabilia, Liz had penned the words, *But You, O Lord, are a shield about me, my glory, and the One who lifts my head.*[8]

"I'd just been thinking so much of Psalm Three after you guys figured out that someone deliberately caused the landslide that hurt Dan," Liz explained. "It's like, who can we trust? The Psalmist

---

[8] Psalm 3:3 (New American Standard translation).

answers my question, that's why I included the full text of it on the final page. I still can't quite believe what happened when we shared this with Dan and Beth."

Jack turned the page and read,

O Lord, how my adversaries have increased!
Many are rising up against me.
Many are saying of my soul,
'There is no deliverance for him in God.'
But You, O Lord, are a shield about me,
My glory, and the One who lifts my head.
I was crying to the Lord with my voice,
And He answered me from His holy mountain.
I lay down and slept;
I awoke, for the Lord sustains me.
I will not be afraid of ten thousands of people
Who have set themselves against me round about.
Arise, O Lord; save me, O my God!
For You have smitten all my enemies on the cheek;
You have shattered the teeth of the wicked.
Salvation belongs to the Lord;
Your blessing be upon Your people![9]

Jack took Liz's hand. "This is a perfect way to end the album. We have a mighty God, don't we? I didn't think Dan, at least, would listen any more than he did the last time I tried to talk with him about faith, not too long after Steve baptized me. My ears are still ringing from that conversation, so when you read that Psalm, I have to admit I'd kind of braced myself for an explosion or for them just to leave the room."

"I know," Liz said, "but I also know that both Dan and Beth were worried by what happened the day after Christmas, especially after officers went to the scene."

---

[9] Psalm 3 (New American Standard translation).

"Dan and Beth aren't the only ones worried, Liz." Jack squeezed his wife's hand tightly. "We still don't know the why's and it could have been you buried under all that snow and rock. Had it not been for Dan's quick thinking, it *would* have been all of you."

"Jack, it wasn't all of us," Liz said soothingly, "but that worry may have been what made them listen. That's a start and God doesn't waste His Word."[10]

"You're right," Jack acknowledged. "I've known Dan for a very long time and all he's ever been is antagonistic when it comes to God, religion, or the faintest hint that someone else is in control of his life other than him. So the fact that he just listened and asked a few questions is as close to a miracle as I've witnessed since you almost died."

Jack smiled. "I think that God has a hold of my friend and I hope I'm there when Dan finally caves into what he's known for almost a year—that a God Who can work a miracle of faith in my life is worth learning about. Dan met Reverend Dad a long time ago and knows about our dysfunctional relationship. That's why Dan figured with me, he had lifelong company on the agnostic train. My 'finding religion,' as he calls it, took him by surprise."

Liz's expression grew sad. "Your dad and his way of life have done a lot of damage to a lot of people. What makes me so unhappy is that he's done it all while claiming to serve God. I need to let go of my dislike for the man and commit to praying for him on a regular basis, because despite his profession, I don't believe for a moment that Lloyd knows God, at least not in any real sense of the word."

"Don't be so hard on yourself," Jack said soothingly. "He's not an easy man to be around, let alone like."

"Neither were the tax collectors or prostitutes of Christ's day, but Christ sought them out anyway," Liz pointed out. "Jack, we haven't even tried to call Lloyd since we stayed with him before the trial."

"I know," Jack muttered, "but if you recall, we did try to call him after I proposed, we did invite him to the wedding, and we did

---

10   Isaiah 55:11 So will My word be which goes out of My mouth; It will not return to Me empty, Without accomplishing what I desire, And without succeeding in the purpose for which I sent it. (New American Standard Translation)

send him a thank you after he sheltered you last winter. We've heard nothing from the man apart from his ministry's annual letter asking for money. Let's face it, he's not going to change."

"Isn't that what we were just saying about Dan? And we both know God's working on him."

"Yeah, but…"

Liz shook her head and said adamantly, No 'yeah buts,' Jack. God loves your dad as much as He loves you, me, Beth, and Dan. And if God hasn't given up on Lloyd, then who are we to give up on him? It's New Year's Day, the anniversary of another miracle." Liz touched the diamond band on her left hand and took Jack's hand. "Let's pray for the year ahead, for our friends, our families, and for God to use our love and our home as a beacon for Him and a shelter for those who need a home, in whatever sense of the word."

PART 3

The God on the Mountain Is Still God in the Valley

CHAPTER 36

SINGING SKIES AND DANCING WATERS

Be Thou my vision
O Lord of my heart.
Naught be all else to me
Save that Thou art.
Thou my best thought
By day or by night.
Waking or sleeping
Thy presence my light.

Riches I heed not
Nor man's empty praise.
Thou mine inheritance
Now and always.
Thou and Thou only
Be first in my heart.
High King of heaven
My treasure Thou art.

High King of heaven
When vict'ry is won.
May I reach heaven's joys
O bright heaven's Sun.

Heart of my own heart
Whatever befall,
Still be my vision
O Ruler of all.[vi]

Liz played a few more chords then put her guitar down, ignoring the requests for more from those sitting around the campfire. "Enough, guys, enough." She speared Dan, the loudest of the bunch, with a glance. "If you want music so badly, take the guitar and make it yourself. We've done everything from *Three Dog Night's* greatest hits to my favorite hymns and choruses and my formerly-frostbitten fingers are sore."

Dan put his hands up in the air and shook his head. "No way, not me, all that happens when I sing solos is I scare the wildlife."

Jack guffawed, "True that." He looked around the campsite illuminated by the flickering flames. "This is the good life, isn't it? The rest of the world is celebrating Labor Day by partying and eating too much, and here we are…"

"Partying and eating too much," Liz giggled. "That was a great dinner, husbands. I'm so full I could burst."

"Too full for one of these?" Beth removed the top from the box she held, revealing her homemade turtle candies and offered one to Liz.

"Um, no." Liz helped herself. "Yum!"

Jack took a candy and laid back, resting his head in Liz's lap and his feet on a nearby rock. The four of them had enjoyed an idyllic week in the BWCA. The early September weather had been spectacular, the unseasonably warm temperatures allowing for dips in the clear, cold lakes followed by resting or paddling in the sun. Indeed, it had been a reflection of their year, thus far.

After Dan's mishap the Christmas before, life had been almost perfect for the four of them. No more "accidents" had plagued their outings or their everyday lives. Although the county sheriff's department had investigated thoroughly, they'd reached no conclusions about who'd orchestrated the explosion near Basswood lake, or why. Life continued, Dan recovered from his injuries, and the incident was all but forgotten. Even Jack, worrier by nature that he was, had slowly relaxed.

Taking a bite of Beth's homemade candy, Jack closed his eyes, relishing the treat. "Mmm, this is fabulous. Thanks, Beth."

Beth smiled. "You're welcome. Hey, how did your trip to Toronto go?" she asked Jack, spearing her husband with an irritated glance. "I asked Dan and he told me we'd talk later. That was almost a week ago."

Dan looked sheepish. "Sorry, wife, but we've been a little busy since then and I forgot. It went well. Ontario wants to contract with our teams for Search and Rescue in the Quetico Provincial Park Wilderness and also work with Jack and me to create their own program. So we'll be doing a lot of hiring and consulting on both sides of the international border this winter. It's been a great year for the BWSRU."

"That's terrific news." Although, thanks to Jack, Liz was privy to the news about Ontario, she still had excitement written all over her face. "I'm so proud of you both!"

—~⌣~—

Later, alone in their tent, Liz snuggled closer to Jack and draped her arm over his hips. "This is so nice. I think we should make it an annual event."

Turning into Liz's embrace, Jack kissed her, caressing her lightly. "I agree. We've had a lot of fun on this trip and Dan's right, it's been a great year all around. This agreement with Ontario is just another highpoint. We'll be expanding our program, training new responders for here and in Ontario. That means more press, larger budgets, and more lives saved."

Kissing Liz again—this time deeply and with more fire—Jack whispered, "By the way, have I ever educated you in the finer points of how to safely make love in the wilderness?"

Liz grinned in the dark. "Several times in fact, but my memory's a bit fuzzy." She kissed him back. "I think I need a refresher course."

Jack had just pulled her closer, his kiss alive with passion when someone slapped on the zipped door of the tent.

"Hey, you two, are you asleep?" Dan called.

Jack counted to five and cleared his throat, striving for civility. "Asleep? Why no. Is something wrong?"

"Not exactly, Beth and I just wanted to ask you guys something."

Jack was busy counting to ten when Liz broke in, "Can it, um, wait until morning?"

"I guess. It's not critical or anything. It's about that song you sang right before we called it a night. So yeah, I guess it can wait. Sorry."

Dan jumped back in surprise when Jack unzipped the tent fly and muttered, "We'll be out in a minute. Why don't you make yourself useful, heat up the coffee, and stir the fire back to life?"

A few minutes later, the four of them sat huddled around the flickering fire pit because the night had gotten colder. Jack sipped his coffee and looked at Dan. "You said something about a question?"

Dan must have heard the remnants of annoyance in Jack's tone because he said, "Hey, I'm sorry because I think I interrupted something. When you hear this, don't forget that we're friends."

Liz patted Dan on the shoulder. "Don't worry about it, hon, he's fine. Just tell us what you guys are wondering."

Dan looked at Jack intently and asked, "Do you really love God more than Liz?"

Jack was confused. "Huh?"

"That last song Liz sang," Beth explained, "it says, 'Thou and Thou only be first in my heart.' Does that mean you love God more than Liz?"

"Or more than me, or Beth, or your families, excluding your father, of course," Dan added.

"Actually, it's because of God that I can love my father, or at least try to like him a little." Jack smiled faintly. "You know our history."

Dan grimaced and nodded. "I thought it would take a miracle for you to have a civil conversation with him, but after what he did for Liz, I guess things are better between the two of you."

Shaking his head, Jack tried to explain, "Dan, Lloyd hasn't changed, he helped Liz and me because he'd hoped he could use that as leverage to get me to change my last name back to his." Jack smiled wryly. "At least he helped, even if now we're back to generic Christmas letters and money requests from his ministry."

"When you decided to ask for his help, I couldn't believe it," Dan admitted, "and when you called him 'Dad' on the phone that day, I just about dropped my teeth. That was the first time I'd ever heard you call him by anything other than his first name or um, something worse. So yeah, your civility and willingness to ask him for help was a miracle; I'll grant you that. Let's go back to our original question. Can you honestly say that you love God more than you love Liz?"

Jack frowned, his brow creasing with thought. "I hope that it never comes down to making that kind of choice." He took Liz's hand and held it tightly. "The kind of statement I'm about to make comes easier in the light than in the dark—and yes, I'm speaking metaphorically.

"Dan, whatever you may think, I know that Liz came into my life by God's appointment," Jack asserted. "The chances that something like what happened would happen by accident are vanishingly small. God put her into my life for me to love, yes, but also to steer me toward a heavenly appointment that He orchestrated before the beginning of time. To that end, she was God with skin on to me. She spoke for Him. And thanks to God's mercy, she's here with me now, my love and the most important rock of my Earthly existence. Honestly, I've never even considered the question of who I love more, God or His cherished daughter, Liz."

Seeing the sardonic smile on Dan's face, Jack snapped, "If you want me to say another word, you'll wipe that idiotic grin off your face and listen. Fine, so it's sappy, but it's the truth. I can't imagine my life without Liz, or without you and Beth, for that matter. God knows how much I love each one of you, but He loves the three of you more than I ever could. He holds all of us in His hand and is going to allow events—both good and bad—through His fingers for our good, our growth, and His glory. I trust Him to do that. In fact,

I trust all of you sitting here, my chosen family, completely and absolutely to God. So yes, when it comes down to it, I love Him more than I love my wife and you, my best friends, because of that trust."

The only sound was the crackling of the fire. Beth and Dan sat there with their mouths open. Liz wrapped her arms around her husband and said, "C. S. Lewis is one of my favorite authors. He was one of the foremost Christian apologists of the twentieth century after his conversion to Christianity from atheism in 1931. He taught at Cambridge University and was a prolific writer. He addressed just what you're asking about, concluding,

> *When I have learnt to love God better than my earthly dearest, I shall love my earthly dearest better than I do now. Insofar as I learn to love my earthly dearest at the expense of God and instead of God, I shall be moving towards the state in which I shall not love my earthly dearest at all. When first things are put first, second things are not suppressed but increased.* [11]

"I agree with Lewis," Liz emphasized. "I wouldn't want Jack to love me more than God, because then we'd both suffer the consequences of having our priorities wrong in life. It's hard to imagine loving anyone more than I love Jack, but like Jack, and because of my trust in God, I love Him first."

"Wow," Dan, clearly uncomfortable with the emotional tenor of the conversation, managed after a few minutes, "that's some God you two have." He got up and pulled Beth to her feet. "Thanks for answering our question. I know it couldn't have been easy for either of you."

Jack got up and gave Beth a hug and shook Dan's hand. "You'd be surprised, and you're welcome. We appreciate your questions. They make for interesting and important campfire conversation between friends. Sleep well."

---

[11] C.S. Lewis, *The Letters of C.S. Lewis* (1952).

Waiting until after their friends retired to their own tent, Liz pulled Jack down beside her. "You okay?"

"Fine," Jack put his arm around Liz and stared into the flames. "I just thought, well, I thought this was going to be it. God gave us such a perfect opening and I assumed that Dan and Beth were going to…to…"

"To meet Him tonight?"

"Yeah."

"Jack, you know that God doesn't work in our timing but in His. Still," Liz leaned into him, "I know what you mean. You did a wonderful job with a really hard question. I know the way you answered that question is something they'll both be thinking about for a long time to come. Maybe it will even keep them up for the next few hours."

"I just hope I answered it honestly. I meant what I said about it being easier to answer in the light than in the dark."

"From the sounds of it, it was an awfully dark time that first morning you met God in my hospital room."

"I know, but that was different, somehow. I didn't know God in the same way I do now. I hadn't made a commitment to Him, like I did a year and a half ago." Jack smiled and shook his head. "It's hard to believe it's been that long."

The stars spun overhead in their slow, majestic dance and in that moment, both Jack and Liz knew that their friends had taken another step toward home. They didn't know the end of the story but could rest in knowing that what Jack had said was true—that God loved Dan and Beth more than they ever could. The deep peace of God's creation sang the four of them to sleep that night.

CHAPTER 37

A SPECIAL GALA

"Do you really want to go tonight?" Liz asked Jack, fidgeting uneasily. "It's not that big a deal if you don't go with me, and I know you have a lot going on, preparing to train those new doctors from Canada."

Jack wrapped Liz in his arms and kissed her on the end of her nose. "There's no way I'm missing this and it is a big deal. I can't remember the artist's colony ever celebrating a local artist with a one-woman show before."

"That's only because we're hosting a benefit for the colony and you know that. It's just a one-night thing, dinner and a silent auction with 50 percent of the after-tax proceeds going to benefit scholarships for artists new to the colony."

Jack didn't let go of Liz. Smoothing her hair away from her face, he said, "I'm very proud of you. The benefit was your idea and is your way of supporting the organization that helped birth your career."

Liz made a face. "I hope you'll be just as proud when you see how much of a hit my earnings take."

"Hey, why the sourpuss?" Jack was confused. "We talked about this before you ever proposed it to the board. You know that the money's not an issue. So what's wrong?"

"I'm nervous," Liz confessed, "and I have no idea why. Earlier I was wondering what will happen to my career and my association with the colony if no one bothers to bid on anything."

Stepping back, Jack looked at her incredulously. "What? You're one of the best-selling artists in the state. Why would you even think something like that?"

"I didn't say it made sense," Liz replied defensively, "I'm in kind of a tizzy, that's all. I want tonight's benefit to be a success for the colony. It's not about me," pausing, she frowned, "at least I don't think it is. Could it be that I'm afraid that my art has run its course, and no one will be interested?"

"Liz, love, if you can ask that question, the answer's no," Jack reassured her. "I want to be with you tonight, to be the proud husband who gets to introduce you to your admiring public. I plan on telling anyone who'll listen that you're the most talented, most groundbreaking, most versatile artist I know. And," he spun her away from him, hanging on to her hand, "the prettiest." That dress is beautiful. Did you make it?"

Her cheeks reddening, Liz nodded. "Yes, I did."

"I thought so." Jack drew her back into his arms, kissed her, then smiled against her lips. "It's perfect and it should garner a high bid, which is fine, so long as you don't plan to sell it off your back without having something else to wear at hand."

Liz laughed merrily, the sound a far cry from her morose imaginings. "You're awfully silly sometimes. The dress or one just like it, winner's choice, is included in the silent auction but I promise not to give my colleagues a glimpse of me in my underwear." She looked at Jack in his tuxedo. "You look mighty fine, too. I'm glad the committee insisted on black tie."

"Only for you would I don a monkey suit in the middle of the most beautiful September on record." Seeing a frown start to reappear on Liz's face, Jack took her wrap from the back of a dining room chair and held it out to her. "Hey, I'm teasing. Let's not undo all that hard work we just did finding your smile. It's time to celebrate you, artist wife, so let's go celebrate."

Jack leaned against a support post in the gallery, having a marvelous time watching his wife. Surrounded by well-wishers, Liz was smiling and nodding. Those patrons who weren't waiting to talk with her were, by and large, bidding on the items scattered around the room. Bids ranged between three and five digits before the decimal point. Jack's bid was no exception. Unbeknownst to Liz, he was currently the high bidder on the dress she wore. He didn't want someone else to have it.

The lustrous black satin gown highlighted Liz's curves and coloring, the V-neck and long sleeves showcased her tone-on-tone beadwork and embroidery of her own creation. To his amazement, she'd also embroidered a wave pattern suggesting Lake Superior around the hem of the dress with iridescent black, midnight blue, and silver beads. Jack couldn't imagine the hours of work that element alone represented. It was beautiful and perfect for her.

"Hey there, are you going to sleep?" Liz's teasing voice interrupted his musings.

"Hardly," Jack winked at her. "I just couldn't get a word in edgewise, so I thought I'd leave you to your adoring fans." Looking at Liz seriously, he asked, "So how's that tizzy now? Things appear to be a great success."

Liz nodded, a happy smile on her face. "Better than I'd ever imagined. Everybody's been very generous both with their praise and their pocketbooks. We have about an hour left before the auction ends, and the colony is already calling the fundraiser a great success." Her forehead creased. "But…"

"What's wrong, Liz?" Jack asked, concerned by her sudden change of mood.

"I still feel stressed, like something's wrong," Liz admitted.

Jack pulled her into a loose embrace. "Love, that's Satan talking. He doesn't want you to feel good about using God's gifts in your life. I can guarantee he didn't like you giving God the glory for your talent in your speech. Just take a deep breath, ignore the whispers, and enjoy this evening God has allowed us to experience together."

Liz's smile blazed back to life. "You're right, and I'm sure that Satan didn't appreciate your comments about God either. I hope they make the newspaper tomorrow."

"Me too, so long as they don't take liberties with the scripture that I quoted. Feeling better?"

Nodding, Liz took his hand, "Come on, I want to introduce you to some friends."

⁓

"Thank you, Phil, for the chance you took on me tonight and for letting Jack and me do this," Liz said as she slipped into the full-length cape Jack held for her. "I'll never be able to repay the debt I owe the colony."

"No, Liz," Phillip Stanford, the chairman of the nonprofit ArtForce—the company that operated the colony—said, "thank *you*. It was never about taking a chance on you. Your art has a large following and we're thrilled that you're a part of our community. This was a great idea and we hope to make it an annual benefit, showcasing an artist each year. You're welcome back anytime you're willing to participate."

Liz sucked in her breath; this was exactly the outcome she'd hoped to see. Hugging Phil excitedly, she said, "Thank you so much, and I'd love to participate again sometime. First, let's allow others an opportunity to give back to this amazing community and be celebrated by our equally amazing patrons."

Phil nodded then smiled. "You look great tonight. Did someone win that magnificent dress?"

Liz glanced up at her husband. "Uh, yes, Jack did, so I guess it's going home with us. However, we talked to the second-place bidder who's agreed to make her promised contribution if I'll make her one in dark purple. So we ended up collecting twice on it, with the bidders' full knowledge and consent." She giggled. "I don't think that bidder number two was worried about Jack showing up to a formal event in the same dress."

Phil hugged Liz back and shook Jack's hand. "Thank you for your work and generosity, Liz and Jack. I take it the two of you are calling it a night?"

"Yes," Liz responded, "we're going to take a short walk, then head home. I had a great time, Phil. Thank you again for giving me the opportunity."

＊

"What an absolutely superb way to end this day," Jack murmured, his lips against Liz's ear.

Liz snuggled back into Jack's body as she enjoyed God's benediction on the evening. They stood under the lighthouse at the end of the east breakwater—one of two that protected the small Grand Marais harbor. A full harvest moon hung low on the horizon, its light reflecting gold sparkles on the myriad wavelets at their feet. "Yes, it is. Thank you for thinking of it and for helping me over the hard parts getting out here." She lifted one foot. "I might have killed myself in these heels without you."

Turning in his arms, Liz kissed Jack. "Thank you, too, for chasing my attack of the heebee jeebies away. Tonight was wonderful, and I'm so glad you were there to share it with me."

"Thank you for sharing your life with me, Liz." Jack caressed her upturned face. "You've made my world so joyful and fun that I don't know what I'd do without you anymore."

"I'm glad to hear that," Liz smiled, "since you've done the same thing for me and I don't ever plan to let you go, at least not until I'm 103 when God calls us home together." She squeezed his hand. "What say we take the rest of this celebration home?"

CHAPTER 38

IN THE SPACE OF A HEARTBEAT

"Are you tired, Jack?" Liz asked, stretching in her car seat.

Jack shrugged, "Not particularly." He looked sideways at his wife, trying to figure out what she had in mind while keeping the car on the road. "What are you thinking?"

"I don't want this evening to end and I've changed my mind about going right home," Liz said. "Let's stop along the shore somewhere and enjoy the moon, the lake, and the quiet. I have a blanket in back, so we won't freeze."

Jack squeezed her hand. "That's a great idea and I don't think we'll freeze; it was still over sixty degrees when we left Grand Marais. As for being tired, it's still a little before ten and neither of us has to get up early. Do you have anyplace particular in mind?"

"Driver's choice, just nothing too rough or steep," Liz specified. "I changed into my flats, but you still might have to help me over the rocky spots."

After driving for several more miles, Jack made a left turn and pulled the car to a stop at the end of a long driveway. Just ahead of them, the lake sparkled in the moonlight. "How's this?" he asked.

"This is great!" Liz said enthusiastically. "I never thought of driving down to the Pearson place." Ted and Barb Pearson summered at their home on the lake and had just closed the place for the season a week ago. Liz and Jack kept a watch on their friends' summer home when no one was there, making sure that the contracted company plowed the driveway, that the heat remained on, and the security alarm armed.

Jack, carrying the blanket over one arm, opened Liz's door and extended his hand. "I seem to recall a bench with a beautiful view just ahead, but first…" Jack took her in his arms and spun her into a slow waltz. They danced together in the moonlight, needing only the music of the wind in the pines. After a few minutes their movements slowed and finally stopped, and they stood together, wrapped in each other's arms, their kiss deep and sweet.

Their dance and snuggling together enjoying the moon over the lake on a glorious mid-September night was an interlude that Jack would always remember. Here, off the highway, it was quiet except for the schussing of the waves on the rocky shore. They were warm, and neither of them felt the need for words. Jack was content to absorb the beauty around him while holding his wife. The rapt expression on Liz's face spoke eloquently of her delight.

They might have stayed there all night, but for a shift in the wind that raised goose bumps. Kissing Liz's temple, Jack finally said, "I think it's time to head back. That wind's a little raw. Okay with you?"

Nodding, Liz got to her feet and wrapped the blanket around her. "Brrr, you're right, and we still have a seventy-mile drive home. Thank you so much, Jack, this was wonderful."

Liz was asleep before Jack pulled the car into the garage. He reached over and gently shook her awake. Coming around to the passenger side of the car, he helped her up and held her close for a moment. "Thank you for a wonderful evening, love." His kiss started soft and sweet, but she returned it with an intensity that drove all thoughts of sleep away. He chuckled softly, "Why don't we take this inside?"

"That's a superb idea, Dr. Lockwood." A male voice with a heavy Hispanic accent came out of the darkness. Before either Jack or Liz could move, four large men surrounded them, holding each of them by both arms. Jack struggled to free himself but accomplished nothing more than irritating the men holding him. One of them drove a punch into Jack's gut, leaving him gasping for air.

"Please don't do that again, Dr. Lockwood, otherwise I'll be forced to move up my timetable for the evening." The man stepped out of the shadows. Both Liz and Jack gasped, their faces blanching when they recognized the intruder.

"Reynoso," Jack began.

"Spare me the obvious comments, Doctor. We all know I was incarcerated a long way from here which means that I must have engineered a successful prison break and garnered some transportation." Reynoso looked down at his fingernails, buffing them on his jacket. "It's amazing how persuasive the almighty dollar can be to those who don't have enough almighty dollars."

"What do you want?" Jack could think of nothing to do, other than to keep Reynoso talking. News as big as a felon escaping a maximum-security Federal penitentiary would be all over the news and law enforcement blotters. Hopefully Dan wasn't sleeping.

"I believe your wife and I have a score to settle—the small matter of spending over a year of my life locked away thanks to her testimony." Reynoso nodded at the two men holding Jack. Both of them moved at the same time, one driving a fist into Jack's kidneys, the other hitting him in the gut. Jack sagged in their grasp, barely hanging on to consciousness.

"Stop it," Liz implored, "please, you want me, don't do this to him."

"Our time will come, Ms. Lockwood. However, I can think of no more effective way to hurt you than by causing the good doctor here pain." He nodded and both blows fell again. Jack lost his battle to stay conscious.

Reynoso took an automatic from his pocket, aimed it at Jack, and checked the sight. "Bang. I think I can dispense with a suppressor all the way out here. No one from town's going to hear a thing."

"No," Liz whimpered, fighting the men who held her. "What kind of coward beats a man unconscious and then shoots him?"

Reynoso spun and back-handed Liz, striking her so hard that he split her lip. "The same kind of man who'd hit a defenseless woman. Now be quiet."

Reynoso started to check the sight on the gun again but stopped when an approaching siren became audible. Listening intently, he rattled off an order in Spanish, and the men holding Liz dragged her toward a car parked back in the trees. The men holding a barely-conscious Jack stayed where they were.

Smiling at Liz, Reynoso said, "One moment, gentlemen, I want to give Ms. Lockwood something to remember before we take our journey." Taking aim, he calmly shot Jack in the chest. Then as Jack fell to his knees and blood mushroomed around the wound, Reynoso took aim again, and pulled the trigger.

Tilting his head, the felon listened to the approaching sirens, then looked at the sobbing Liz. "It's your turn, but we need to take this party elsewhere." He hit her on the back of her head with the butt of his gun, and she dropped like a stone.

CHAPTER 39

THE DARKNESS DEEPENS

Dan held Jack close to his body, trying desperately to keep his friend's head elevated while staunching the flow of blood from his chest. He'd arrived on the scene just minutes before. Despite the after-midnight hour, he'd wanted to warn Liz and Jack about Reynoso's escape, and to schedule some time with them the following morning to discuss security. When neither of them answered their phones or the radio, something pushed Dan to call for backup and drive out to the Lockwoods' home.

When they got there, they'd found Liz gone and Jack in a crumpled heap on the lawn, bleeding out from a double tap to his chest. Tearing off his jacket as he ran, Dan rammed it against the heavily bleeding wounds.

"Dan," Blood bubbled from between Jack's lips, the blood vessels on his neck standing out as he forced the words from between his lips, "Rey…Reynoso, Liz."

Jack fell back against Dan's arm, unconscious and fighting to breathe. "Where are the medics?" Dan called, pressing harder on his blood-saturated jacket. "I'm losing him!"

"They're here, sir."

Dan became vaguely aware of the whuff-whuff-whuff of rotor blades and the wind picking up around him. Gus stood in the center of the front yard with a spotlight, illuminating the only fully cleared space on the property, sized especially for the models of helicopters used by the BWSRU.

Moments later, much to Dan's relief, Jack was in Zach Birch's hands. Dan stayed with Zach and the two EMTs, helping where he could, but mostly holding tightly to Jack's hand, hoping to anchor his friend in the world of the living. Zach slapped a chest-seal patch over the bullet wounds on Jack's chest and Dan heard his friend's labored breathing ease. Finally, Zach got to his feet, "Let's get him in the chopper."

"Anderson," Zach looked at one of the EMTs, "get on the radio and tell them I need Theresa Paschal up here now. If Jack makes it that far, this is going to be a risky surgery, and I want the best surgeon available."

"Yes, sir." Anderson took off running for the helicopter.

When they were in the air, Zach asked the other EMT to get Jack's vitals.

Listening carefully to the reply, Zach shook his head worriedly. "His breathing's getting worse. I'm going to insert a chest tube."

Observing the change in Zach's body language, Dan asked anxiously, "Zach, how's Jack doing? I know it's bad, he lost a lot of blood."

"Dan, I don't know how he's made it this far," Zach said tersely

Christine Anderson slid into her place beside Zach and reported, "Paschal's on her way."

Not looking up, Zach acknowledged the EMT, "Thanks, Anderson. Now get EBCH on the radio and tell them to have an echocardiogram set-up and their best tech in ER when we get there." Without waiting for an answer, Zach made a surgical incision in Jack's chest then watched as blood spurted from the small diameter tube he'd inserted.

Zach had no more than set down his scalpel when Dan tried again, "It looks like we got to Jack just a couple of minutes after Reynoso left with Liz. Zach, I need to call their families when I get back to the hospital. What can I tell them? What are his chances of pulling through?"

Zach looked up at Dan, irritation and grief warring in his expression. "Dan, I need to focus on Jack, so please stop asking me questions I can't answer. According to all the medicine I know, Jack shouldn't be alive right now. He's hypovolemic. He's having trouble breathing. One of the bullets nicked his left lung, he's bleeding into his chest cavity and into the pericardium—that's the sack around his heart. His vitals indicate a cardiac tamponade, something we can't begin to treat until we get him into surgery. If we can get him that far, then he has at least a chance of surviving the next two hours. I have the best thoracic surgeon in the northern half of the state flying in from Duluth. But given the severity of the chest injury and the blood loss, Jack could die at any time. So please, leave me alone and let me try to keep that from happening."

Dan shut his mouth, not angered by what Zach had to say, but scared almost out of his skin by the physician's abrupt responses and the thought of losing both Jack and Liz in one horrible night. He had a BOLO out on Reynoso but having seen only the taillights of a car half a mile away, he couldn't be certain it would do any good. His information about Reynoso's mode of transport was far too generic in terms of both the make of the vehicle and its direction.

His team had notified all law-enforcement entities in Minnesota about Reynoso and sent both the US and Canadian Border guards a "capture and detain" notice, adding that the suspect was not only armed and very dangerous, but also that he had a hostage. They'd also notified all local bus stations, airports, and the Grand Portage Indian Reservation council of the same information. Finally, they'd set up roadblocks on the major routes into and out of the area. That was all Dan could do for the moment, that and call Liz and Jack's families when they landed. How he was going to break this kind of news to them, he had no idea.

For a moment, Dan wondered what Jack would be doing were their positions reversed and without even giving it much thought he knew that both Jack and Liz would be on their knees or sitting in chairs with bowed heads, pleading with their God to keep their friends alive and safe through the dark night. For moment Dan considered it, then wondered if God even listened to the prayers of unbelievers. Deciding he had nothing to lose, he whispered, "If anyone's out there, please don't let Jack die and keep Liz safe in Your care. Help us to find her and catch the people who did this. Thanks."

CHAPTER 40

VALLEY OF THE SHADOW

The darkness surrounded Jack, pressing down on his chest, making it hard to breathe. He moved his lips, silently mouthing a cry for help. For him, yes, but mostly for Liz. Reynoso? They'd thought themselves free of him, but he'd appeared out of nowhere at the end of one of the most wonderful evenings of Jack's life. Despite his impotent struggles and Liz's pleas, Reynoso had shot him and taken his beloved wife.

Somehow Jack knew he hung suspended in a nether world between life and death. He couldn't sense God's presence but neither could he open his eyes and answer the friend who'd just broken his life-time rule by reaching out to God on Liz and Jack's behalf.

The shadows deepened and Jack heard Zach talking to someone. "Bag him, start chest compressions. Charging. Clear." Jack felt his body arch in response to the current. "Again," came the voice and Jack's body repeated its peculiar dance. Curiously, he didn't feel anything, but slept for a time out of mind.

CHAPTER 41

FIRST STEPS

"Chief Harrison, wake up, Chief."

Dan sat up, blinking his eyes. He was sitting in the surgical waiting room at EBCH. Sitting next to him was Doctor Theresa Paschal. She wore light blue surgical scrubs and looked exhausted. "Uh, yeah, um, what time is it? How's Jack?"

"It's 6:30 a.m. and Jack came through surgery. He's in recovery right now."

Dan noticed that she hadn't really said anything about Jack's condition, only that he'd made it through surgery. "Dr. Paschal, how is Jack?"

Theresa Paschal looked at him with compassion in her eyes. "Not good. He coded twice before we made it to the OR, and once more while I had him on the table. I was able to get him back, drain and repair the pericardial sack, and close the bullet wounds, but his heart and lungs suffered a sustained trauma."

When the doctor left, Dan woke his sleeping wife. "Hey, Jack made it through surgery, but his prognosis, according to Dr. Paschal, is very poor. She doesn't think... "Dan choked on both his words and the tears he was trying to hold back.

Beth hugged him close. "Don't give up hope, DH, you know how strong Jack is."

Dan took a deep breath and shared his greatest fear, "I know Jack's strong, but I also know that the last thing he saw was his wife in the hands of the man who nearly killed her two years ago, a man who's set on revenge. What's that going to do to Jack's will to fight for his own life?" His voice quavered as he confessed, "I don't know what I can do for him or even how to share this news when their families get here. What do I say?"

In the end, Zach Birch and Theresa Paschal handled the medical explanations, leaving it to Dan to express the pain they were all feeling about what had happened. Dan also explained the law enforcement piece, what they were doing to find Reynoso and Liz.

It was at this point that Todd, Liz's sandy-haired, green-eyed brother, spoke up, "Dan, when we're done here, can I have a minute? I might be able to offer some assistance and I feel pretty helpless just sitting here."

"Of course," Dan acknowledged, "anytime."

"Why don't you let me get Mom settled in our hotel room, then I'll come back—here?"

Nodding, Dan indicated Jack's family. "Yeah, I've kind of set up shop here for the moment. I want to stay close to them and to Jack."

"Totally get it," Todd said. "I'll check for you here first then in Jack's room, if they'll let me into the critical care unit. Otherwise, I'll ask a nurse to let you know I'm here."

Dan found Zach and asked for and received permission to sit with Jack, who rested in a room in the CICU. To his chagrin, he found Theresa Paschal already there. "I'm sorry, Doctor. Zach told me I could sit with Jack, but I didn't know you were in here with him. I'll come back."

"Chief Harrison, wait." Theresa got to her feet. "I'm finished here. I was just hoping that maybe this good doctor had decided to join the party," she shook her head sadly, "but he's still enjoying the good life, wherever he is."

"Call me Dan, Doctor Paschal. I was wondering something," Dan began. "Jack's last memories will be of his wife in the hands of a very bad man who has hurt her in the past. Could that impact Jack's recovery?"

Theresa nodded. "Yes, Dan, it could. You need to understand that Jack shouldn't have made it this far. The fact that he's done so is a tribute to his spirit, his fitness level, and the fact that help was almost immediately on the scene. The good news is, he's off the vent and breathing on his own. However, we still have a long way to go and with the amount of blood loss he suffered, I'm not only worried about his heart but the possibility of brain damage brought on by hypovolemic shock. So far he's not responding to any environmental stimuli."

Dan looked confused. "I don't understand. What are you talking about?"

"Jack spending the remainder of his life without the full use of his brain," Theresa said bluntly.

His eyes widening, Dan gasped, "You're talking about the broccoli plant scenario."

It was Theresa's turn to look confused. "The...The *what?*"

Having the good grace to look a bit embarrassed, Dan explained his comment, "I hold Jack's health-care power of attorney in the event his wife can't make decisions for him. The broccoli plant scenario—that's what we called Jack's aversion to machines keeping him alive if he's only going to be a living, breathing husk. Is that what we're talking about?"

Theresa Paschal nodded. "It could be, but that's the worst-case scenario. To get back to your earlier question, Dan, Jack's battling for his life right now on several fronts. I can't say with any certainty that he will fight like he needs to fight if he believes that Liz is dead."

Theresa reached down and squeezed Jack's hand. Turning back to Dan, she said, "I'll leave you two to have your own conversation." Just before walking out of the room, she turned her head, "Jack can hear you, never doubt it." With that, she was gone.

Walking back to the bed, Dan sat down next to Jack. Despite his pallor, the IV's feeding fluid and whole blood into his arms, and the large dressing covering his chest, Jack looked almost peaceful. Reaching out, Dan took Jack's hand then almost dropped it when Jack smiled and whispered, "I love you."

Dan bent over his friend. "Hey, brother, you awake? I love you too and if you'll open those baby blues, I'll even give you a big ole kiss." Jack didn't respond, the smile on his face fading to a faint shadow of what it had been.

"Jack," Dan tried again, "Jack, don't worry, I'm kidding about the kiss thing, but you need to wake up. Come on, as you once told me, it's time for you to join the party."

Jack didn't respond, and Dan finally sat back in his chair. Wherever his friend was, it was a lot better place than here. And that's what had them all so scared.

CHAPTER 42

PERCHANCE TO DREAM

"This is so nice, Jack, I'll never forget tonight." Liz rested her head on his shoulder as they moved in time to the music.

With a start, Jack realized they were still dancing on the lawn at the Pearson home. Yet something was different. There was music flowing around them. Music with words that spoke eloquently of his feelings for the woman in his arms.

Liz started to sing softly as they moved together,

> I cherish the treasure
> The treasure of you
> Lifelong companion
> I give myself to you
> God has enabled me
> To walk with you faithfully
> And cherish the treasure
> The treasure of you.[vii]

Jack smiled down at Liz. "That's beautiful, but are we dancing to Christian music? Isn't that a no-no?"

Liz shook her head. "It might be a bit unconventional, but I think God will forgive us this once."

Jack brushed Liz's lips with his, "I cherish the treasure of you."

Liz put her hand behind his neck, drew him closer and sang,

As I obey the Spirit's voice
And seek to do His will
I then can see the wisdom of His plan
For as He works His will in me
I then can love you selflessly
And by His grace, can pledge my love to you.

Jack took his wife's hand and placed it over his heart. "My heart beats with yours, Liz, and I pledge my love to you."

"His heart rate just increased to 145, blood pressure's dropping. Doctor, he's in v-fib." A terse voice interrupted their dance.

Jack frowned, whoever they were talking about was in trouble. He wondered for a moment if he should step in to help, but when he tried to move, he couldn't. Looking down at Liz curiously, he asked, "What's going on, love?"

Liz stroked Jack's cheek, "I'm not sure, Jack. I think this interlude was to keep us from that place where something's happening to both of us. I can't stay, I'm sorry."

Letting go of Jack's hand, Liz backed away, leaving him alone. "No, Liz, please stay with me," he begged.

Before Jack finished his quiet plea, she was gone, leaving only an echo behind, "Be strong for me, dear Jack. I love you."

Jack listened intently in the sudden silence and heard her voice echoing out of the darkness.

This sacred vow I make to you
Does not contain an "if"
Though I'm aware that trials lie ahead
I will love you and pray with you
And through it all, I will stay with you
Our home will be a refuge of
Unconditional love.

"I love you more than life, Jack. Wherever you are and wherever I am, I will be praying for you. Come back to our home—our refuge, and to me."

Jack closed his eyes, thinking of happy and peaceful times in their home. He was tired and wanted nothing more than to follow his wife back to that joyful place, to once again live with her in the here and now. The darkness beckoned him, sweet with promise.

CHAPTER 43

THE HERE AND NOW

"Dan, wake up."

Dan stirred and looked up at the woman shaking his arm. It was Vicky, Jack's sister. "Um, yeah, I'm awake." He blinked, trying to figure out where he was but wished he hadn't as his memory quickly returned. He was lying on a couch in the CICU waiting room. "Uh, Vicky, how's Jack?"

Jack's sister's face fell. "He made it through another night, but I can tell the doctors are worried. They think he should have regained consciousness hours ago." Tears trickled from her eyes. "Everybody keeps saying what a miracle it is that Jack's made it this far, but his vitals keep falling and it's like my brother is just, well, fading away."

"Have you reached your father yet?" Dan asked, not certain if he wanted to know.

Vicky sighed. "I talked to him, which is not the same thing as reaching him."

"Does he understand how bad things are with Jack?" Dan snapped. "He needs to get his butt off that nice soft throne of his and get up here, sooner rather than later. I'd arrest him and drag him here if I could."

Tears welled in Vicki's eyes again. "I told him, Dan. I even asked Dr. Paschal to talk to him, but Dad was at his noncommittal best. So I don't know if he plans to show up or, if the worst happens, if he'll get here before Jack dies."

197

Dan tried to tamp down the anger he felt with Lloyd Beckett. What kind of man would behave like that? Worse, Beckett was a preacher, his son was close to death, yet he couldn't be bothered to change his schedule.

Taking a deep breath, Dan reminded himself that he could only control his own behavior, not Lloyd Beckett's. There'd be time for recriminations later, right now what mattered was Jack and Liz. It was hard for Dan to believe that just a little over fifty hours had passed since Reynoso had shot Jack and taken Liz.

Although Dan had spent most of that time at the hospital, law enforcement from several agencies, including the FBI, were investigating Liz's disappearance and had people spread out over the state in an ever-widening search pattern. They'd alerted and updated the international borders and all airports, including the small private fields; expanded the roadblocks; and were investigating all the motels, hotels, and lodges in the area. Reynoso's photo and photos of his known associates were all over the news. They were doing everything humanly possible to find Liz. All to no avail, at least not yet. Still, six people didn't just disappear, that number coming from the forensic evidence at the scene, and they would find them. It was just a matter of whether or not they found them in time to do Liz Lockwood any good.

"Anyway," Vicki continued, "Todd Hanley wants to talk with you. He thinks they might have a lead on Liz's whereabouts. He's in with Jack right now, but he asked me if I could come and get you."

When Dan opened the door to Jack's room, he found Jack's brother-in-law praying. Although he stood in silence waiting for Todd to finish, Dan was annoyed by the delay. As soon as Todd lifted his head, Dan stepped over beside Liz's brother. "I'm here, I understand you wanted me for something. Something other than some supernatural mumbo-jumbo, I hope?"

"As a family, we'd welcome your prayers for both Jack and Liz," Todd responded calmly. "I know Jack would as well. We certainly believe in that power. However, I do have something else on my mind which I hope you'll find useful and that will bring my sister home alive."

"You know the doctor said that Jack can hear us." Dan looked uncomfortable. "I'm sorry about what I said. I know you all believe in God and I didn't intend any disrespect. It's just," rubbing his forehead, Dan admitted, "I feel pretty useless right now."

"All the more reason to talk with God." Todd smiled faintly. "Let's just forget the beginning of this conversation and start over, shall we?" At Dan's nod, Todd motioned him to a chair. "I'm sorry this has taken me so long to acquire, but I have something for you."

"And you want to do it here?" Dan was surprised. "If this is about Liz, shouldn't we talk elsewhere?"

"If Jack is listening, I want him to hear this." Pulling a flash drive from his pocket and handing it to Dan, Todd explained, "I don't know if Liz or Jack ever shared with you that I work for the Directorate of Operations branch of the CIA. Whether or not either of them shared that fact, I'd ask you to keep it and any mention of my involvement to yourself and out of any press releases."

Dan nodded. "Yes, I knew, but I flew recon missions for the Navy in Gulf War One—pretty secret stuff—and I'm used to keeping any intelligence types out of the conversation." He lifted the flash drive. "So what's this, what does it have to do with Liz, and what am I supposed to do with it?"

"Eduard Reynoso is a foreign citizen and an enemy of the United States," Todd said significantly.

Dan nodded, that's why Todd could even be involved in this kind of conversation, "I'm with you so far. So this," tapping the flash drive, Dan continued, "is the information you have on Reynoso?"

Todd nodded. "In part, but also something far more important. Three years ago, when Reynoso first started recruiting in this area, we spent a lot of time up here, trying to locate his base of operations. As you can imagine, that was challenging. He didn't spend much time in northern Minnesota, as his preferred base was in the Minneapolis area. Being from Columbia, the weather up here wasn't his cup of tea.

"For a while we thought he might have abandoned his operation in the northern tier of the state. We were wrong. When the Minneapolis cops arrested Reynoso, he sent locals after Liz and ended up nearly killing her. The FBI got involved at that point, helping to hide her at Lloyd Beckett's place. After that we never stopped following the local foreign nationals with a known connection to Reynoso."

"This," Todd tapped the flash drive, "is last night's satellite footage of a small cabin in the BWCAW that shouldn't be there at all. It is also a place that Reynoso's lackeys used from time to time to meet. While it's been dark and quiet for the past two years, we're actively watching the area now, because Reynoso doesn't have many options when it comes to running. We've got the borders, the airports, and the roads covered. It's possible, even likely, that Reynoso might return to this place to lay low for a few days. I wanted to invite you to the party tonight when I share this information with the FBI. They've got a live infrared satellite feed and I have a hunch that we might see some activity in this area later tonight. A helicopter will be here at 1930 to fly me to Duluth. You in?"

Dan nodded. This was the first good news in more than two days. "Yeah, I'm in."

CHAPTER 44

No Longer the Struggle

Jack was alone in the dark. His pain was worse now—it was harder to breathe and even harder to think. Yet he wanted to think about what was happening to him. It was outside his experience. The Bible said that 'to be absent from the body is to be present with the Lord[12],' but this certainly didn't feel like Heaven and Jack couldn't sense God's presence at all.

Jack guessed he was still bound by mortal life, guessed that all the flashes of hospital equipment and the medical jargon meant someone was treating him for life-threatening injuries. Perhaps he was in a coma. That would explain the strangeness, but how did it explain Liz and being with her in a place he knew they'd shared?

Moreover, he'd heard Liz's brother talking. Jack felt sudden fear constrict his chest even further. Todd had sounded worried, so had Dan for that matter. They'd talked about Liz like she was in trouble. There was another name they'd mentioned, a name Jack both feared and despised—Reynoso. That was it.

Out of the darkness came a whisper, "I think that's a superb idea, Dr. Lockwood." Images of Liz in Reynoso's grasp brought terror in their wake. Terror so profound that Jack couldn't breathe.

Once again, Jack heard Liz's voice, beckoning him, drawing him away from the terror and pain. Her whisper, sweet with prom-

---

[12] 2 Corinthians 5:8 (Paraphrase).

ise, comforted him. "Remember, my love, and hang on through this trial. Our home awaits both of us." Her arms held him close as she sang,

> *This sacred vow I make to you*
> *Does not contain an "if"*
> *Though I'm aware that trials lie ahead*
> *I will love you and pray with you*
> *And through it all, I will stay with you,*
> *Our home is our refuge of unconditional love.*

Suddenly, excruciatingly, Jack was torn away from his wife and that familiar, beautiful place that they shared. He opened his eyes and found himself alone in a hospital room. Well, not alone—Dan sat by his side in a glass-walled room. His friend looked worried and held his hand.

"Dan," Jack choked on his whisper. His throat was sore, his head ached, and his chest felt like someone was standing on it. Still reeling from the shock of regaining consciousness, Jack squeezed Dan's hand, trying to get his attention. That worked.

"Jack," Dan leaned over his friend, "Jack, are you awake?"

"Yeah," Jack whispered hoarsely, "I think so. I remember," his eyebrows furrowed, then he hummed a melody. "I cherish you, love."

Dan hit the call button. Wherever Jack was he wasn't all here and Dan didn't have much time. Bending over his friend again, he said, "Jack, it's Dan."

Jack looked up. "I know. It's been strange. What's happened and where's Liz?" The minute Jack spoke his wife's name all the images he'd seen before came back to him. He put his hands up as far as he could, trying to ward off the memories. "No, that can't be! He's in prison."

Dan sat back and eyed Jack sadly. "You do remember. I'm sorry Jack, but Reynoso has Liz, at least for the moment. You're at EBCH. Reynoso shot you twice in the chest and we've all been waiting for you to come out of it. You're lucky to be alive. I need to leave in a few minutes. Thanks to Todd, we think we've got a solid lead on Reynoso's location."

Zach Birch banged the door open and was at Jack's bedside in two long strides. "Hey, welcome back. Can you tell me your name?"

"We've already covered that, Zach," Dan unceremoniously interrupted the physician. "Jack knows who he is, what happened and who I am. So maybe you can start your exam from there?"

Zach looked at him sourly. "I don't tell you how to be police chief, don't you tell me how to practice medicine." Returning his attention to Jack, Zach asked, "Apart from the obvious, how do you feel? What's your pain like?"

Jack felt lost. "I want to go back to that place, with Liz and the music."

"Jack," Zach asked urgently, "Jack are you with us?"

"Yes, I'm here," Jack struggled to pull himself together. "Zach, I hurt, my chest is about a twelve. Everything is kinda hazy, but I need to go with Dan. I need to help Liz." Jack tried to sit up and swing his legs over the edge of the bed, but only succeeded in sliding sideways.

"Hold it." Both Zach and Dan reached for Jack, settling him back against the pillows, then Zach continued, "Jack, you're not going anywhere. You couldn't walk out of this room without support if you tried. We had to go into your rather mangled chest and that meant cracking the breastbone. You tell me when you're going to be walking around without support again. Best case scenario."

"Then bring me a walker," Jack insisted.

Dan reached down and grasped Jack's shoulders. "Jack, you're my best friend. Trust me to get the information I need to bring Liz home. You know I love her too. You focus on staying conscious and following doctor's orders so that when she comes home, she won't have to worry about you."

Dan's eyes met Jack's. "Brother, I give you my word. I won't stop looking until I find Liz, and I'll keep you informed every step of the way."

Jack stared at him for a long moment, then slowly nodded. "I know." Zach injected some medication into Jack's IV and his eyes started to close. "I want to dance with Liz when she gets back."

Appalled, Dan speared Zach with an irritated glance. "What did you just do? We've spent the last two and a half days hoping Jack would wake up and now you put him back to sleep?"

"Still telling me how to do my job, Dan?" Zach had a faint smile on his face. "All I did was medicate Jack for pain. We can wake him easily if we need to, but for him to admit he hurt like that, it's got to be bad. His recovery will go more smoothly if we can manage his pain. Besides, you heard him. He's still a little out of it and the rest will do him good."

———※———

In the deep quiet of the after-midnight hour, Jack tossed, unable to get comfortable, unable, even, to pray. There was nothing he could say to God that he hadn't already said. Still, the Bible promised that when Jack couldn't find the words, God knew the cries of his heart[13]. Everything inside him screamed a prayer that they'd located Liz tonight and that she would soon come home to him, safe and unharmed. Yet he knew that was unlikely in the extreme. It wasn't that he didn't believe God could work that miracle, it's just he'd seen what Reynoso was capable of, and he remembered Liz caught in the cruel grip of two of Reynoso's men.

Jack had then pleaded with God to bring Liz home, even if it was only her body that came home. He needed both the closure and to know that Liz was no longer in Reynoso's hands. At least she'd be at peace. Tears trickled from his eyes. He was nowhere near ready to say goodbye to his wife, but he knew God loved Liz more than he did. The best thing he could do right now was to leave her in the hands of her Heavenly Father.

---

[13] "In the same way the Spirit also helps our weakness; for we do not know how to pray as we should, but the Spirit Himself intercedes for us with groanings too deep for words" (Romans 8:26 New American Standard translation).

Jack had just closed his eyes again, trying to find rest, when the door to his room opened.

"Son, are you awake?

Jack raised the head of the bed slowly, not believing his ears. "Dad? What the devil are you doing here at three in the morning?"

Lloyd Beckett turned to address someone Jack couldn't see. "It's okay, he's alone."

Then, walking into the room, Lloyd stopped by Jack's bedside. "Mind your tongue. I'm here because your sister called and told me that you'd been badly hurt. I've come to pray over you."

Before Jack could begin to process that statement, another man stuck his head through the door and asked, "Okay for me to come in, Reverend?"

Lloyd beckoned him forward before Jack had a chance to say anything. "Yes, yes, I'm ready to get started." Not bothering to introduce Jack to the newcomer, Lloyd put his hands over his son's form, looked toward Heaven, and began in a theatrical voice, "Oh Lord God, hear me…"

Jack lay there stunned, trying to absorb what was happening. He was still confused and weak. His mind was on Liz, not on his surroundings, so for a moment, he didn't respond. It wasn't until the third man switched on a video camera and began filming Lloyd's ostentatious prayer that Jack pressed the call button, held the heart-shaped pillow they'd given him after the surgery on his chest, and exclaimed in the loudest voice he could manage, "Stop! Dad, what in blazes are you doing?" Jack turned to the man who was still filming and managed to yell, "No more! Stop that camera now."

The man looked at Lloyd, who nodded, "Go ahead and stop, Marcus." Then Lloyd swiveled back to address his son. "I'm praying for you, Jack, can't you see that?"

"With your own personal camera man filming it all?" Jack asked, unbelievingly.

"We at the ministry film as many miracles of grace as we can," Lloyd said proudly.

"Get out! Both of you," Jack wheezed, "and if you use a moment of that footage, I'll sue you, Reverend Dad, your ministry, whoever that is with you, and anyone else I can think of! This isn't some kind of bizarre photo op. My wife is missing and in the hands of some very bad people, including the man who nearly killed her a couple of years back."

"And Jack, here, is in critical condition. Neither of you have clearance to be in this room at this hour." Dr. Andrea Barstow and one of the male RNs on duty, stood in the doorway with a security guard. "You both need to leave now, and next time, if there is a next time, check in with the nurse's station before you barge into a patient's room. Do I make myself clear?"

Lloyd stood his ground until the security guard moved toward him, then turned back to Jack. "We flew all the way up here from Chicago, in the midst of my very busy schedule, and this is how you thank me? No wonder God is bringing His judgement down on you." Spinning on his heel, Lloyd motioned to the other man, "Come along, Marcus, God's not wanted in this room."

Jack sat there glaring until the two men left, then fell back, his body shaking with expended effort and pain. Andrea was at his side in seconds. "Are you okay, Jack? I'm so sorry they got in here. It was one of those fluke intervals when everyone was away from the desk. Those two must have been watching for an opportunity."

Jack pressed the pillow to his breastbone, trying to ease the ache, and shook his head. "Not your fault, Andi, Dad can be determined when he gets an idea in his head. I supposed he looked at this as a way to meet an obligation and garner more contributions by filming a little drama—Daddy flying to his injured son's bedside to perform a miracle."

Andrea turned to the nurse and asked, "Tom, will you please get Dr. Lockwood three milligrams of morphine, the order's already in the system."

A few minutes later, Jack could feel the medication taking effect, sweeping Lloyd, Liz, and his pain away into healing sleep.

CHAPTER 45

THE AGONY OF WAITING

It was late afternoon that same day that Dan returned to Jack's bedside. He was amazed and pleased to find his friend in a regular room outside of the CICU. When he arrived, Jack was sleeping so he sat down and thought about how to tell him what they'd seen the night before on the FBI's satellite feed.

Todd's surmise had been correct, timing and all. Up until yesterday there'd been no activity at the cabin for two years. Last night, there'd been six heat signatures plus a fire or wood stove showing up on the feed.

"Now what, I ask you, could be a reason for that?" Todd had posed the question to the group. "Maybe Reynoso's not running, at least not yet. Further, if he has to run, would he really kill his only bargaining chip?"

Todd's logic had been flawless and Dan was now a believer. Tonight, the FBI was sending in an HRT[14] by helicopter. Dan and BWSR Team One were flying in right behind them—in their capacity of search and rescue only. The FBI would do the rest. Dan had objected to that caveat and Todd had responded curtly, "Those are the terms. You know that area better than anyone and there's a good chance we're going to need medical help. Do you want to go or not?"

---

[14] The Hostage Rescue Team (HRT) is an elite tactical unit of the Federal Bureau of Investigation.

Dan had agreed reluctantly then asked, "Are you going?"

"In an observational capacity only. I have to," Blinking back tears, Todd clarified, "Liz is my sister." Then, getting to his feet, he'd added, "Wheels up at 2030. Pick your team, Chief, and we'll see you tonight. Oh, and feel free to talk to Jack about this."

So here Dan sat, waiting to talk with Jack. Unlike Todd, Dan was afraid that the stress of the night ahead could severely compromise Jack's progress. Perhaps it would be better to share everything when the teams returned. Still, he'd given his word to Jack that he'd keep him posted. Taking a deep breath, he shook Jack's shoulder gently. "Hey there. Wake up."

Jack opened his eyes. "Uh, yeah, I'm awake. Tough session with the respiratory therapist. Who would have thought breathing could hurt so much. What, um, what time is it anyway?"

"About 5:00 P.M. on Thursday. I just got back from Duluth a little while ago."

Jack swallowed hard. "What did you find out?"

"Remember that cabin Todd told us about that was dark and quiet on Tuesday night? Well, last night we found evidence of a hot fire or wood stove and six people at the place. So tonight, the FBI's finest Hostage Rescue Team and yours truly along with our Team One will be paying this group a surprise visit. We're going to bring Liz home."

Jack collapsed back against the pillow and asked anxiously, "Rescue or recovery?"

Dan reached out and squeezed Jack's arm. "As of less than twenty-four hours ago, it was still rescue and my money's on Liz. So don't you go leaving her alone, understand?"

"Dan, I need to go with you." Jack sat up slowly and carefully moved his legs toward the edge of the bed, but Dan stopped him.

"Just a minute," Dan said. "Let's not ruin all the progress you've made. Keep this up and you'll be back in that glass-walled prison known as CICU. You can't walk the length of the hallway without support, so you'll be no good to me or to Liz out there. Zach is going in your place tonight. Trust us to bring her home."

Jack fought him for another moment, then fell back against the bed. "I hate this! I should be going with you and instead, I lie here useless."

"No. You need to be here and well on the mend when we bring Liz home," Dan said forcefully. "Jack, you may have the most important role of all in this. Pray, buddy. Talk to your God about what we're doing and about your wife. You've told me that your God can be depended on absolutely and that you trust Him. So help us tonight by doing your thing with heaven, okay?"

It took time, but Jack finally nodded, "Okay. Be careful and bring her home. Please."

"How do you feel, Dr. Lockwood? Are you ready to go back to your room?" Maggie asked as she gripped the gait belt and walked beside Jack. It was after two in the morning and the halls were quiet.

Jack leaned heavily on the walker but shook his head. "No, anything but that." He looked at the nurse, who was a long-time friend. "How about if we go down a floor to the ER, so I can walk around some familiar stomping grounds."

Maggie frowned and shook her head. "Dr. Birch specified a short walk up and down the hall."

"I know, Mags, but I'm going stir-crazy in there," Jack waved at the door to his room. "Please, I can't sleep anymore, and Zach and Theresa will know this was my idea. I just need to convince myself that things," Jack choked, "I just want to remember what normalcy looks like. Please. I'll tell you if it's getting to be too much and you can go in search of the nearest wheelchair."

Jack waited in silence while Maggie considered his request. The truth was the teams had been gone for over six hours. There was no reason for it to take so long, at least none that his imagination hadn't run wild speculating over.

In the hours since Dan and the teams had left on their rescue mission, Jack had prayed for their safety, and for God to bring Liz home. As the hours passed, he went from hopeful, to resigned, and finally to terrified. Now he had to do something, anything, but lay in his bed and focus on the pain he was in and the fear escalating in his spirit.

"Okay, just behave, so you don't end up falling on your face." Maggie smiled at him, as she walked him to the elevator.

Maggie didn't know anything about what was going down tonight, and she would never know the immense favor she was doing Jack just by allowing him off the floor. However, by the time they'd greeted the staff at the Emergency intake desk and walked part of the hallway that circled the ER treatment rooms, Jack was panting and hurting. He stopped and gasped, "Mags, do you think we can sit down for a minute?" He waved a hand at some chairs just down the hall from the double intake doors. Jack looked sheepish. "Then I guess it's time to go back upstairs, sorry."

Maggie took Jack over to the chairs, helped him sit, then sat down beside him. "Dr. Lockwood—Jack, you're doing great. Just rest for a minute and we'll go back. I'll even find you that wheelchair if you'd like."

Jack smiled faintly. "No. No wheelchair. I'm determined to do this under my own power. Thanks for letting me sit for a minute first." He leaned his head back against the wall, for the moment too tired to dwell on anything but breathing.

CHAPTER 46

A Sojourn in the Shadow

Jack was just about ready to ask Maggie to help him back to his room when the doors to his left burst open. A stretcher surrounded by four people in scrubs started down the hall in the other direction. Jack didn't think much of it until Dan and Todd followed the group through the door.

Paling, Jack struggled to his feet. "Liz?"

Grabbing the walker in front of him, Jack called out, "Dan!" Pushing Maggie aside, Jack staggered down the hall. "Harrison!"

Dan turned, his own face paling when he caught sight of Jack. Turning around, he caught his friend by the shoulders. "Jack, why are you awake and what are you doing down here?"

"Liz, is that Liz? Is she alive?" Jack struggled to push Dan out of the way. "Let me through."

"No," Dan responded calmly. "Jack, I need you to come with me. I promise I'll tell you everything."

Jack hit Dan shoulders with his fists before slowly collapsing to the floor, pleading with his friend, "Let me go to her, please."

Half-conscious, Jack continued to argue with Dan all the way back to his room, where two orderlies lifted him into bed. Maggie hit the call button and a few seconds later Andrea Barstow came into the room at a run. She took one look at her patient and ordered medication to ease Jack's pain and put him to sleep.

Dan put his hand on the doctor's shoulder and said, "Don't do that, Doc. I need to talk to him now and I need him to have a clear head. Is there anything you can give him that will help his pain but not put him to sleep?"

Andrea nodded and a few minutes later, Dan and Jack were alone in the room. Pulling up a chair, Dan shook Jack's shoulder, "Are you with me?"

Jack nodded, he was calmer, but the lines of pain in his face made him look old beyond his years. "Why did you stop me? I need to see Liz."

"Jack, the only thing that you can do in that room right now is harm. The docs need you out of their way and you know that. Think about how you feel about having family members in a room when you're working on a patient."

"That's different, I'm a physician."

"Jack, you're a physician who can't stand up straight and you're the patient's husband. You don't belong in that room any more than I do."

Jack struggled to sit up. "Then you better tell Andi to go ahead and sedate me, because while I can stand, walk, crawl, or scoot, I'm going down there. I belong with my wife."

Catching Jack by the shoulders, Dan held him tightly. "Jack, listen to me! No one wants to sedate you because Liz needs you conscious and aware. If you'll sit back and shut up, I'll tell you about everything. I'll even show you the photos I took at the scene. I give you my word, Liz was alive and holding her own when we brought her in, and Zach thought that there was a very good chance they could keep her that way. That's a lot more than he thought about your chances of survival when we brought you in a few days back. He will be up here as soon as he can be to update you. Now, buddy, will you please let them do their jobs and let me tell you about Liz?"

Jack slumped against Dan, all his fight gone. "She's really alive?"

Dan nodded. "Yes, and she gave Reynoso a run for his money."

"Reynoso?"

"In the wind for now but lost in the BWCA with a bullet wound in his side. He's not going far."

"Who's bullet?"

Dan smiled faintly. "Need you ask?"

Jack sank back against the pillows. "Thought you weren't supposed to do any shooting."

"Why don't you let me tell you about this from the beginning?" Dan asked softly. "Things might make a little more sense that way."

Jack nodded. "Okay but give me the abridged version please. I don't like the look in your eyes. It tells me that there's more to this than you've shared."

"Of course there's more to it, since I haven't shared much of anything yet." Dan snapped. "Anyway, by the time we landed the HRT had secured the cabin. We found the four stooges there that you described, and they are now all incarcerated just as uncomfortably as the Feds can manage. When we questioned them about Liz, it was like we were missing the punchline of a joke. It seems that your wife escaped the cabin by clobbering one of those four, presumably the one with the big bruise on his head, with the chair from the room they'd locked her into."

"Reynoso asked for her, and when neither the guard nor Liz was forthcoming in a timely fashion, Reynoso went storming down the hallway and found the guard unconscious and Liz gone. Reynoso took off after her himself and the guards hadn't seen him since. We searched the cabin and didn't find Reynoso or Liz, but," Dan scrounged in his pocket and pulled out a paper wrapped bundle, "here, these belong to you and Liz."

Jack slowly unwrapped the paper and Liz's wedding rings tumbled into his hand. Blinking back tears, Jack looked at his friend pleadingly. "Dan, I appreciate the play by play, but I need to know what's happened to Liz. Please."

Dan's face darkened, but he nodded. "Okay, I'll tell you the rest later. Jack, when we landed at the cabin, Liz had been there and in Reynoso's hands for over fifteen hours before she escaped. I don't know how to tell you this, but in that time, he tortured her."

Pulling out his phone, Dan showed Jack the first photo of his wife. Her face was almost unrecognizable under the swelling and bruising. "Reynoso hit her hard enough to break her right orbital bone and cause bleeding inside her right eye," Dan explained, "and to split her lips in several places."

The next photo was of Liz's hands both of which were swollen and discolored. "Reynoso broke all four fingers on her right hand and one—her ring finger—on her left. The final photo was of her back. Several bloody welts stood out against her pale skin. "It looks like he whipped her. There's evidence of more beatings on her torso. From what one of the flunkies said, when she passed out, Reynoso would stop, only to resume after she regained consciousness."

"Was she raped?" Jack asked in a scarcely audible voice.

"The flunky that was singing from the time we arrived hoping for a deal says no. He said Reynoso kept telling Liz it was nothing personal, he just had to be sure to send a message. I guess rape was too personal. However," Dan looked at Jack, hoping this wouldn't be the last straw, "Zach ordered a rape kit, and once we get Liz's okay, we'll run it."

"Run it," Jack insisted. "You have my permission."

"Sorry, but your permission won't do. Without a court order, we need Liz's permission, and I think you know that."

"What else?" Jack asked, not looking up.

"In order to answer that, I need to finish what I was telling you before, okay?" Dan asked. Seeing Jack's nod, Dan picked up where he'd left off. "Reynoso and Liz were nowhere to be found inside the cabin, so our team took over. It was clear that Liz had gotten out of the room where they'd imprisoned her and went out through the window in the bathroom. I found her trail right away. Unfortunately, I also found Reynoso's, but his trail wandered all over the place, while Liz headed in a straight line away from the cabin. I found where she'd stopped to rest." Dan neglected to tell Jack that she'd fallen, not just stopped.

"I came to a spot where I couldn't find any sign of Liz and was getting ready to bring in the dogs when it hit me—something was familiar about the place. Jack, I was back on Little Gabbro Lake and I remembered the cave you took refuge in a couple years back. It took me a while to find it, but when I did, I found Liz, huddled on the dirt floor. I thought she was unconscious, but when I put my arms around her, she moved."

Dan sat silent. He didn't know how to tell Jack the rest. He remembered his own horror when Liz had turned in his arms, flinching away from the contact, and, he swallowed hard, the mewling noises she'd made. That was the only way Dan could describe them. They hadn't been language in any sense of the word. Holding her close to him, he'd whispered soothingly, "Shhh, honey, it's Dan. Everything's going to be okay."

Liz had no more than pushed him away, shaking her head violently, when another voice echoed from behind him. "I'm afraid you're wrong, Mr. Chief of Police." Reynoso grabbed Liz, shielding himself with her body and in a single motion raised the knife he held and brought it up in a fierce thrust. She'd cried out in pain, then slumped to the ground.

Reynoso had just raised the knife again, now dripping with gore, when a shot rang out. Dan stood, holding his gun rock steady on Reynoso.

Getting to his feet, Reynoso moved toward Dan, Liz once again held firmly in front of him. When he reached a point even with the cave entrance, Reynoso shoved her at Dan and took off, "I believe I've settled our score, Ms. Lockwood."

From then on, it had been the same fight with blood loss that Jack had fought several nights before. Even while working on Liz, Dan couldn't clear his mind of the image of her face when he'd first found her. Reynoso had beaten her almost beyond recognition. How could he share with Jack, that as soon as the team found them and Liz was in Zach's hands, Dan had retreated behind a stand of trees and vomited until there was nothing more in his gut.

"Dan," Jack touched his shoulder, making him jump. "what happened after you found her?"

Swallowing the bile in his throat, Dan continued, "I'd just gotten to Liz when she pulled away from me. Reynoso had beaten me to her and was hiding in the back of the cave. Before I could do anything, he grabbed Liz and pulled her in front of him, shielding himself. I didn't have a clear shot."

The distress Dan felt must have shown on his face, because Jack reached out and squeezed his shoulder. "I know you did your best to protect her. Just tell me."

"Reynoso stabbed her under her arm. Deep enough to nick an artery. I shot him when she fell. He dropped the knife but managed to pick her up again and use her as a shield until he was even with me and the cave entrance. At that point he shoved her at me and took off. I'd already radioed our location, so the team was on the scene within just a couple of minutes, but Jack, it's my fault that Liz is down in ER with one more battle to fight. I let Reynoso get the drop on me and he stabbed her."

Dan hung his head. "I'm so sorry. I'd give anything to change the way it went down."

<hr />

Jack was silent for a few moments, trying to process everything, especially after seeing the almost-unrecognizable photos of his wife. Still, he couldn't let Dan carry this kind of guilt around. "Brother, don't do this to yourself. You had no way of knowing that Reynoso was in there with Liz. You know what she'd say, don't you? She'd say…she'd say…"

Jack made a small gagging sound in his throat, grabbed Dan's shoulders, and bowed his head. "God, please help my wife. Don't let the darkness win. You put Liz into my life, don't take her from me, not now. Please keep her alive, give those caring for her wisdom. Give her body and mind the strength to heal from the evil that surrounded her and from her injuries.

"And Lord, please take any misplaced feeling of guilt away from any in the rescue teams who are feeling it. The only ones responsible for what's happened are Reynoso and his group. I pray Lord, I pray…" Jack's hands knotted into fists. "I pray that Reynoso won't die alone in the woods but will be brought to justice to answer for what," choking on unshed tears, Jack struggled to finish, "what he did to my wife. I pray Liz and I will both be there to see that day. I…I…"

Pulling away from Dan, Jack, in Dan's parlance "lost it." Dan could do nothing but sit with his sobbing friend and wonder at his strength. Jack was just four days out of major surgery and recovering from wounds that should have killed him. His wife had been in the hands of a man who nearly killed her almost two years before and they were now treating her for life-threatening injuries one floor below where Jack lay. Yet he was the one praying not only for Liz, but for others, including Reynoso.

Jack sat up slowly, wondering what had awakened him. He was suddenly afraid Liz had taken a turn for the worse and someone had given orders that he shouldn't be disturbed. Yet he knew Zach wouldn't do that after giving his word that he'd wake Jack if Liz's condition changed.

Zach had come up earlier, just after Dan had finished telling Jack about Liz's rescue. Pulling up a chair, Zach asked Jack if he was ready to talk about his wife's condition.

Liz was doing better than anyone had expected. They were replacing the blood she'd lost with whole blood, Jack's, as it happened, as he was a universal donor who'd been giving blood since he arrived in Ely. They'd sutured the knife wound under Liz's arm closed and treated the contusions and lacerations. An orthopedic specialist would be in tomorrow to look at her hands and face. Zach also wanted to call in an ophthalmologist to look at her right eye, just to make certain surgery wasn't necessary for the hemorrhage. Medicated for pain, an unconscious Liz rested comfortably in ICU, just down the hall from where Jack lay.

Jack looked carefully at his colleague's face. He could see something was bothering him. "Zach, what is it you're not telling me?"

"I'm worried because Liz hasn't shown a single sign of consciousness. She's not that heavily medicated and there's no medical reason why it should take her this long to come out of it."

"Are you concerned that the beatings caused some kind of brain injury?" Jack asked. He'd been worried about that same thing.

Zach shook his head. "I thought of that and ordered a CT scan after we finished in the ER. It's negative for bleeds and that's good news. No, what I'm worried about is Liz's mental state. I don't have any experience with torture victims, and if we're honest with ourselves, that's exactly what Liz endured. It could be that she wants to stay in that place where she doesn't have to deal with pain or with what was done to her."

"She was conscious when Dan found her." Jack pointed out

"Was she?" Zach challenged. "I know she pulled away from Dan and hid from Reynoso, but according to Dan she didn't really recognize him, flinched away when he touched her, and didn't verbalize anything beyond, in Dan's words, 'a few mewling cries.' Does that constitute awareness in Liz?"

"She was aware enough to make it six miles through the woods, aware enough to recognize where she was, and aware enough to remember that there was a hiding place in those rocks," Jack snapped.

"How could she remember that place, Jack?" Zach countered. "You carried her in there when she was unconscious, and she was unconscious when we carried her out."

Jack sat back, unable to argue with Zach's logic. Jack had never made that connection. He was so certain that Liz had volitionally headed for a place she knew she could find shelter. "I...I," suddenly dizzy, he fell back against the raised head of the bed, "Zach, I don't know."

Zach leaned forward as a monitor alarm went off, warning of a fall in Jack's blood pressure. "Jack, you need to call it a night, or in this case a morning."

Jack shook his head vehemently, "No, I need to see Liz. They've moved her out of ER and I was on my feet earlier today, no, yesterday."

Zach's expression communicated what he was thinking long before his words. "Jack, I can't let you do that, not with your blood pressure in the cellar. It's been a nightmarish week for both you and Liz. Maybe I'm wrong about all this and what the two of you really need is some rest, and then time together to recover.

"The other thing that occurred to me was the same thing we were afraid of with you when you were slow to regain consciousness." Zach continued. "Liz's last memory before Reynoso hit her and took off, was of him shooting you in a way that she must have assumed was fatal. Frankly, it should have been fatal. Your life is still at risk and if you die, I won't give a plugged nickel for Liz's chances. You need to rest for a bit."

"Zach, I *need* to see my wife," Jack insisted. "I don't want to be asleep if things go sour, I want to be with her. Besides, if you're correct about what's going on with Liz and she thinks I'm dead, won't it help her to know that I'm very much alive?"

"Not if you fall on your face in front of her." Zach held up a hand. "Enough. You know this is the same call you'd make if I was your patient. If you'll rest for the next few hours, I give you my word I will wake you if her condition changes or if she regains consciousness. When you wake up, I will take you to her room myself, because that's exactly where I want you, after I'm certain you're going to stay on your feet."

In the end, Jack agreed to Zach's conditions and fell asleep almost immediately after Zach medicated him.

When Jack woke the room was dark and quiet. One of his favorite Bible verses was ringing through his spirit.

O Lord, You are my God;
I will exalt You, I will give thanks to Your name;
For You have worked wonders,
Plans formed long ago, with perfect faithfulness.[15]

---

[15] Isaiah 25:1 (New American Standard translation).

Jack felt better and more in control of himself. He could rest in the knowledge that no matter what, God was faithful. Knowing that there was no way they'd let him see Liz at this hour of the very early morning, Jack settled himself to pray. In that way he could be there for his wife until he could hold her hand.

CHAPTER 47

ANSWERED PRAYER

Nevertheless, I am continually with Thee;
Thou hast taken hold of my right hand.
With Thy counsel Thou wilt guide me,
And afterward receive me to glory.

Whom have I in heaven but Thee?
And besides Thee, I desire nothing on earth.
My flesh and my heart may fail,
But God is the strength of my heart and my portion
forever. [16]

The door to Liz's hospital room opened, startling Beth, who smiled when she recognized the visitor. "Hi, Jack. I was just keeping Liz company, but look at you, sans walker and everything."

Jack smiled. "Well I'm not going to break any land speed records, but yeah, it feels good to be able to walk down the hall on my own again. That Psalm you were reading, Psalm Seventy-Three, is one of Liz's favorites."

Beth nodded. "I thought it might be, given how she's marked it up." Her eyes growing sad, Beth sighed, "I keep hoping that doing

---

[16] Psalm 73:23–36 (New American Standard translation).

this might help, but she's as far away as ever. It's been over a day since they moved her to a regular room and nothing. I'm so sorry."

Jack sat down next to Beth and hugged her. "Honey, that's not your fault. Thank you for staying with her while I was with the Cardiac Rehab folks. Thank you, too, for reading God's word to her. I know that's not really your thing, but it means so much to Liz and to me."

Beth frowned and admitted, "I'm not certain where Dan and I are with this whole God thing, but it makes me feel better when I'm reading to Liz from her Bible. I just pick out some of the passages she's marked, but it's like the words make me feel closer to her, wherever she is."

"Me too," Jack said, "just as praying for Liz while holding her hand helps me. The only difference is, I know and trust the God Who's word I'm reading and Who I'm petitioning."

"What will happen to that trust if Liz dies?" Beth asked softly.

Jack took a deep breath, wanting to answer truthfully. "Beth, both Liz and I have been awfully close to death all week. All I can say is even when I thought Liz dead, I trusted God to bring her home. And yes, my grief will be all consuming if she dies, but God is still the only one Who can bring sense out of the senseless. If she lives but never regains consciousness, then I'll trust Him to help me make the right decisions for her—but I pray that won't happen."

"Are you going to pray now?"

Jack nodded. "I was going to wait until we finished visiting, but yes, I'm going to pray. I love praying with my wife, and even if she doesn't know I'm here, it makes me feel that our cord of three strands is intact and strong."[17]

"Cord of three strands? What's that?" Beth asked curiously.

"In a marriage between Christians, there are three covenant partners, the man, the woman, and God. It is the God strand that gives such strength to our bond. You and Dan know that, you've

---

[17] Ecclesiastes 4:12-And if one can overpower him who is alone, two can resist him. A cord of three strands is not quickly torn apart. (New American Standard translation).

seen it at work in us in the good days and in the bad days. Even with Liz unconscious, I need to seek out that bond to give me strength, because," Jack swallowed hard, "God knows how much both Liz and I need Him right now."

"Would it disturb you if I stay while you pray?" Beth asked. "At least for the out loud part. I've watched you enough to know that you do a lot of your praying silently."

Jack took Beth's hand and said, "You're welcome in this circle." Then he took Liz's hand and bowed his head. "Father, we thank You for the bright sunshine outside this room on this beautiful autumn morning. We thank You, the Master Artist, for creating all this splendor for us to live in and enjoy. I thank You for keeping my dear Liz safe through another night. I thank You for our friends, Dan and Beth, who have cared for us in thought, word, and deed through this awful time. I pray that You will draw them close and protect them until the day they seek You out and long past."

Beth peeked when Jack paused and watched him place Liz's bandaged left hand on his heart.

"Abba[18], I beg You to bring Liz home to me," Jack continued, "I long to see her smile and hear her voice in our home again. I pray that wherever she is, she can hear my words and know that we still have a beautiful life ahead of us. I pray that she knows beyond the shadow, how much I love her. And Lord, if Your will is to call your daughter home, then I pray that You will do it quickly and without more pain. She's already suffered so much. If that's the way things must be, then help me, in my grief, to find a way forward in a manner that honors You. I pray for her family, Father, that You will surround her mom and her brother and his family with Your love and comfort. Help them to know that, somehow, You are in this. I pray in Christ's name and for His glory, Amen."

Beth's eyes filled with tears as she watched Jack bend over and kiss Liz.

---

[18] Aramaic for "Father"—a familiar term for Father, connoting both love and deep respect.

Jack whispered, "Good morning, love. It's a beautiful day."
Then he turned to Beth, "Thank you for sharing our prayer time."

Beth nodded. "Thank you, Jack, for..."

They both jumped when Liz cried out, "Stop it! Jack's dead!"

Jack and Beth were both stunned. Liz lay motionless, just as
she had been, but tears seeped beneath her eyelids. Jack recovered
enough to hit the call button and when the nurse responded he said,
"Page Doctor Birch to Liz's room immediately." Then he bent over
Liz and cupped her cheek with his hand. "Liz, love, I'm not dead. I'm
right here. Come back to me."

Liz was silent for a moment, then shook her head without
opening her eyes. "No. You killed Jack. Please, just...just let me die."

With a start, Jack realized that Liz didn't know that she was no
longer Reynoso's captive. Bending closer, Jack kissed her gently, then
rubbed her nose with his. "No Liz, Reynoso tried to kill me, but I'm
very much alive and I need my little pooky-nose to come home to
me. You know that's something I only call you in our most private
moments, something that Reynoso couldn't possibly know, so push
away your fear and open your beautiful eyes."

"I'm...I'm afraid," Liz whispered.

Jack nuzzled her cheek, "There's nothing to be afraid of, Liz,
trust me." Then he sat back, watching his wife closely. Her eyelids fluttered and he saw pain form in her expression. After a few
moments, Jack's prayers were answered when Liz opened her eyes
and looked up at him.

When Zach burst through the door, he found Jack sitting on
the bed, holding Liz in his arms. Beth sat wide-eyed in the bedside
chair.

⌒〜⌒

It was dark by the time Jack was alone with Liz again. He sat
beside her as she slept, trying to settle himself after the emotional
upheavals of the day. There was nothing but gratitude in his heart
to God for bringing Liz home alive. That, in itself, was a miracle
enough for a lifetime. There was no reason to expect her to return

and just pick up where she'd left off. No one, not even battle-hardened soldiers trained for such an eventuality, walked away from torture unscathed.

What frightened Jack was that Liz was trying to do just that. From the time she'd come to, Liz had graciously put up with all manner of poking and prodding by her doctors and had even greeted a few visitors, including her mother, who'd driven up from Duluth as soon as she'd gotten the news that Liz was awake.

Late in the day, Liz had asked Jack for a mirror. He'd given her one, knowing that she needed to begin coping with what Reynoso had done to her. After examining herself, she'd looked at him calmly and asked, "I assume my back looks pretty much the same?"

When Jack asked her for permission to run the rape kit, Liz had given it, adding only, "Don't worry, Jack, it will be negative. Reynoso didn't get that far before I got out of the cabin." She was matter of fact and calm, too calm.

Jack couldn't have asked for a smoother, more textbook day for Liz's first day conscious. The problem was, he didn't believe any of it, not for a second. He knew his wife and he knew her unwavering strength, especially when it came to protecting her loved ones.

Deep inside himself, Jack knew that Liz was playing a part—showing her caregivers and those who loved her exactly what they wanted to see. She'd played the part well, except Jack could see gaps in her performance. Every time someone got too close to her, she flinched. She covered it nicely, but Jack was closer to her than anyone and he'd felt it every time he touched her.

Jack understood enough psychology to know that Liz couldn't continue as she had today. Sooner or later, all the pain and stress would come out sideways and she'd be in a far worse place.

CHAPTER 48

AN UNFORESEEN TURN

A week went by and Jack's concern for Liz only grew. Physically, she was doing well—in fact, she'd thrown herself into healing. Her goal was to get out of the hospital and back to a normal life.

Zach had released Jack two days earlier and he was staying with the Harrisons until Zach cleared him to drive. He was at the hospital for most of the day and evening anyway, so Dan took Jack there in the mornings, visited Liz, then went to work, leaving Jack with her until he returned.

The ice in Jack's gut was starting to take its toll on him and even on their marriage. He couldn't have imagined a circumstance where Liz would come home only for them to lose what was so precious between them. But she wasn't interested in reading the Bible or praying, she wasn't interested in talking about what had happened to her, and if he asked her questions about how she was coping with the emotional trauma, she either responded with icy silence or shoved him away angrily. He couldn't even touch her without her pulling away.

It had gotten so bad that yesterday, Jack had walked upstairs to discuss Liz's behavior with Ronda Stafford, a PhD psychologist specializing in trauma. She'd agreed to visit Liz this morning and Jack was anxious to see if his wife had connected with her and how Liz felt about ongoing sessions. He would go with her, if she wanted him—if not, he would pray that the time would come when they could talk together with Ronda.

Dan walked beside Jack that morning, bringing Liz a favorite treat from Beth. Jack slowed as they approached Liz's room, sudden trepidation dragging at his feet like sticky molasses.

Pulling his friend to a stop, Dan asked, "Jack, are you okay?"

Jack shook his head and answered truthfully, "No, not really."

Dan steered Jack over to a small waiting area and they both sat down. "What's going on? Apart from the obvious, is something wrong with Liz?"

Jack thought about whether or not to share his concerns with Dan. If he was going to share them with anyone outside of Liz and her doctors, it would be Dan. He was closer to Jack than Jack's own brother. Jack wouldn't even be here today were it not for Dan.

"Jack, what's going on?" Dan's concern was evident in his eyes.

"Have you noticed anything odd about Liz?" Jack asked.

Dan shrugged. "She's too cheerful and I know enough medicine to know that isn't good. I also see a difference in the way," he took a deep breath, "um, in the way you two are when you're together. It's like there's an invisible wall between you or something. I just assumed that you guys would work it out. What you went through was bound to make things back in Normalville a bit wonky."

Nodding slowly, Jack responded, "Yeah, wonky's one word for it. Dan, you're right, Liz can't possibly be as unaffected by all this as she acts. It's medically impossible. They don't even know if she'll regain the full use of her right hand. What does that mean for the future when you're a right-handed artist?"

Jack rubbed his forehead tiredly and confessed, "As for us, I don't know what to do anymore except pray. Liz keeps me at arm's length. We can't seem to have a serious discussion without arguing, and when I try to put my arms around her or squeeze her 'good' hand gently, she flinches away. I know that might be entirely normal and I may just have to get used to it for the time being, but it's hard."

Dan shook his head sadly. "I'm sorry, Jack. I won't say I understand, because I can't imagine what it must be like to feel distance between you after what you both went through. Still, you said that nothing can happen to Christians except what God allows to happen for, how did you put it? 'For our good, our growth, and His Glory?' Do you still believe that?"

"I also said that statement is easier to make in the light, than it is in the dark," Jack reminded Dan, "but yes, I still believe it. In fact, I'm counting on it, because it's only in that context that I can understand God allowing what happened to Liz." He stopped to clear his throat, trying to keep it together. "What other explanation could there be for allowing Reynoso to torture my wife? Why would God allow that to happen to His beloved daughter?"

Dan was clearly out of his league with Jack's questions. "I don't know, Jack. I just know that your faith has carried you through before and I think you need to hang onto it right now. Your God doesn't seem to be the kind of God who deserts you when things go bad."

"Unlike your father, God will never walk away from you. He will never disappoint you. And He will always be there for you." The echo of Liz's words on that long-ago night came back to Jack, bringing comfort and the courage to get up and move forward. His wife was safe, and they would find a way to make it through. God hadn't deserted them and would continue to center their lives and their marriage on the third strand of their covenant bond. Despite the circumstances, Jack was certain of that.

Slinging an arm around Dan's shoulders, Jack grinned faintly. "You sure are one spiritually smart guy for an agnostic. What do you say we go say good morning to my wife?"

Jack's improved mood lasted until just after they walked into Liz's hospital room.

Dan walked over to the bed and gave Liz a kiss on the cheek, "Good morning, hon. How are you doing today?" He handed her the box he held. "These are from Beth, with her best wishes for a wonderful chocolate high."

Liz smiled faintly. "Please thank Beth for me. I'm fine and can't complain, since I'm looking down at the ground, not up at the roots. I have a big day of physical therapy ahead of me and I'm raring to go."

Jack smiled and moved to Liz's bedside. "Good morning, love." He leaned down to kiss her, but she pulled away.

Her smile disappearing, Liz looked up at him and asked, "Did you send Ronda Stafford down to talk with me this morning?"

Jack, puzzled by Liz's tone, nodded. "Yes. Ronda's a friend and a colleague, she goes to our church, and I've been talking through some things with her. I just thought maybe…"

"Maybe you need to play god where I'm concerned." Liz's tone went from calm to icy. "I keep telling you I'm fine. Do you have any idea of how embarrassed I was when Ronda walked into my room this morning thinking otherwise?"

"Liz!" Jack exclaimed. "You're *not* fine. You *can't* be fine. Or at least not as fine as you claim. I can see it. Others can see it."

"Jack, you aren't my physician and I'd thank you to keep your opinions out of my medical needs and prognoses. I believe that your involvement actually constitutes a breach of medical ethics. I *am* fine. I *am* doing very well according to my doctors." Liz looked at him with fire in her eyes. "I don't want you interfering again. In fact, I don't want you here at all, because all you do is mess up my forward progress. Go away and stay away! Once I get out of the hospital and get myself set up somewhere, I'll be in touch, or rather, my attorney will be in touch. This, our marriage, all of it, was a huge mistake. Now leave before I have to call someone to make you leave."

Liz glared at Jack, then yanking at a chain around her neck, she broke it and threw her wedding rings at him. "Here, now go!"

Stunned, Jack caught the rings and managed to respond, "If that's what you want, Liz, I'll go. Remember that I love you, and I won't give up until these are back on your finger where they belong. I'll be here for you, even if the only thing I can do is pray and ask God to bring you home."

Trying to stop shaking, Jack walked over to Liz's bedside and handed her the rings. "No matter what, these were gifts and belong to you."

Gulping, Liz took the shimmering bands. "Fine, thanks, but I'm not wearing them ever again. They're nothing more than a pretty reminder of a mistake. I am home, I simply don't want anything more to do with you, or with God for that matter. I can take care of myself. Now I'm going to ask you one more time, go away. Dan, you go with him. I don't want you here either, or Beth. I think we all know who's side you're on." Liz tossed the box of goodies Dan had given her back to him. "Here, I don't think I could stomach these right now."

Dan, looking shocked, said heatedly, "I'm sorry you feel that way, Liz. Beth and I love you, but Jack loves you so much more. You're a lot less healed than you think you are if that doesn't mean anything to you."

With that, Dan took Jack's arm and pulled him from the room.

Liz waited until she was certain that they were both gone before she slumped back against the pillows. She'd never be able to forget Dan's angry words or the stunned expression on Jack's face when she'd announced that their marriage was over. Still, the important thing was that he was gone and gone on her terms. Now he could begin to heal on his own without her holding him back.

Liz took a steadying breath. She knew that if she started to cry now, she'd never stop. Jack was better off without her; he was alive and had his life ahead of him. That's what really mattered, well, that and freeing him to live without having to look over his shoulder for the rest of his life. Now, if she could only be strong until he gave up on her.

CHAPTER 49

THE WASTELAND

Jack sat in his living room, holding Binx and watching the wind blow the few remaining leaves from the trees. It was the end of October. He was home, mostly recovered from the physical wounds he'd suffered back in mid-September. His fifty-second birthday had come and gone, and he'd barely noticed. He was back to work on a part-time basis, both in his search and rescue capacity and as a staff physician at EBCH. He was grateful for the hours he spent working, they kept him grounded. He'd almost thought "sane," but insanity wasn't what was wrong with him.

Picking up the sheaf of papers on the back of the sofa, Jack could scarcely believe it had come to this. From the moment he saw the legal firm name printed in the upper left corner of the envelope, he'd known what it contained. Liz had carried through with what she'd threatened the last time she'd spoken to him, that morning in her hospital room. She was proceeding with the dissolution of their marriage. Almost two years of their lives that the court would wipe out of legal existence in the space of a thirty-second pronouncement by a judge.

Because of caring friends, Jack had been able to follow Liz's progress from afar. He knew that three weeks ago, Zach had released her to a rehab facility. She was healing well and Jack was grateful. Still, the email he'd received from her a week ago had caught him off guard. He was still reeling from the news that she'd leased a furnished home in Grand Marais and would be stopping by the house tonight to collect her clothing, her cat, and her car. According to her, the rest could wait until she settled into her new place and their divorce was final.

Apart from signing a piece of paper, Jack didn't have to do anything—what he wanted was irrelevant. In the state of Minnesota, no-fault divorce made it easy and quick. He could contest the divorce, slowing down the process, but it would move forward with or without his signature on the papers.

Bowing his head, Jack's heart cried out to God. Why was their Abba so silent at a time when they both needed Him so badly? When Jack had awakened that September morning that Liz had regained consciousness, he'd never expected to have to cope with God's silence or his wife's determination to end their marriage for reasons Jack couldn't begin to understand. He still loved her with all his being. Had she really stopped loving him?

All afternoon, Jack had been reliving their last evening together in Grand Marais. It had been wonderful, right up to the horrific ending. He remembered how pretty Liz had looked, wearing that beautiful dress of her own design—a dress that was now in shreds, the remains of which had fallen victim to shears in the ER. He especially treasured the memory of dancing with her in the moonlight and of their kiss that had left him breathless just before their evening together shattered into terror.

"Abba," Jack whispered brokenly, "You're the anchor of our marriage. Please, I'm lost, I need You to show me what to do. All I know is that everything inside me is rebelling against this—separation. I want and need my wife back in our home, to live with, to hold, and to love. Our wedding vows ended with the phrase, 'what God has joined together, let no man put asunder.' Are those just words? Meaningless and trite in today's world?"

Wiping his eyes, he continued, "I don't want to hold Liz here if she truly needs to walk away, but God, You know that she hasn't recovered fully, at least not in her beautiful spirit. She's loved and depended on You for years, yet she's walked away from You too. We both know that's not Liz, Father. This can't be the right time to make a decision as important as ending our marriage. Please, heal her. Bring her back to You," Jack choked, "and to me, I beg You. Please give me the wisdom and grace to get through tonight. Give me the words You would have me say and please, Lord, show me what to do about these." He touched the divorce papers, sitting by his side.

Jack fell silent, unable to say anything more. Tears welled in his eyes again, sliding down his cheeks, as they had so often in the past weeks. Binx head-bonked Jack's hand, and Jack took comfort in her presence, as he rested his head against the sofa cushion and cried.

Getting out of the car, Liz thanked her friend for the ride home. Except, it wasn't her home anymore. Looking at the house she and Jack had shared since they were married, she knew this was going to take every ounce of her strength. Squaring her shoulders, she walked up on the porch, but instead of using her keys, she knocked.

Jack answered, holding the door open for her with a faint smile. His appearance scared her. His face was gaunt, he looked tired, he'd lost a lot of weight, and his wonderful blue eyes were dull and red, telling her that he'd been crying. The thought of Jack, her Jack, in tears because of her, nearly broke Liz's resolve, but she had to do this—for her, yes, but especially for him.

"Hi, love," Jack said and moved to hug her. "It's so good to see you."

Liz backed away. "No! No pet names, no touching, let's just do this." Her tone of voice was colder than the wind blowing through the open door.

Jack stopped where he stood. "As you wish, Liz. I have your things packed in your car, except for," he held up a soft sided kennel with Sierra in it, "her. I, um, I'll miss this sweet girl," he swallowed hard, "and I'll miss her mom even more. If you decide you want Lazarus, just let me know. I'll carry Sierra out to the car for you, since I'm sure they're still restricting your lifting. Between the cat and the kennel this weighs in quite a bit over ten pounds."

"Thank you." Liz said coolly.

Jack walked her outside. Earlier he'd pulled her car out of the garage, so she wouldn't have to contend with the memories of the last time she was in there. Putting the cat in the passenger seat, Jack straightened and said quietly, "I've tried to abide by your rules, Liz, but I have to say this. I'm sorry for whatever I've done to hurt you. I love you and no court or circumstances will change that. I will always be here for you. Please be well. Goodbye, my love."

"You be well too, and please, make this easy on both of us and sign those papers," Liz said curtly, then turned on her heel and walked away.

Starting the car, Liz pulled ahead down the drive. Glancing in the rear-view mirror she saw Jack fall to his knees and bury his face in his hands.

Liz gasped, suddenly back in this same place, but it was dark, and someone was holding her. Slamming on the brakes, she shoved the car into park. Everything she'd felt that night when she'd watched Reynoso calmly shoot her husband came crashing back into her consciousness. He'd forced her to watch as two bullets slammed into Jack's chest. She couldn't look away as her husband fell to his knees; his eyes fixed on her. Then, blood staining his white shirt, he'd toppled sideways and lay motionless on their lawn.

Finally, Liz remembered waking up a prisoner in the cabin where they'd taken her and her despair when she realized that her beloved Jack was gone, taken from her in the space of a heartbeat. The never-ending agony of that realization made what Reynoso did to her in the coming hours pale in comparison. All she'd wanted was to die and join Jack. The memories from those hours came faster, each one worse than the last, battering at her until finally the world faded to black and she screamed.

CHAPTER 50

A LIGHT IN THE DARKNESS

The bright morning sun flooded the room where Jack sat, once again keeping a vigil over his wife. She looked peaceful now, but he had no idea what had happened to her the night before. By the time he'd gotten to the car, Liz was sitting in the driver's seat screaming and beating on the steering wheel with her still fragile hands. Little of what she was saying was understandable, but he'd heard his name and Reynoso's, so at least he knew where she was in time. He'd done his best to calm her, but to no avail, so he'd called 911 and they'd dispatched an ambulance. He'd sat in the car, holding her tightly, letting her blows fall on him, until help arrived.

By the time Zach had finally examined Liz, she was exhausted and hoarse, but no closer to reality. Hoping rest was the answer, he'd sedated her and admitted her to the hospital, at least for the night. Jack had been with her the entire time, staying beside her and praying; wondering if this was the breakthrough he'd prayed for or some other terrible incarnation of Liz's experience. If that was the case, would it take her further away from him?

Jack remembered snatches of the night they'd airlifted him to this hospital. The echo of Liz's voice telling him to be strong, but in this moment, he had no strength left. The fight for his life had been painful and exhausting—a fight that had taken everything he had to win. Then came that long night and the days following Liz's rescue, as he'd prayed her home. Most unexpectedly, there was the schism in their marriage, culminating in the court serving him with divorce papers. Now there was this, her breakdown in the midst of leaving him. What was he supposed to do with any of it? He wished God would speak audibly, like he had when Liz was fighting for her life after her first encounter with Reynoso. He needed that kind of assurance and he needed the direction.

The door opened and Dan walked into the room. "Okay for me to be here?"

Jack shrugged. "As far as I'm concerned, you're welcome, and Liz," he tilted his head toward the bed, "is still too out of it to have an opinion."

Dan sat down. "What happened?"

"She came by the house last night to collect her clothes, toiletries, some personal stuff, and Sierra. When she pulled out of the driveway something happened." Jack swallowed hard. "She stopped the car and by the time I got to her, she was hysterical. I couldn't bring her out of it, so I called 911."

Closing his eyes, Dan squeezed Jack's shoulder. "Tell me what you need, brother, what can I do?"

Jack shook his head sadly. "That isn't on you. I need God to tell me what to do, because I don't know what to do anymore. I don't know what's best for her."

"What about what's best for you, Jack?" Dan asked. "How much more of this can you take?"

"That's the difference between us." Rubbing his brow, Jack struggled to find the words. "I can't just think about me. Our marriage isn't just about what's best for me, or what's best for Liz, it's about what's best for both of us. It's about what God created our covenant bond to be and I can't believe that plan involves divorce. For right now, at least, Liz and I are still married, so I need to figure out how to help her heal. I don't know what to do, I don't even know what's going to happen when she wakes up. I'm not certain I can handle watching her walk away again."

"No," Liz whispered, sniffling, "no, please, I'm so sorry."

Jack raised the head of the bed, so he could look at Liz without having to touch her. "Liz, are you okay."

Liz looked at him sadly and shook her head. "No. I'm not. I'm not okay at all, but I'm so sorry, Jack, for putting you through this. Please give me another chance."

Swallowing hard, Jack could only pray he wasn't misinterpreting her words. "Liz, I'm not leaving you. I love you. I want nothing more than for you to be well and for us to live out our lives together." He took a deep breath. "May I touch you?"

Not bothering to answer, Liz leaned forward and wrapped him in her arms. "I saw you die again last night, and everything came crashing back. When…when Reynoso shot you, my life ended. Dear Jack," Liz buried her face in his chest and cried like her heart was breaking. "Please be real, please be here."

Looking out of the window into the dark night, Jack watched the first snow of the season fall softly on the hospital lawn. Liz was now peacefully asleep, still hospitalized, but Zach planned to release her in the morning. It had been a challenging day and Jack's heart ached for his wife. She was so unhappy, not because of something he'd done, but because of what she'd done to him over the last month. She'd tried to explain the whys and he understood them to a point. Somewhere in her hurting psyche, she'd been trying to protect him and maintain the fragile, unreal world she was living in—a world that helped shield her from the reality of what Reynoso had done to them.

Liz had asked Jack to contact Ronda Stafford and Ronda, in her gentle way, had drawn out of Liz heretofore unknown details of her capture, flight, and rescue. Some of those details Jack had never heard and with a start he realized that he wanted to kill Reynoso with his bare hands. That thought had frightened Jack. What kind of a Christian and what kind of a physician would want to take a life like that? It went against everything Jack believed. But listening to his wife tell Ronda that Reynoso had systematically worked his way down her body, beating her, breaking bones, all the while telling her it was nothing personal, had driven Jack to the edge of control. Just before Liz had escaped, Reynoso had started threatening her with rape. It was nothing personal he'd asserted again; it was just the next stop on his torturous journey down her body.

On Liz's first day conscious, when she'd told him so calmly that the rape kit would be negative because Reynoso hadn't gotten that far, Jack hadn't paid much attention to her words, hadn't understood the magnitude of what she'd meant. Had she not escaped when she did, she would be dealing with yet another violation and another loss.

Reynoso's final act of cruelty before beating Liz unconscious for the last time, was to explain carefully that he planned to leave her alive—to live with what he'd done to her and, because of her, to Jack. Even now, Jack had to swallow bile just thinking about it.

After Ronda left and Liz was talking with Zach, Jack had run to the nearest restroom and locked himself in—vomiting until all he could do was lay on the cool tile, too exhausted to move. Later, while washing his face and hands, he'd looked in the mirror and almost hadn't recognized his own reflection. His face was thinner than he remembered it being with more lines engraved into its surface. Thanks to the guilt he carried, he looked older than his years, older than he had just a few short weeks ago. How could he live with what had happened to Liz, let alone help her live with it, when he was the one who'd failed to protect her?

"Jack," Liz's voice came out of the dark, "please, come back over here."

Returning to the chair beside Liz's bed, Jack covered her hand with his own. "I'm right here, love."

"What were you thinking about just now?" Liz asked. "You looked so sad."

Jack shook his head, determined to be honest with Liz. "Not sad so much as trying to cope with what Reynoso did to you. I'm so sorry." He put his arms around her. "I couldn't stop them from taking you."

Liz stroked the back of his neck soothingly. "I'm sorry too, Jack. Reynoso's a part of our lives because of me. Honey," she waited until his eyes met hers before she continued, "Ronda said the guilt stuff was poison for both of us and that we need to concentrate on moving forward. But you need to know that I've never blamed you for anything that happened to me. Watching Reynoso fatally shoot you, or so I thought, will forever be my definition of the worst moment of my life. Do you understand what I'm saying? It wasn't what Reynoso did to me that I'm struggling with so much as what he did to you in the name of payback for my testifying against him. I thought you were dead.

"Then, when I came back and found you'd survived, I couldn't quite believe that we'd been given another chance at life together. It scared me, loving you so much yet knowing this could all happen again, because Reynoso's still out there. What if next time, he succeeds in killing you to get back at me? As I told you before, that's why I shut you out. I'm not saying it was right, but that's why. Somewhere in the functioning part of my brain, I came up with the idea that leaving you would be the best thing for you." Liz put her palm on his cheek. "I'm so sorry for the pain I've caused you over the last month. I wish I could take it away from you, so that you'd feel better."

Jack leaned into her touch. "Liz, I do feel better. I feel like a hundred-pound weight has rolled off my chest. I can breathe again, knowing that you're with me and plan to stay that way." He backed away and looked at her intently. "Right? You do plan to stay with me?"

A single tear slid down Liz's cheek as she nodded. "Forever and beyond if you'll have me."

"I've already told you I'll love you for eternity and a day and that hasn't changed."

For long moments, Jack just sat with her in his arms, but finally, he asked, "Liz, what about God?"

Liz sighed deeply. "I never stopped believing in God, Jack. I've just been running from Him—taking a side trip into Babylon if you will. I knew that filing for divorce was the wrong choice, just as I know the way I treated you was terribly wrong. Still, it's hard to understand why God would allow Reynoso into our lives again. Wasn't once enough? Am I that dense that I missed some lesson the first time around? The problem is, I still don't know what I'm supposed to be learning from all this. Reynoso's still out there, at least he is if he isn't dead. If I'm missing what God is trying to tell me again, will some worse lesson come along in order for Him to get through to me? That scares me, and it makes me wish God was in the room, so I could give Him a good talking to and get some answers."

Jack laughed quietly. "Liz, love, God *is* in the room. Will you talk to Him with me? I've been feeling much the same way as you and I think it's time we clear the air with our Abba. You know from reading some of David's Psalms that David felt like God abandoned him at times. He expressed his anger, even recording it for all succeeding generations. I'm convinced that God can take whatever we throw at Him, but we need to start the conversation." Jack took Liz's left hand gently in his. "Pray with me? Please."

Hours later, they woke to the early morning sounds of the hospital coming to life around them—food trays rattling, nurses fresh from the shift change taking patients' vitals, and doctors on their first rounds of the day. Zach stood in the doorway of Liz's room with a huge grin on his face. "Well," he drawled as he walked over to the bed, "it looks like you're both feeling better." Then he shifted his gaze to Jack and cleared his throat. "Uh, boss, you do know that this is technically against regs?"

Not quite awake, Jack realized that he and Liz had fallen asleep, their arms wound tightly around each other. "Um, yeah, so, report me. We were praying and fell asleep, that's all." He focused on his wife who hadn't moved out of his embrace. "Are you okay, love?"

Liz nodded sleepily. "I'm fine. I was just waiting until Zach finished lecturing you. I feel so much better now that we've talked to each other and together talked to God." She sat up and stretched. "Let's go home."

CHAPTER 51

GOD'S APPOINTMENTS

Later that same afternoon, Jack pulled the car up in front of their house. It was a beautiful, unseasonably warm, end of October day in the northland. The air was crisp and fresh, redolent with the aroma of dried leaves. He walked around the car, helped Liz up, and stood holding her. Today was a new beginning for them. Today marked the rebirth of their marriage and their relationship with God. Both he and Liz were well on the mend physically and Ronda, a fellow believer, was going to help them heal emotionally, together.

God was no longer silent, and Jack doubted that He'd ever really been silent but rather hard to hear over the clamor of pain and willfulness. The night before, Jack and Liz had prayed, yelled, pleaded, and bargained with God until finally, they could acknowledge that it was enough that God was still on His throne and held all things in His hands. That knowledge was sufficient to calm their spirits into listening.

Kissing his wife tenderly, Jack hugged her close. "Liz, I love you. I love you more than the day I married you. Thank you for being here with me."

Liz cuddled into his body and smiled. "Following Ronda's affirmation advice, huh?"

Jack squeezed her gently. "No, just heartfelt words from a deeply grateful man."

"Wow," Liz sniffed, "Thank you. I'm so grateful too." She wound her arms around his neck, looked into his eyes, and repeated, "Jack, I love you. I love you more than the day I married you. Thank you for being here with me."

Jack knew that he wouldn't be so quick to take Liz and what she brought to his life for granted in the future. He wouldn't take the gift of his own life for granted so easily either. He knew that Liz felt the same. He smiled down at her and asked, "Are you ready to come home?"

Liz pulled out of Jack's embrace and took his hand. "Let's get the stuff out of my car, make some coffee, and sit out on the porch. It's so beautiful and peaceful today. I know Dan and Beth will be here with supper in a bit, but we have time."

Thirty minutes later, Liz leaned back against Jack's shoulder, her knees raised in a vee in front of her. The porch swing moved back and forth, and she closed her eyes. Three cats shared the swing with them. The screened room where they all rested allowed them to be together outside, while protecting the cats from predators, insect bites and other dangers. "Mmm, this is nice," she murmured, contentment on her face.

Jack rubbed Liz's shoulders gently. "Are you happy?"

Liz nodded. "Very. I feel like I can breathe again."

"Isn't that what I said yesterday?" Jack asked, smiling.

"Yep, and it was pretty darn good, so I decided to reuse it." Feeling Jack's warmth soak into her tired body, Liz sighed happily. "I love it here. I've always loved it here, even that first week. You make me feel so safe."

Closing his eyes, Jack pushed away the guilt and recriminations Liz's words brought to mind. He hugged her close. "I'm glad you love it here, because I love being here with you. You make me feel safe, too."

When Dan and Beth arrived, they found the Lockwood family sound asleep in the fading light. Dan looked at Beth. "Now what? Do we wake them up?"

Beth smiled and shook her head. "They look so peaceful. Why don't we let them rest a bit more, while we get dinner on? Then you can wake them up."

"Why me?" Dan sputtered.

"Because you're my hero, you're brave and strong, and I can talk Jack out of being angry with you by showing him dessert." Beth lifted the box she carried.

"Fine." Giving in, Dan pulled out his key to the house.

"Where in the world did you find fresh blackberries at this time of year, Beth?" Liz asked later that evening, as she spooned the last bite of cake from her bowl. "This was such a treat."

Beth smiled. "I have to confess something, I used frozen berries that we picked last summer. It still turned out okay, didn't it?"

"Okay? No, it's fabulous. Just look at my health food nut husband, helping himself to a second piece." Liz teased, jabbing Jack in the side with a gentle finger.

"This is good. Really good," Dan said with satisfaction.

Beth turned around. "Thank you."

"I didn't mean the cake, although that was really good, too, babe. I was talking about being here together like this. Just a few days ago, I didn't know if, well, if Jack's and Liz's God was going to come through or not. I guess He did."

Jack put his arm around his wife's shoulder. "He came through, but it was more in spite of us, than because of us. The two of us needed to start listening rather than talking. Part of my problem was that my behavior wasn't rooted in my love for Liz, but in shame," Jack confessed. "After I began to recover, I felt like I'd failed the most important person in my world, so when she regained consciousness, I went into overdrive, trying to control both the situation and her recovery. I didn't realize how much pressure that put on her, especially at a time when she was just beginning to cope with the magnitude of what Reynoso had done to her."

"And I," Liz said, squeezing Jack's hand, "gave into fear. First, I was convinced that Jack was dead. Between that knowledge and being in Reynoso's hands, I couldn't see any future free of torment and I was terrified. That's why I ran. I believed that dying alone in the woods was better than being in Reynoso's hands or living with the knowledge that I'd caused Jack's death.

"Then, after you rescued me and I found out that Jack was alive, I didn't know what to do with that knowledge or with him. I'd already declared him dead. At the same time, I found out that Reynoso might still be alive. At that point, fear consumed me. I had to manage every little detail of my life just to be able to put one foot in front of the other. I somehow convinced myself that the only way Jack would be safe and fully able to recover was to leave him. The problem was I didn't talk to God, I just listened to the voice of fear."

"Between us, we were pretty much poster children for how not to handle dark times as believers," Jack said sadly. "I'm sorry Liz had a flashback the other night, because I know how much that hurt her. Yet I'm also grateful, because it got our attention. It focused us on what was really important in our lives and what we needed to do to recover fully. Most importantly, it led us back to our Lord."

Dan frowned. "How can you say that? I was here for most all of this and I know you prayed, Jack, pretty much constantly for those first few days."

Nodding, Jack agreed, "You're right. I prayed pretty much constantly when the only thing I could do was pray. I was fighting for my own life and no one knew where Liz was or if she was still alive. I could barely move, I couldn't be out there with you when you went after her, and so I prayed. The problem started after that, when Liz came back with you and against all odds, she was alive.

"From the time you and I struggled down in the ER corridor until the morning Liz told me to leave and not come back, I followed my own lead. I thought I prayed a lot during that time, but most of the time I spent on my knees, I spent telling God what I was going to do for Liz. I lost my way and I lashed out at God, but I never really calmed down enough to listen. My certainty that I knew what was best for Liz drowned out God's still, small voice. Psalm 46, verse 10 says 'be still and know that I am God' and I forgot how to be still."

"I think that you're being way too hard on yourselves," Beth said. "Is that what Your God demands?"

Both Jack and Liz smiled. "No, that's what He forgives," Liz said softly. "Because of His mercy, not our actions, Jack and I sit here tonight, alive, still married, and enjoying time with dear friends." She looked at Jack. "Honey, will you please bring me my guitar, I have this song in my head. The last verse is so powerful and tonight I want to share it as my hope for our future. I think I can manage the chords."

Jack got up, found her guitar among the boxes stacked in the corner and handed it to her before sitting down. He looked at their friends. "Is this okay with you?"

Both of them nodded and Dan said, "You don't need to ask. You don't need to ask, this your home. Besides, after what's happened, hearing Liz sing again will be a privilege," his cheeks reddened, "anyway, honey, please sing for us."

Liz smiled and strummed a few cords, testing the strength and flexibility of her fingers. They felt okay and even if she made some mistakes, God wouldn't care, He knew her heart. She closed her eyes and sung her prayer.

I once was lost in darkest night
Yet thought I knew the way
The sin that promised joy and life
Had led me to the grave

I had no hope that You would own
A rebel to Your will
And if You had not loved me first
I would refuse You still.

But as I ran my hell-bound race
Indifferent to the cost

You looked upon my helpless state
And led me to the cross
And I beheld God's love displayed
You suffered in my place
You bore the wrath reserved for me
Now all I know is grace.

Hallelujah! All I have is Christ
Hallelujah! Jesus is my life.

Jack put his arm around Liz's shoulder and sang the third verse with her, their voices blending in sweet harmony, lifting their prayer to Heaven.

Now, Lord, I would be Yours alone
And live so all might see
The strength to follow Your commands
Could never come from me.
O Father, use my ransomed life
In any way You choose
And let my song forever be
My only boast is You.

Hallelujah! All I have is Christ
Hallelujah! Jesus is my life.[viii]

Jack whispered, "Amen." Sitting with his eyes closed, he felt the Spirit of God descend so powerfully that he would happily have stayed in that time and place forever. Then a odd sound, like a cross between a gasp and a soft cry brought him back and he opened his eyes at the same time Liz moved. Dan was on his knees, his eyes filled with tears.

Liz reached him first. "Dan, what's wrong? What can we do? Are you in pain?"

Dan made a strange noise. "Of course I'm in pain! I'm an idiot. I've wasted so much time. You two have been through a horrific experience yet here you sit, on your first night home together, praising God and telling Him that He can do with you as He pleases. How is that even possible, especially for two self-confessed, Type A, control nuts?"

A lone tear trickled down Dan's cheek, "I want to have that kind of rock steady faith in something bigger than myself, my decisions," he put his arm around Beth's waist, "and even my marriage."

Lifting his eyes to Jack and Liz, Dan said, "Show me how to meet this God of yours. I don't think I can be the man I need to be for me, for my wife, or for anyone, now that I've seen Him at work in your lives and felt Him here tonight." He looked up at Beth. "I'm sorry, babe, but I have to do this."

Beth took Dan's hand. "No, DH, *we* have to do this—together. I want to be able to sing that song and not feel like a fraud."

<hr />

Blinking sleepily, Jack extricated himself from Liz's arms and rolled out of bed. He stretched and started for the bathroom, but her soft murmur stopped him. He hadn't understood a word she'd said, but she sounded happy. Sitting down in the chair beside the bed, he just watched her. She was on her side facing him, sound asleep, a serene expression on her face. He had to smile because all three cats were in their usual places. Binx lay in the crook of Liz's arm, under the covers with her head on Jack's pillow. Sierra had curled up in the bend of Liz's knees, and Lazarus, the free spirit of the bunch, slept on top of her head. Jack soaked in the peace and normalcy of the moment.

Breathing a prayer of gratitude, Jack thought about the night before. It was Liz's first night home and in their bed in almost two months. He would have been content to simply hold her as they slept, but because of her courage, those hours had been healing far beyond sleep. Because of her, they'd plumbed the depths of renewed closeness and restored intimacy.

At one point, Jack could see the courage that loving him had taken. He'd been resting, touching Liz, just enjoying the feel of her body next to his. She'd caught him looking at her and at once he'd seen her uncertainty. He couldn't quite believe that she was worried about the scars or that her body would be a disappointment to him, but he'd finally coaxed that confession from her. All he could do was hold her close and tell her the truth—that she was more breathtakingly beautiful in his eyes than ever before. Physical perfection meant little to him. Having Liz warm and alive in his arms after all that had happened, was one of the most extraordinary experiences of his life. It was a gift from God that he could never repay.

After bowing his head and thanking God again for the twin miracles of the last forty-eight hours, Jack returned to his morning routine.

"Good morning, love. I..." Jack stopped and looked around. Liz was no longer in their bed, where he'd left her a little over an hour before. Puzzled, he peeked into the library area, but she wasn't there or in their bath. She hadn't been in the kitchen or living areas of the house either. Just when he was going to call out, he heard a thump and a muted exclamation. She was upstairs.

The light was on in Liz's dry studio, so Jack opened the door quietly. Liz sat at her worktable, beads scattered on the table and all over the floor at her feet. Her eyes were dry, but she was twisting her hands together as if they pained her.

Walking over, Jack crouched by her chair and gently folded her hands in his. "Good morning, love. Something tells me it's not all sweetness and light up here. Are you hurting?"

Liz took a deep breath. "No, I'm just frustrated. These," she pulled her hands from his and waggled her fingers at him, "aren't doing what I want them to do, yet. I can't seem to handle the beads without spilling them, dropping them, or dropping the needle. I know I need to give it time, but this is what I do." Liz looked up at Jack sheepishly. "Sorry."

Putting his arms around her, Jack said soothingly, "There's nothing to be sorry for, Liz. Your art is central to your life, and I respect you for all the work you're putting in, so that, one day soon, you'll be able to get back to doing what you love. Can you embroider without adding the beads?"

Liz nodded, "I tried that first and did this." She handed him a bit of fabric.

Taking the piece in his hands, Jack studied the fine stitches. To his eyes, it was flawless.

"There are a few mistakes in it," Liz admitted, "but I don't usually have a problem with the stitches, especially if I use a frame."

Jack smiled. "This is beautiful. I hope it made your heart happy to work on it."

"It did and," Liz's frown was replaced by the hint of a smile, "my agent has a great idea about what I can do when my fingers aren't cooperating."

"What's that?" Jack asked

"She wants me to write a book. I'll start with photos of some of my favorite pieces then add text that shares my inspiration for the piece, the materials I used, and the technical challenges I faced in its creation."

"Wow, I'd buy that book, and I'm married to you," Jack said enthusiastically. "What do you think?"

"I think I've got a new project. I'm excited about getting started."

Jack hugged Liz tightly. "I'm excited for you and to see what projects you include. If I can do anything to help, just tell me."

Liz giggled. "Even proofreading?"

Jack winked at Liz. "Even proofreading. I'll be ruthless, I promise. Love, I really want to talk more about the book, but I came to get you because our guests are finally awake. They'll be over in about half an hour for breakfast. Does that work for you?"

Liz pulled out of their embrace. "That's fine, but don't berate them for sleeping until after ten. It was quite a night last night and we were all up really late. I'm glad they decided to crash in the guest house rather than driving home. Besides, I slept late, too, I just woke up when you got in the shower and couldn't get back to sleep. I showered and dressed while you were out walking."

A shadow crossed her face and was gone, but Jack saw it. He looked at Liz quizzically. "What were you thinking about just now? I saw something in your expression."

Shaking her head, Liz smiled. "Nothing, really. I'm probably just being paranoid and we don't need that in our lives right now."

"Tell me," Jack urged.

"Okay, it's not like it's a big secret. They never found a trace of Reynoso. Not him, not his body, nothing. When you went out in the woods by yourself this morning, I worried. I know I'm not supposed to, I know that he's probably dead, but sometimes it just happens, sorry."

"Love," Jack held her close, "please quit apologizing. The fact that none of the search teams found Reynoso or his body bothers me too. Just wait until the next time you want to go shopping or teach a class and I can't go with you. I'll probably want to call out the National Guard." He grinned. "Although, the last time that happened, a momentous occasion occurred—I found you in my front yard."

Caressing Jack's cheek, Liz smiled at the memories. "You saved my life and then you kissed me."

Jack made a face. "Um, please make certain that when you tell that story in that way, your audience understands that by the time I kissed you I was no longer your physician. Otherwise, they're going to pull my license."

"Silly man, no one would believe you're capable of such impropriety, or for that matter, for ever taking advantage of a vulnerable woman." Liz eyed him coyly. "I know that for a fact. I was the one who had to take advantage of you last night, remember?"

Jack flushed as his thoughts reverted to the night before. It had been after midnight before the Harrisons had retreated to the guest house. Liz was already in bed when Jack finished in the bathroom. He crawled in beside her, rolling over to kiss her goodnight. His fingers met nothing but skin. She turned to face him, put her arms around him, and kissed him breathless. He remembered her soft touch as she traced the scars on his chest with a gentle finger. Before long, the sweet memories dissolved into fire when her lips had touched those same scars. Their loving had been long and intense—a welcome home to a place of love and safety.

The last thing Jack remembered seeing before falling asleep was a blush tinge in the eastern sky. They'd loved the night away, something new in Jack's experience.

Swallowing hard, Jack nodded. "Um, yes, I remember. I remember so well that I want to start all over again." He kissed Liz slowly and deeply. "Thank you for last night, all of it, but especially for that last part."

Liz giggled. "Are you saying that getting lucky was better than watching our two best friends meet God?"

"No," Jack said, "I'm saying that yesterday was a day of miracles and of those miracles, our lovemaking was the closest to my very human heart. Liz, love, please don't take this wrong, but just a couple of days ago, you were here collecting your belongings and asking me to sign divorce papers. Then last night, you were in my arms, loving me so senseless that I can't even find the words to tell you how incredible it was.

"As grateful as I am that Dan and Beth have joined us as eternal family and as honored as I am that God allowed us to witness that moment, I'm still a man—a very human man." Jack pulled Liz into his arms and whispered, "A man who still doesn't know how to thank God for bringing you home to me."

Kissing him, Liz murmured, "He knows, Jack."

After a few minutes, Jack helped Liz to her feet. "I'll help you clean up all these beads later, but right now, let's go rustle up some breakfast for our friends. I want to hear what their first hours in the kingdom have been like." Jack smiled. "You know, for many years, Harrison and I have occasionally referred to each other as brother, but now that's true in the most eternal sense of the word. I have another brother and sister and, a Father, a real Father."

Downstairs, Liz plunked herself on a counter stool and patted the stool beside her, watching as Jack sat. "Speaking of fathers, there's something we should talk about before Dan and Beth join us."

Jack's face fell. "Uh-oh, why is it I don't think I'm going to like this?"

251

Liz shrugged. "Probably because you won't. Dan told me what your dad did while you were in the hospital. I'm so sorry, Jack. That was the last thing you needed."

"Tell me about it," Jack said.

"Honey, I understand your feelings, but he's still your dad. More importantly, God hasn't given up on him. That means we shouldn't give up on him, right?"

"I want to say let's go ahead and give up on him," Jack muttered.

Liz's eyes met Jack's. "Do you really mean that?"

It was very quiet in the room. Then Jack shook his head slowly. "No, I just don't know what more to do."

"I do," Liz responded. "The holidays are almost upon us and we have a lot to celebrate. Let's invite Lloyd up here for the week between Christmas and New Year's. I assume he can't come for Christmas, because he's the pastor of his own church."

Laughing cynically, Jack shook his head. "You don't know the Reverend Dr. Dad very well. He takes Christmas off to 'meditate and pray' and puts one of his underlings in the pulpit."

"Okay, then let's invite him up for Christmas," Liz responded evenly. "He can meditate and pray in the beauty and quiet of the north country."

"He'll say no."

"If he does, then he does, at least we will have tried. I'll write him a note, on real paper, asking him to come join us. Then I'll call him. I really want him to come, Jack. Not to reopen old wounds, but to be a part of our family, because he is a part of our family. We're going to invite Mom up, too, so at least we'll have a buffer."

Jack snorted. "Unless he hits on her."

Frowning, Liz exclaimed, "Stop it, Jack! You're not this kind of man, and your bitterness only hurts you. I know your dad has done some terrible things, but look how often you and I need to ask God for forgiveness. God will know what to do with Lloyd, when it's time. Your dad needs to meet the God he claims to be serving. Besides," a faint grin crossed her face, "my mom will put Reverend Dr. Dad in his place if he so much as suggests something inappropriate."

Jack took a deep breath. "Okay, let's invite him. Only," he stroked Liz's back, "promise me you won't be too disappointed if he can't be bothered."

Ignoring Liz's unhappy look, Jack stood and pulled her to her feet. "Come on, we've got other family coming to breakfast."

CHAPTER 52

THE ALPHA AND OMEGA

"Merry Christmas, dear family," Pastor Steve Lynch said as he stood to close the Christmas Eve midnight service. "I hope that this season has been a blessing for you. Before we pray and say goodnight, we have a special benediction to this service. Our friends, Jack and Liz Lockwood, are going to share a very special song.

"Not everyone who comes to church on Christmas Eve is joyful, not everyone who sits beside you knows Christ, and not everyone who walks out of our door tonight is at peace. Looks can be deceiving. Tonight our Savior invites you to become a member of an eternal family, with a Father Who loves you more than you can imagine. During this interlude, if you want to become a part of that family, join us at the front of the church and let us pray with you. Come and meet the Author of peace, joy, and family. Nothing in your past matters—no sin or wall can stand against the power of Heaven. The babe whose birth we celebrate tonight has covered every debt you owe. Together let's celebrate the sufficiency of God's Christmas gift to us."

Jack and Liz walked onto the platform and Lloyd Beckett prepared to leave. He would wait in the narthex. He knew what it meant to be a Christian and he certainly didn't need to sit through one more altar call. Something kept him in his seat. He told himself that he didn't want to embarrass his son by getting up and walking out while their friends and Liz's mother sat next to him, but deep inside Lloyd knew that wouldn't have stopped him in the past. The truth was, he'd never expected his son to take part in a church service and he was curious. He folded his hands and watched as his daughter-in-law began to sing.

> *All is calm and all is bright*
> *Everywhere but in your heart tonight.*
> *They're singing carols of joy and peace*
> *But you feel too far gone and too far out of reach.*

Something caught Lloyd's attention. The lyrics weren't that of the "Silent Night" he could sing from memory by the time he was four. He focused just enough to listen as his son's voice joined Liz's for the chorus.

> *Somewhere in your silent night*
> *Heaven hears the song your broken heart has cried.*
> *Hope is here, just lift your head*
> *For love has come to find you,*
> *Somewhere in your silent night.*
>
> *From heaven's height to manger low*
> *There is no distance the Prince of Peace won't go...*

Lloyd sat up straight, realizing that Liz had stopped singing. His son was now performing solos in church? What kind of a miracle was that? Lloyd had tried to get him to participate in his services since he was a child, but Jack had always demurred. Studying his son, Lloyd watched as Jack closed his eyes and lifted his hand toward Heaven as he sang. Was this really the Jack—the son—that Lloyd knew? Lloyd felt a pang in his chest. Jack looked happy and peaceful. How was that even possible after what had happened earlier in the fall? Liz had the same expression on her face. What did they know that Lloyd didn't? Shifting uncomfortably, Lloyd listened carefully to his son's words.

> *From manger low to Calvary's hill*
> *When your pain runs deep*
> *His love runs deeper still.*

Was that the answer? Had God's love somehow erased their pain? In Lloyd's experience that kind of thing didn't happen. It was one-part wishful thinking and one-part self-delusion. A man had to stand on his own and solve his own problems. God helped those who helped themselves, right?

> *He has always loved you, child*
> *And He always will.*

Liz's voice joined Jack's on the chorus. By this time, Lloyd was feeling uneasy indeed. Something in the words of this song was causing him distress in the deepest part of his being. He knew God, right? He was a minister, therefore he had to know God. He had a church and a lot of people who listened to him, right?

Even as he reassured himself of his qualifications, Lloyd remembered all of the times he'd dragged Christ's name through the mire, doing things that even the secular world considered wrong. The images of his failures were unrelenting, coming one after the other until he wanted to scream "stop."

Instead of screaming, Lloyd tried again, really tried, to listen to the words of the song Jack and Liz had chosen for this time. Somewhere in those words was the secret of peace.

> *Somewhere in your silent night*
> *Heaven hears the song your broken heart has cried.*
> *Hope is here, just lift your head*
> *For love has come to find you*
> *Somewhere in your silent night.*

Wait, love had come to find him? The Reverend Dr. Lloyd Evert Beckett, the minister with the PhD in Divinity? But who was he really?

In that moment, Lloyd recognized the lie that he'd bought into—a lie that came from the pit of Hell. Knowing God wasn't about the size of his ministry, it wasn't even about running a ministry. It wasn't about his television ratings, his altar call numbers, his education, or his title. It was about meeting the God of the universe on His terms and living life for His glory, not Lloyd's own. God was using this song to shout over the clamor of Lloyd's own self-importance and with that taken away, he had nothing to his name but a string of broken relationships, alienated loved ones, and misled followers. Was there anything left to him?

> *Lift your head,*
> *Lift your heart,*
> *Emmanuel will meet you where you are.*
> *He knows your hurt,*
> *He knows your name,*
> *And you're the very reason that He came.*
>
> *Somewhere in your silent night*
> *Heaven hears the song your broken heart has cried.*
> *Hope is here, just lift your head*
> *For love has come to find you.*
> *Somewhere in your silent night.*
>
> *Love will find you*
> *Love will find you.*[ix]

After the last notes faded into silence, Liz covered the microphone with her hand and touched her husband on the shoulder. "Jack, look, in the aisle," she whispered, her expression caught somewhere between amazement and disbelief.

Like Liz, Jack couldn't believe his eyes. Lloyd was now standing at the altar, patiently waiting his turn to talk with someone. Jack was confused, there were several problems with what he was seeing. First of all, Lloyd never waited for someone, at least not patiently. Second, and most amazing of all, when a friend of Jack and Liz's came alongside him, Lloyd sank to his knees, tears spilling from his eyes. Jack had never seen his father cry, not even when he'd left his children behind. Jack stood there, stunned into immobility.

Liz took Jack's hand and urged, "Come on, we need to pray with them." By the time they reached Lloyd's side, Nancy, Dan, and Beth were also there. They all knelt around Lloyd Beckett. Jack put a hand on his father's shoulder as Lloyd finally met the God he'd spent years claiming to serve. In that moment, the angels danced and God smiled.

***

Liz sleepily opened her eyes when her alarm chimed. They'd all been up so late the night before that in another three hours the sun would have been up on Christmas morning. She rolled over in her husband's embrace and shook him awake. "Merry Christmas, dear Jack."

Jack opened his eyes and pulled Liz closer. "Merry Christmas, dear Liz." He nuzzled her neck. "Our third together and the happiest Christmas of my life. I love you!"

"I love you, too." Liz kissed him gently.

"Liz, did what I think happened really happen last night?" Jack was still in awe of what God had done.

Liz smiled. "We have a mighty God. And yes, it did."

That realization kept both of them warm as they showered and dressed on this sub-zero morning. Walking downstairs from one of the two new bedrooms created when they'd redone the loft, they met Nancy coming out of the master suite. She smiled and greeted them, "Good morning, children. Merry Christmas!"

Liz hugged her close. "Merry Christmas to you too, Mom. I love you."

"I love you too, dear daughter," Nancy looked up at Jack, "and you too, dear son. How are you both this morning?"

Jack smiled broadly. "We're fine. After last night we're better than fine actually. What a Christmas gift." Jack hugged Nancy close. "Thank you for praying for Dad all this time. You and Liz were so faithful in that, even when I wasn't."

Nancy reached up and cupped Jack's cheek in her palm. "We had the advantage of not growing up with Lloyd, my dear. Years of disappointment and sadness take their toll, especially on a child. But now, Lloyd's come home, and we all are truly family."

"Did the two of you stay up a long time after the rest of us went to bed?" Liz asked.

Nancy shook her head. "Only about an hour, dear. Lloyd wanted to talk about, well, I'll let him tell you about that. Now, are those friends of yours awake? Because I'm going to start breakfast. Corn fritters and bacon coming up."

Much later in the afternoon, replete with Beth's Christmas ham and potatoes settling in their stomachs, they all sat around the tree, sipping eggnog and listening to Handel's Messiah.

> *For unto us a Child is born, unto us a Son is given,*
> *and the government shall be upon His shoulders:*
> *and His name shall be called Wonderful, Counselor,*
> *the mighty God, the everlasting Father, the Prince*
> *of Peace.*[x]

"You know," Dan said, "I must have heard this piece a dozen times in my adult life, yet I never really heard it at all. Christ was so much to so many. He was a Jew and he came to fulfill the Messianic prophecies for the Jews. When the religious authorities of the day didn't accept Him, Christ opened his arms to everyone. Because of that," he took Beth's hand, "He's our Wonderful Counselor and Prince of Peace. Because of Him," Dan looked at Jack and Liz, cuddled together on the sofa, "health and peace have returned to this home. That's…"

Dan's phone buzzed. He pulled it from his pocket and then excused himself. "Sorry, I have to take this."

He came back to the room with a stunned expression on his face. "Uh, sorry for the interruption guys. I don't even know whether or not to share this today, but I think Jack and Liz will want to know."

Jack looked up curiously. "What is it, Dan?"

"The Cook County Sheriff's department has Eduard Reynoso in custody. They found him last night, injured and hiding in a cabin up on the Gunflint that the owners closed for the season several months ago. He's being treated in the hospital right now, but he's asked to see you both before he's remanded into Federal custody and transported back to the Twin Cities."

"When is that going to be?" Liz asked quietly.

"Tomorrow evening." Dan eyed his friends with concern. "You know that you don't have to do this."

Liz looked at Jack and seeing his nod, she replied, "Yes, I think we do."

CHAPTER 53

FULL CIRCLE

Liz held tightly to Jack's hand as the deputy escorted them back to the small visiting area. Reynoso sat under the watchful eye of both the sheriff and FBI Agent Bornell. Shackles attached to the table bound his hands. Reynoso frowned when Liz and Jack walked into the room together. He said nothing until they sat down across from him, then he smirked. "How are your hands, Ms. Lockwood?"

Laying her hand on Jack's arm, Liz responded, "They're improving, thank you. How are you?"

Reynoso obviously hadn't gotten the rise he was looking for, so he tried again. "Recovering from a bullet wound in my side. It was there thanks to your friend Chief Harrison. No matter, if we can find him on a ski trail in the wilderness, we can find him anywhere. You both look well. Better than I'd hoped, but then again, I was unaware, until just recently, that the good doctor managed to survive our party. I should have done a better job killing him."

This time Jack rested his hand on Liz's arm. "Reynoso, one of my prayers in the darkest time after you shot me and took Liz, was that you would survive. Do you know why?"

"Enlighten me."

"Because the best ending to this story will not involve another death, but rather it will encompass justice and you finding life."

Reynoso made a face. "You're speaking in riddles, Dr. Lockwood, at least in part. I understand what your 'justice' entails. If I'm shivved in prison, it keeps your hands lily white, but for now, I'm still alive."

Jack smiled sadly. "There was also a time when I didn't care about my lily-white hands. All I wanted to do was kill you. That's not what either Liz or I want anymore."

"And what, pray tell, do you and your dear wife want?"

"We want you to find peace. Peace that's not rooted in drugs, money, or violence. We brought you something."

Jack handed the small package to the deputy, who showed it to Bornell, who shrugged and said, "Yeah, why not? Go ahead and give it to him."

Reynoso took the small package. Inside he found a leather-bound Bible. Realizing what he held, he sneered and spat on the floor. "I'm not the one who needs this. Say your prayers, because you'll be meeting your God long before I will. It's just a matter of time until I find someone else who needs a few dollars."

Liz and Jack both stood and looked down at Reynoso, sadness rather than fear in their eyes. Taking one last look at the man who'd terrorized the two of them, Jack said, "Goodbye, Eduard. For our part, we forgive you and hope, one day, that you'll be able to do the same for us. You'll be in our prayers."

It was only after they returned home, that Jack realized he'd seen another of his prayers answered.

"No!" Liz screamed. "No! Jack!"

Jack woke up and put his arms around his trembling wife who was now sitting straight up in bed. "Shhh, love, it was just a dream." He held Liz until she opened her eyes, then he smiled at her. "Hi. Everything is fine. In fact, it's better than fine. While it's a bit early, it's still our wedding anniversary." He kissed her forehead. "Happy second anniversary, Elizabeth Lockwood."

Liz blinked, fear still in her eyes. "Jack, dear Jack," she threw her arms around him and cried.

Jack stroked Liz's back soothingly. Her nightmares still came frequently, and Ronda had told them not to expect them to go away anytime soon. Jack understood that his wife's experience at Reynoso's hands was not something that would just 'go away,' but rather something that both of them would have to learn to live with, at least for now. Certainly, things would improve, and they had, but post-traumatic stress had a long half-life and many incarnations.

When Liz's sobs quieted, Jack put a finger under her chin and tipped her face up so he could kiss her. "I'm right here."

Liz managed a watery smile. "I believe you are, since I've never had a hallucination kiss me like that before." Wiping her eyes, she snuggled close to Jack. "I'm sorry I woke you up. I don't plan these things. I don't even know why I would have a dream like that tonight. Everything's been so wonderful the last few weeks, what with Christmas and all."

Jack could still hear the echo of fear in her voice. "Liz, love, I know you don't plan your nightmares, but Ronda said that we both should expect to have them. They're not a reflection of our lives today, but rather memories of some awful yesterdays that our subconscious hasn't forgotten."

Liz held Jack tightly. "I... I know, but I don't want you to get tired of having this mopey woman on your hands. I want to get better. I really do. You've already put up with so much. I'm trying to get through this, really I am."

Jack pulled away until Liz could see his face, then asked quietly, "Why would you even think that I could somehow 'get tired' of you? You're my life and, apart from when Reynoso had you, those weeks that I thought that you didn't want me anymore were the worst weeks of my life." Unshed tears glinted in his eyes. "You, here in my arms, is the most precious gift God's given me, apart from His Son. We'll get through this together."

Liz squared her shoulders, looking at Jack with determination. "I'm fine now. I love you."

Jack laid back against the pillows, drawing Liz with him. "I love you, too. Let's get a little more rest before I tell you what I've got in mind to help us celebrate our anniversary." He stroked her hair as she cuddled close. "And we are going to celebrate because, against all odds, God has brought us to this day, together. Do you know what verses I was thinking about when I was planning things for later?"

Liz shook her head. "No. Which ones?"

"Ephesians 3, verses 20 and 21.[19]"

After thinking for a moment, Liz said, "One of my favorite songs is based on that verse." She hummed a few bars then sang,

> *More than all we ask*
> *Than all we seek*
> *All our hopes and dreams*
> *You are immeasurably more*
> *Than we can know*
> *Than we can pray*
> *All our words can say*
> *You are immeasurably more.*

> *There's nothing greater than Your love*
> *You're more than we can imagine*
> *There's nothing sweeter on this earth*
> *You're more than we can imagine*
> *Our hearts respond to who You are*
> *It's You, oh Lord, that we adore.*
> *You are more, You are more*
> *You're more than we can imagine*
> *You are more, You are more*
> *You're more than we can imagine.*

> *More than all our sin*
> *Than all our shame*
> *Stronger than the grave*
> *You are immeasurably more*

---

[19] "Now to Him who is able to do far more abundantly beyond all that we ask or think, according to the power that works within us, to Him be the glory in the church and in Christ Jesus to all generations forever and ever. Amen" (Ephesians 3:20–21 New American Standard translation).

I can't help but sing
Can't help but praise
My heart cannot contain
You are immeasurably more.[xi]

Jack closed his eyes and touched his forehead to hers. They sang the chorus together once more, worshipping the God who had touched their lives in ways that were beyond belief. Now they could rest.

EPILOGUE

A YEAR LATER

Leaning on her ski poles, Liz called out to Jack who was about twenty feet in front of her. "Jack, honey, can we stop for a minute?"

Jack turned around and snowshoed back to her. Listening to Liz's heavy breathing, he said, "Of course. I'm sorry, I should have slowed down a bit after that uphill run."

Liz laughed merrily. "It's all uphill from the lake, Jack, but I'm fine. I just need to catch my breath."

"Do you want to go back to the lodge?" They were celebrating their third wedding anniversary with a long weekend away at one of their favorite lodges on Lake Superior, just north and east of Grand Marais.

"No, I do not want to go back to the lodge. I *want* to see Devil's Kettle in the wintertime. Right now, I just need to rest for a minute. I'm afraid I'm still a little soft."

Leading her over to some rocks on the bank of the Brule River, Jack plunked down, pulling Liz down beside him. "Me too. This run used to be a piece of cake, but today it's more like work. It's worth all the sweat, though, I promise. The view from the bottom of the falls is spectacular. Then, if you're up to it, we can leave our snowshoes behind, climb about six million steps, and see the view from the top."

"Oh joy." Liz rolled her eyes and got to her feet. Holding out her hand, she helped Jack up. "Well, if we want to get back to the lodge before dark, we'd best be going."

Jack looked around happily as he followed Liz up the river, letting her set the pace. It was a beautiful January morning in the north. The sun was shining in an azure sky, it was above zero, and there was no wind. This was a new adventure for Liz, who had never seen Devil's Kettle in the winter or from the bottom. They'd started down at Lake Superior and were snowshoeing up the Brule River to the falls.

A half hour later, they were both staring up at the ice-fringed falls, still flowing at this time of year. They'd moved nearer to shore, as the river ice was thinner here, so close to the bottom of the falls. Jack had his arm around his wife's waist as she stood staring at this marvel of nature. After a while, he asked, "Do you want to go up top or just head back?"

"I want to go up top. This is incredible!" Liz replied enthusiastically. "You may have to drag me back to civilization by my hair, but I wouldn't miss this for the world."

Six million, give or take, slippery wooden stairs later, they stood watching the roiling river tumble over a rock ledge and then disappear into the "kettle"—a large hole in the bedrock. Despite years of research, no one knew exactly where the water came out or how long it took to reappear. It was a breathtaking sight, the sun glinting off the bare ice-frosted branches and the open water foaming as it tumbled over the rocks.

Cuddling close to Jack, Liz whispered, "Wow, this is incredible. Thank you!"

Turning to face Liz, Jack kissed her deeply. "You're welcome. Being here today with you is a perfect beginning to the year." Tilting her face up with a gloved hand, Jack looked into his wife's beautiful eyes. "Happy Anniversary, my bride."

Liz touched his cheek. "Happy Anniversary. I love you, Jack, and I'm so grateful you're still by my side. I know it's been a bumpy ride."

Jack tightened his hold on her. "Where else would I be, Liz? You're my life and I made a promise, remember? It went like this: I, Jack, take you Liz, to be my wife. To have, and to hold, from this day forward, for better, for worse, for richer, for poorer, in sickness and in health, to love and to cherish, forsaking all others, till death do us part."

Liz smiled and replied, "You're my life too, Jack, and I made the same promise. I, Liz, take you, Jack, to be my husband. To have, and to hold, from this day forward, for better, for worse, for richer, for poorer, in sickness and in health, to love and to cherish, forsaking all others, till death do us part."

The music of the rushing water was the only benediction needed to the impromptu renewal of their wedding vows. They'd made it through the darkness and thanks to God, once again stood together in the sunshine. They'd put Eduard Reynoso into the hands of their Lord and continued to pray for him. Best of all, their love and their faith in God was stronger than ever before.

Liz squeezed Jack's hands. "I look forward to sharing the years ahead with you in this beautiful place, Jack. I love my life and I love you."

AUTHOR'S NOTE

Hi. My name is Joy. I'm a woman of a certain age, similar to, okay, let's be honest, a little older than Liz. Being a woman of that age, I like to think that what I have to say has some relevance in this world and so I write. This story, while fictional, has its roots in reality. I grew up in Duluth, Minnesota. I love Lake Superior and its moods. I've been canoe-camping in the Boundary Waters wilderness. (Like Liz, I was a bit uncertain, but had a wonderful guide in my husband) I've enjoyed pizza at Sven and Ole's, and doughnuts in both Grand Marais and Ely. One day, my beloved and I hope to return to that area to live.

After reading this book, you know that I'm a Christian. Sadly, like my characters, God often needs to use a heavenly version of a two-by-four to teach me important lessons. Thankfully, none of these lessons have been as painful as what Liz and Jack went through. Still, they were all painful (or scary) enough to get my attention. Have any of you been through that kind of experience? As with Liz and Jack things often get to a point where I end up shouting at God (He doesn't shout back but speaks in a still, small voice) before I decide it's time to listen. I'm hoping that with age comes wisdom.

The skeleton of this story, it's framework if you will, is rooted in my deep love for the north shore of Lake Superior and the Boundary Waters Canoe Area Wilderness, the practice of medicine, and my belief that there are still heroes in this world. Then there's the non-fiction book I read several months ago about a man stranded alone in the BWCAW and the team that saved him. Put these together and you have a place for a man like Jack Lockwood to live his life.

Grand Marais is home to a thriving art colony and to the North House Folk School—a nonprofit community committed to passing on heritage crafts. It's my place for Liz to become and grow in her post religious-liberty law years. Like her, I consider Grand Marais, Minnesota, one of my favorite places on Earth. It's beautiful and peaceful, yet energetic and fun.

You may have also noticed a rather liberal use of song lyrics as I build to the denouement of the story. I did this because music is a powerful path to God for me. I like to think it's God's own way of drawing us into worship. After all, song fills the Bible—the Book of Psalms comes to mind. I want to thank those songwriters who gave me permission to use their beautiful lyrics. I have no claim to their great gifts apart from being a grateful listener.

Perhaps you think I've tied things up too neatly, and perhaps you're right. I'm a sucker for happy endings. However, bear this in mind—the thing about God's lessons is they don't end until we're taken home to God's side. I'm also a firm believer in God's sense of humor, especially when He's teaching us important life lessons. Besides, I'm not leaving things tied up as neatly as you may believe.

While Liz and Jack have weathered a storm, there are other storms ahead. Because they married so quickly, they're still learning about one another. In stressful times, like the one they just came through, the unknown will cause its own problems. I left Reynoso alive and still filled with hatred for a reason. Jack and Liz realize, as they leave Reynoso alive in prison, that an awful chapter in their history may yet come to haunt them. Still, they choose to forgive.

As for the others, Lloyd Beckett finds God—the real God—but his scorched earth policy in the past will forever affect his relationships in the present—relationships with his children, his ex-wives, his paramours, his church, and his conscience.

Dan and Beth? They will find their own challenges as their families and friends react to their newfound faith. That transition is still ahead of them, but consider that they spent their first Christmas as believers with their chosen family and not their birth families. Being close to Jack and Liz, they've certainly seen that life as a believer isn't perfect.

That's where I want to end this note. Life as a Christian isn't perfect. Bad things happen to God's people—you have only to look at current news to know that for a fact. (Or read the Old Testament book of Habakkuk) Christ told his disciples, his closest friends, that, as believers in Him, the world would persecute them. That persecution would, in fact, be the norm, until the day their earthly lives ended. Comfortingly, Christ also left them with His beautiful prayer recorded in John 17 and the promise that He would be with them always. That's also our promise to claim—the promise that we are never alone. What a comfort that is.

The other, harder thing I want to share is that Christians— Lloyd, Jack, Liz and me included—are not perfect. We hurt those we love, judge those we don't know, and drag Christ's name through the filth. The only thing I can offer to those of you who judge Christians because we aren't perfect is this: Christ didn't die for the perfect— He died for the intelligent, willful, imperfect race of man. Can you imagine the mercy it takes to forgive so many of so much? Please look beyond our failures and see our great God.

Thank you for sharing this journey with me. I have prayed for you, even though I don't know you. I pray that you will have your own meeting with the Lord of all Creation and that He will bless you in an immense way.

Look for more of the BWSRU, Liz, Jack, Dan, and Beth in the near-term future. I believe that they have more stories to share—God willing.

I leave you with this, a familiar but favorite verse that speaks volumes about the character of our God:

> *"For God so loved the world, that He gave His only begotten Son, that whoever believes in Him shall not perish, but have eternal life*[20]*"*

---

[20] John 3:16 (New American Standard translation).

MEDICAL GLOSSARY

(IN ORDER OF APPEARANCE)

Hypovolemic shock is a life-threatening condition that results when more than 20% (one-fifth) of the body's blood or fluid supply is lost. This severe fluid loss makes it impossible for the heart to pump a sufficient amount of blood to the body. Hypovolemic shock often leads to organ failure.

Intravenous therapy (IV) is a therapy that delivers fluids directly into a vein. Intravenous infusions are commonly referred to as drips. The intravenous route is the fastest way to deliver medications and fluid replacement throughout the body, because they are introduced directly into the circulation. Intravenous therapy may be used for fluid volume replacement, to deliver medications, and for blood transfusions.

An *electrocardiogram, abbreviated as EKG*, is a test that measures the electrical activity of the heartbeat. An EKG gives two major kinds of information. First, by measuring time intervals on the EKG, a doctor can determine how long the electrical wave takes to pass through the heart. Second, by measuring the amount of electrical activity passing through the heart muscle, a cardiologist may be able to find out if parts of the heart are too large or are overworked.

A *Rape Kit* is a package of items used by medical personnel for gathering and preserving physical evidence following an allegation of sexual assault. The evidence collected from the victim can aid the criminal rape investigation and the prosecution of a suspected assailant.

Tachycardia is a common type of heart rhythm disorder (arrhythmia) in which the heart beats faster than normal while at rest. It can be caused by low blood pressure or enduring sudden stress or fright.

A *chest tube* is a flexible plastic tube inserted through the chest wall and into the chest cavity It is inserted to remove air, fluid (such as blood), or pus.

Metabolic syndrome is a cluster of conditions that occur together, increasing the risk of heart disease, stroke and type 2 diabetes. These conditions include increased blood pressure, infertility, high blood sugar, excess body fat around the waist, and abnormal cholesterol or triglyceride levels.

Stockholm Syndrome is an emotional attachment to a captor formed by a hostage as a result of continuous stress, dependence, and a need to cooperate for survival. In this case, Jack wasn't holding Liz captive, but the weather stranded them together, and he was in a position of power over her.

Chronic migraine is defined as having at least fifteen headache days a month, with at least eight days of having headaches with migraine features, for more than three months.

Fibromyalgia is a disease of the central nervous system characterized by widespread musculoskeletal pain accompanied by fatigue, sleep, memory, and mood issues. Researchers believe that fibromyalgia amplifies painful sensations by affecting the way your brain processes pain signals.

Echocardiogram (echo) is a graphic outline of the heart's movement. During an echo test, an ultrasound provides pictures of the heart's valves and chambers and helps the sonographer evaluate the pumping action of the heart. Those pictures are used to diagnose cardiac tamponade, among other disorders.

Cardiac tamponade is a serious medical condition in which blood or fluids fill the space between the sac that encases the heart and the heart muscle. This puts pressure on the heart and keeps it from filling properly. The result is a dramatic drop in blood pressure that can be fatal. The lack of sufficient blood flow to the rest of the body can also be fatal.

Code—while there's no formal medical definition for a code, doctors often use the term as slang for a cardiopulmonary arrest happening to a patient in a hospital or clinic.

CICU: Cardiac Intensive Care Unit.

Ventricular fibrillation (V-Fib) is a heart rhythm problem that occurs when the heart beats with rapid, erratic electrical impulses. This causes the pumping chambers in the heart to quiver uselessly, instead of pumping blood. Because the heart doesn't pump adequately during ventricular fibrillation, sustained v-fib can cause low blood pressure, loss of consciousness, or death.

ENDNOTES

i   "In Christ Alone" by Keith Getty and Stuart Townend. Copyright 2002 Thankyou Music (PRS) (adm. Worldwide at CapitalCMGPublishing.com excluding Europe which is adm. By Integrity Music, part of the David C. Cook family. Songs@integritymusic.com) All rights reserved. Used by permission. License #1005563.

ii   "Jesus, I am Resting, Resting," by Jean Sophia Pigott 1876. Copyright Public Domain.

iii   "Silent Night," Music by Franz Xaver Gruber, Lyrics by Joseph Mohr 1818. Copyright Public Domain.

iv   "Amazing Grace" by John Newton 1779. Copyright Public Domain.

v   "Good Morning, Life" by Joseph Meyer and Robert Allen, Memory Lane Music. Used by Permission. Capitol CMG Publishing License #1005991.

vi   "Be Thou My Vision," by Eleanor Henrietta Hull and Mary Elizabeth Byrne, 1909. Words and Music: Public Domain.

vii   "I Cherish The Treasure," by Jon Mohr, Copyright © 1988. Birdwing Music (ASCAP) Jonathan MarkMusic (ASCAP) (adm. at CapitolCMGPublishing. com) All rights reserved. Used by permission. License #1006002.

viii   "All I Have Is Christ" by Jordan Kauflin, Copyright © 2008. Sovereign Grace Praise (BMI) (adm. at CapitolCMGPublishing.com) All rights reserved. Used by permission. License #1005563.

ix   "Somewhere in Your Silent Night" by Bernie Herms, Matthew West and John Mark Hall, Copyright © 2017. My Refuge Music (BMI) (adm. at CapitolCMGPublishing.com) All rights reserved. Used by permission. License #1005563.

x   "The Messiah," by George Frederic Handel 1741, Copyright Public Domain.

xi   *Immeasurably More*, Words and Music by Tomlin, Christopher D/Gilkeson, Gareth, Andrew/Llewellyn, Christopher Dean. Copyright © 2014. Thank You Music (PRS) (adm. worldwide at CapitolCMGPublishing.com excluding Europe which is adm. By Integrity Music, part of the David C Cook family. Songs@integritymusic.com)/Worship Together Music (BMI) Six Steps Songs (BMI) S.D.G. Publishing (BMI) (adm. at Capitol CMG Publishing.com) All rights reserved. Used by permission. License #1005563.

Enjoy this sneak peek excerpted from *Boundary Waters Search and Rescue: Beyond Imagination* (Book two in the *Boundary Waters Search* and *Rescue* series). Expected availability autumn 2021 from author Joy Harding and Covenant Books.

PILGRIMS IN AN UNHOLY LAND

Liz Lockwood was in the kitchen making dinner and enjoying the peace of her surroundings. It was a perfect mid-May afternoon, warm, sunny, and the birds sang exuberantly—as if a part of God's choir. She'd had a good day in the studio, her hands cooperating as she embroidered beads onto her newest commission. Despite extensive physical therapy, she still had difficulty working with beads on her textile projects. Some days were so bad that all she could do was wet felt background fabric, write, or if her hands were somewhat cooperative, embroider, but today she'd been able to do the work she loved the most. Finished in the studio, she had one of her favorite CDs playing in the background and all was right with the world.

Liz looked up in surprise as Jack's car came down their road. He was home from the hospital two hours early. She was thrilled; this was the perfect end to her workday. Drying her hands on a towel, she went to meet him when she heard the door open. As soon as she saw him, she stopped short. He looked like someone had hit him over the head, hard.

Her heart pounding, Liz moved forward and put her arms around him. "What's wrong, Jack? You look ill."

Jack embraced her and bent to rest his head on her shoulder.

Liz felt Jack's body shake with suppressed emotion, exhaustion, something. She held him for a long time, rubbing his back and just letting her warmth soothe him.

Finally, Jack took a shuddering breath and straightened. He looked down at her and managed, "I'm okay, Liz. It was just a bad day all around."

Liz led him into the dining room and motioned for him to sit. "That's horse patootie. You're not okay, not even close. Park it and I'll be right back."

Liz returned to the room almost immediately, holding mugs of strong, sweet tea. "It's tea, sorry, but at least it's warm. I've got some coffee brewing." After sitting down next to Jack and handing him the cup, she asked, "What's happened?"

Rubbing his forehead, Jack shook his head. "We are pilgrims in an unholy land, and never have I been more convinced of that than I am right now."

Liz took his hand and squeezed it. "Jack, tell me what's going on. Did you lose a patient?"

Jack nodded, looking almost despondent. "Actually, I lost two patients, a mother and her child. The mother, who was in her second trimester of pregnancy, had gone in to get an abortion at a regional clinic. Something happened during the procedure and the twenty-three-week-old baby she was carrying was born alive. A nurse at the clinic called a friend when the doctor refused to do anything even though the mother pleaded with him to help her child. Her friend called the EMTs, but by the time they got to the clinic, the mother was hemorrhaging, and the baby was dying. Over the doctor's protests, they received permission from the mother to transport her and the baby. Sadly, by the time they got to me, the child was gone, and it was too late for the mother. She bled out within minutes. She kept saying, 'I'm sorry, don't let me die.'"

Jack jumped to his feet. "Excuse me." He ran toward the bathroom.

Liz heard retching as soon as the door closed behind him.

A MILK RUN TURNS SOUR

"I'm going to swing out over the lake and bring us in over Devil's Kettle Falls. It's a sight to see in the springtime." Dan moved the control stick and instead of flying over forest, the four of them were suddenly looking out over the pristine blue of Lake Superior.

Jack laughed from his seat behind Dan. "Isn't this a little out of the way, Harrison?"

Dan eyed his wife, who was sitting in the seat next to him. "Isn't he the one who keeps saying 'everyone's a critic'? Tell the man what we're doing, okay?"

Beth turned to face Jack. "Jack, our pilot here wants us to see a miracle of nature. He knows where and when we're expected at the staging area for training, but since it's a milk run, he figured we could have a little fun on the way."

Dan turned inland as they passed the mouth of the Brule River, his bank just steep enough to force a gasp out of Liz, who sat behind Beth. It was Liz's first time, well, her first time conscious, in a helicopter.

Jack reached for his wife's hand. "Easy, love. Our pilot's just showing off a bit. Humor the old guy."

Liz slapped Jack's shoulder. "You're terrible! Why in the world would you want to tick off the guy who holds our lives in his hands?"

Reaching forward, she patted Dan's arm. "Don't listen to him. He's just jealous."

"Jealous? Of Harrison?" Jack snorted. "Why in the world would I be jealous of him?"

"Because," Beth broke in giggling, "he married the owner of the best bakery in Minnesota, who also happens to make a great cup of coffee."

Jack thought for a moment and said, "Well, there is that. Seriously, Dan, it's a gorgeous day, thanks for thinking of this. Liz and I haven't been up this way in about six months. We snowshoed up the river last January."

Dan pointed out to the left. "There it is. Wow, the water's still high."

Beth and Liz unbuckled their seatbelts to get a better look out of the windows. Liz sat in Jack's lap so she could see the foaming water of the falls and the place where most of the water disappeared into a hole in the bedrock. Jack's arms steadied her as she tried to balance while craning her neck to see more of the landscape.

Beth, unable to avail herself of her husband's lap, leaned forward, using binoculars to help her view the falls. Suddenly, she stiffened, "Hey, there's someone down there, on the bank of the river just above the falls. It looks like he's holding something." Suddenly her face paled. "Dan, he's got a rifle pointed at us!"

"Hang on," Dan yelled, banking sharply as bullets pinged off the canopy. "All of you sit down and buckle in, now! I'm going to…" A red light flashed above him as an alarm sounded. Black smoke started billowing around the aircraft and a few seconds later, the engine noise cut out. Everyone could feel the helicopter begin to shake as Dan tried desperately to level the aircraft and restart the engine. Beth picked up the microphone, her voice calm as she called, "Mayday, Mayday, this is BWSR 3 on a flight plan out of Ely. Complete engine failure caused by ground fire. Mayday, Mayday…" She went on repeating the call for help and alternating it with their location until Dan shouted, "Brace! We're going in. Brace…"

The rotors windmilled uselessly as the helicopter turned end for end twice, tore through the trees, crashing canopy-down in a small lake, bouncing into the air, then splitting in two before it hit the water again.

ABOUT THE AUTHOR

J oy Harding is a Christian, a wordsmith, and a lover of books. She is committed to bringing her readers exciting journeys, uplifting love stories, and family sagas that will touch your hearts. Together with her husband of almost forty years, Joy is a passionate believer in the centrality of God in their covenant marriage relationship. Her characters reflect this passion through good times and bad.

Joy lives in the beautiful state of Minnesota. Her first series, beginning with the novel *Boundary Waters Search and Rescue: Beyond Belief,* is set in the north woods of her home state. She loves to hear from interested readers.

Please visit her website and blog at https://www.joyharding-author.com

CPSIA information can be obtained
at www.ICGtesting.com
Printed in the USA
BVHW030543280721
612812BV00003B/6/J